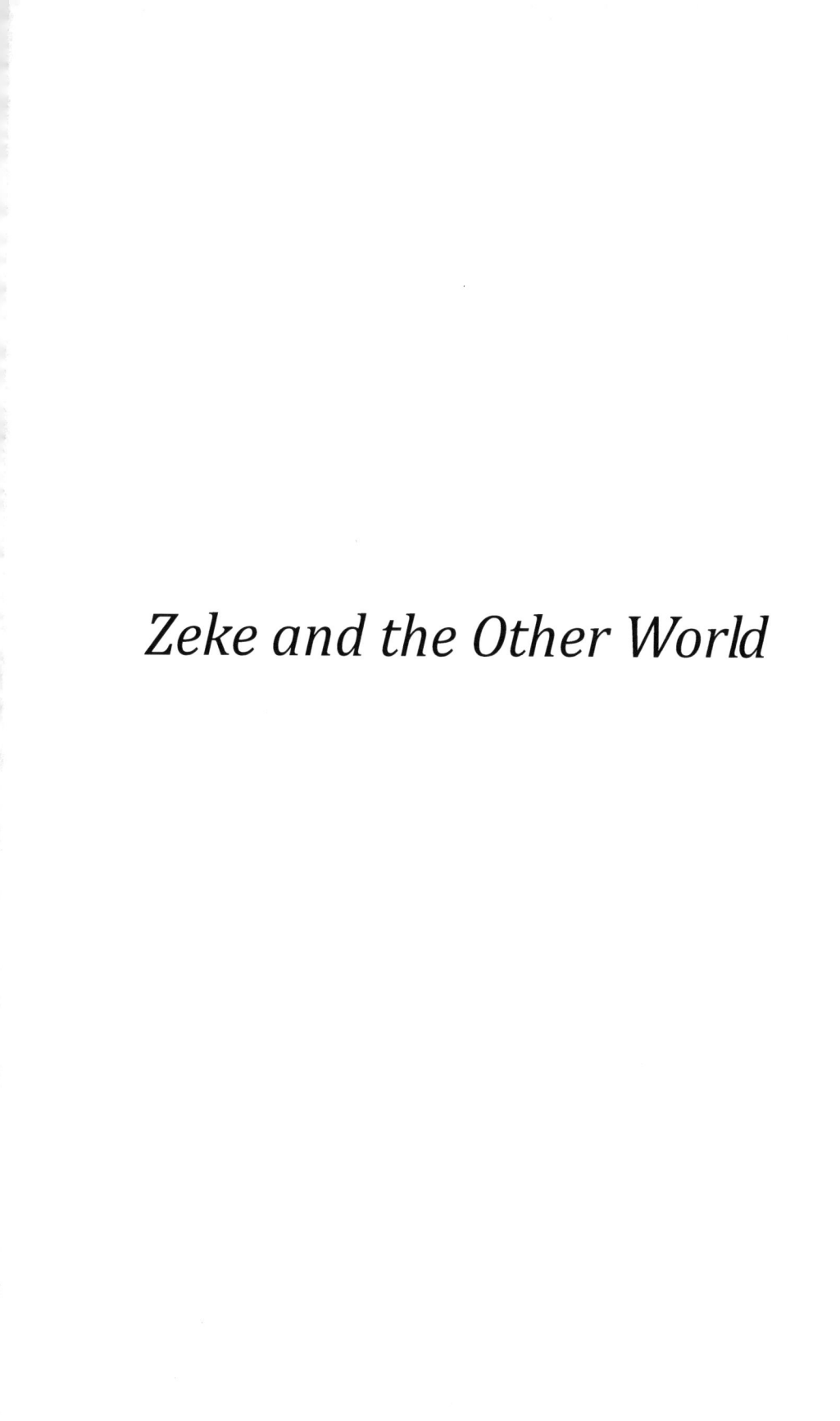

Zeke and the Other World

Books by Leonard Tuchyner

A Journey to Elsewhere: Poetry Through the Seasons of Life (2014)

Merlyn the Magic Turtle: A Story of Love and Trust (2022)

Moon Rising: Stories and Poems (2023)

Zeke and the Other World (2024)

Zeke and the Other World

Leonard Tuchyner

Independently published

Editing, print layout, e-book conversion,
and cover design by DLD Books
Editing and Self-Publishing Services

DLD Books
www.dldbooks.com

Copyright 2024 by Leonard Tuchyner
All rights reserved.

ISBN: 9798324668570

Prologue

One-Who-Swirls-Slowly is on his way to the Other Worlds Exploration Committee meeting. As a human, I would have difficulty seeing One-Who-Swirls-Slowly at all. On this huge planet made mostly of gases, he would seem to be just more gas, indistinguishable from the gases of the immediate environment. If one were to look more closely, one might discern that there is a membrane similar to a transparent jellyfish skin whose shape changes and undulates. It might then be noticed that the phosphorescence that is prevalent throughout the bubble-body is focused in specific places, having semi-permanent shapes and colors. It would be easy to deduce that these areas of concentration and relative stability are the counterpart to human organs.

On this planet, named Gazeon, there is a diffuse ambient light that slowly changes hue, intensity, movement, and pattern. On a planet where there is little more than weather, it is not an insignificant factor.

One-Who-Swirls-Slowly is a healthy member of the dominant species on the planet Gazeon. If a human ear could survive in such an environment, which indeed it could not, it would actually be able to discern the equivalent of spoken language. The Gazeon people are able to vibrate their bodies along a wide range of frequencies, just as human vocal chords do. Although made primarily of gas and coalesced microscopic bits of solid elements suspended electrically within their gelatinous bodies, these gases and suspended solids are able to maintain a discrete and complex organization.

As One-Who-Swirls-Slowly spins his way toward the committee meeting, much like the propeller of a boat, Delicate-Twinkling-Lights spins frantically to catch up with him. She is very attracted to his calm, steady nature. He, on the other hand, is attracted to her ephemeral quality. As on Earth, opposites attract.

He says to her, "I thought you were going to get to the meeting early."

"I was," she says breathlessly. "I got to the coordinates before a line of plasma whirlwinds made the designated place for the meeting unsafe. When the coordinates for the meeting were changed, I was way off course. Plus, there was the need to detour around the whirlwinds."

"You'd think the weather people could get it right," he says.

The people of Gazeon are unaware of the solid surface of their planet. They dwell within a narrow band of its atmosphere. There are no permanent edifices. Everything is floating. Thus, everything is vulnerable to severe weather fluctuations that often displace entire populations from one location to another in very short order. Through millions of years of evolution, the people have adapted. Like creatures on other life-bearing planets, they have built-in global positioning capacities. When a community is moved, it moves as a unit. The movements are similar to those of a school of fish in that they maintain their positions relative to each other.

When buildings are called for, building-entities, bio-engineered for the purpose, unify their bodies into walls and compartments. Such structures may be transient, assembled just before the need for a building and disassembled immediately afterwards. Other buildings are relatively permanent and stand as long as the building-entities survive. All artifacts on Gazeon are living organisms.

"I heard that the team has succeeded in making contact with

the Zeke. Is it really true?" she asks, while the rapid expansion and contraction of her body slows down as she catches her breath.

"Let's just say that we got Strong-Presence's attention for a moment. Nothing more."

"Why, that's wonderful!"

"It's just a beginning."

"But we thought we had lost him forever," she says, her inner lights twinkling rapidly.

"It's promising, not wonderful. The only reason we've been able to get through to Strong at all is because the host's mind is deteriorating. His sense of identification with the creature loosens as that happens."

"You know I don't like referring to the Zeke as a creature. It's a sentient being, not a creature."

"Whatever," he says dismissively.

Ignoring her urge to reprimand One-Who-Swirls-Slowly for objectifying the Zeke, she says, "Then all we have to do is wait until the Zeke's mind deteriorates sufficiently. Then Strong will come back to us. Right?"

"It's not that easy," One-Who-Swirls-Slowly cautions. "The creature's body is deteriorating as well. If the creature's body dies before its mind is sufficiently weakened to free him, he will be lost to us forever."

"How can the mind of a being made of solids and liquids be that strong?"

"I'm afraid that our view of matter is quite colloquial. The density alone would seem to me to have a rather tenacious quality."

"Well," she says, blinking her most beguiling colors, "you're the most solid person I know, and you certainly are the most tenacious. I would like to experience it more intimately sometime."

Suddenly, One-Who-Swirls-Slowly is not swirling so calmly

or steadily. Lights in his reproductive organs start to pulsate involuntarily. He tries to surround them with a fog but does not totally succeed.

Delicate–Twinkling–Lights chuckles. She's pleased by his response to her and finds his modesty charming. Her own lights are quite under control.

They spin their way to the coordinates and find that the building has properly erected itself. Other members of the committee are converging on the access way as they arrive. They exchange the usual pleasantries, made up of the proper words and the proper color patterns, and settle into their appropriate positions within the single hall that is this meeting place. They form part of a floating circle.

The committee chairman leaves the edge of the circle to take her place in the middle of the formation. She officially opens the session. "Dr. Mind–Storm, will you please present your report," she says, and floats back to take her place again on the circle's rim.

A venerable Gazeon takes his place in the center. Although his phosphorescence is bright and organized, his defining membrane shows signs of thinning. No one is concerned that his death is imminent, but when it does happen, as it will happen to all of them, the membrane will break down and the life force will ooze out.

Dr. Mind–Storm is accompanied by a projector entity that provides sensory aids to help the presentation.

"I know that many of you are new to this project," he says. "In fact, there are some here that I cannot recollect seeing before. I am going to assume that there are some newcomers that know nothing of the project's history or its present status, so I'll start from the beginning."

Harmony–Lights and Strong–Presence

Harmony–Lights initially listens closely as Dr. Mind–Storm goes into a long, historical synopsis of the Other Worlds Contact Project. But as he speaks, she remembers. Her mind goes back to those fateful times, full of hope and discovery.

She and her husband, Strong–Presence, had been brought into the team long after the theoretical and technical work had been done. She remembers Strong–Presence as he was then. As all Gazeons are named after certain aspects of their character, so was her mate. Strong–Presence knew who he was. In any place where others were gathered, he stood out. To some he was intimidating, and sometimes he intended to have that effect. To her, his strong presence was reassuring. But he had not always had such a positive effect on her.

She had met him when they were students at the Mind Arts Academy in the scholarly community of Deswald. He was already well known as the academy's premier vortex surf rider. Harmony remembered the first time she encountered him. She was floating leisurely with a female friend toward the nutrition building entity, where she was looking forward to a bubble of methane–based nutritional gases, when she saw a cocky–looking male spinning down the campus as though he owned it. As he passed by a trio of young female students, their internal colors turned two shades toward infrared.

"Flame, who is that guy who seems to think he's a Gazeon god?"

"He *is* a Gazeon god, Harmony. That's Strong-Presence. He's the best vortex surf rider this university has ever seen."

"Big deal. Look at those ditzy females going all pimple-skinned over him just because they think he's so macho. How shallow can you get? He's probably just another jock getting through his education by virtue of his ability to stand on a surf entity." Her voice trailed off at the end as she watched Flame's membranes start to quiver when Strong trained his visual sensors on her for a moment.

Two days later, Harmony floated impatiently toward a crowd surrounding Dr. Crazy-Lights' bulletin entity. Crazy-Lights was her telepathy class professor, and he had just posted a list of which students would be paired as partners for the next semester. She was amused at the various reactions the students had when they discovered who their partners were to be. There were reactions of great excitement and others of abject disappointment. But when she got close enough to perceive that Strong-Presence was to be her partner, her anger was in the red zone. All the harmonious color schemes and rhythms of her internal lights had turned to a boiling dissonance.

"This has got to be a horrible joke," she said out loud.

"I wish someone had played that joke on me," a nearby female exclaimed. "I'm paired with Limpid-Hues. My social life is dead."

Harmony gave her a disdainful look. "Well, I'm not going to accept it."

"What are you going to do?"

"Watch me." She jetted into Crazy-Lights' office entity without requesting permission from the secretary, who tried to stop her.

The professor was floating behind his recording entity, dictating some sort of notes. He looked up, startled, as Harmony burst into his office.

"I'm sorry, Professor," the secretary said, flushed with apologetic embarrassment. "I tried to stop her. She just jetted right past me."

"Jetted, huh? I haven't jetted for quite some time. Not sure I still can. What's the problem, Miss Harmony-Lights? It must be pretty serious to break protocol with such brashness. You know I could expel you for this."

Harmony came to an abrupt halt at those words, suddenly realizing how out of line she was. "I—I'm sorry. But, but—"

"But what? Now that you've done it, you'd better give me a good reason for it."

Harmony expanded her ovoid body in a deep breath, trying to regain her composure. "Professor, there's been a mistake."

"Oh, what kind of mistake?" His mood suddenly seemed to change, his lights glittered with a syncopated rhythm, and she wondered what was so funny.

"You hooked me up with a person totally incompatible with me."

Crazy-Lights juggled through his data entities, scattered about his study space, until he found what he was after. "Hmm, no there's no mistake. I've paired you with Mr. Strong-Presence."

"Yes, yes, that's what I mean. We're so incompatible, I doubt we could share the time of day telepathically."

"You mean you don't share the admiration for our surfing champion that most of your female peers seem to have?" The twinkling pattern had not changed, and Harmony knew he was making fun of her.

"Look, Professor, I know this must seem funny to you, but you could not have made a worse pairing. Please reconsider."

The mocking light show suddenly stopped, and Crazy-Lights' glow took on more somber hues. "Miss Harmony-Lights, I've gone through both of your psychological profiles. I've given the matter serious consideration, as I always do in the pairing. I have quite a few seasonal cycles of experience behind me. You may be surprised by this pairing, and when you realize how foolish you're being, I expect you to be in my office again to apologize. Now, I'm quite busy." He turned end-over-end in a dismissive gesture, and she backed out of his room entity.

She was back the next day. Crazy-Lights peered curiously at Harmony as she floated, motionless, before him. Her countenance flickered light patterns which portrayed disbelief, bewilderment, and humility.

"Well?"

"Wow!" Then she turned around and left.

When Harmony and Strong had touched minds for the first time, they had both been surprised. They most certainly had not expected the breadth and depth of mind that they found in each other once they achieved a complete mind meld. At first, Harmony thought it was just the effect of the intimacy of that kind of encounter, which neither of them had undertaken before. But then, as time went on, and they got to experience the same exercise with many other partners, they discovered that there was something between them that they felt with no one else. With time and practice, their skills grew, and they went deeper and deeper into the mind meld experience. Both exceeded the skills of their classmates almost exponentially. Professor Crazy-Lights theorized that their affinity for each other was at least partially responsible for stimulating this extraordinary talent.

Union as a couple was inevitable. Their affinity manifested not only in telepathy and mind melding, but extended to almost all spheres of life. Their marriage was heralded beyond the academic community because of Strong-Presence's fame as an athlete.

Shortly after graduation, Strong-Presence was offered a position in the United League of Communities in the Mind Warfare Corps. Although Gazeon communities cannot occupy permanent positions on solid land masses, since they are floating entities that are constantly relocating from one global position to another, they do vie for the right to hold or to move to a given place. The need to relocate is a matter of survival. Extreme weather conditions, which might take the form of huge, fiery, whirling cyclones or monstrous updrafts and downdrafts, are often deadly. Therefore, political power is of vital importance.

Communities compete for the safest, most stable locations. Sometimes that means that one community with higher status will supplant another. Depending on the diplomatic relationships between two communities, one group might either move through another or be forced to bypass it. Consequently, diplomacy and community relationships are very complex. They include military options.

Strong quickly lived up to expectations and was regularly promoted to higher ranks.

Harmony was offered a post at a prestigious university in the Mind Arts department and rapidly gained prominence.

Both Harmony and Strong worked privately as a therapeutic team. Since there is no central nervous system among the denizens of Gazeon, there is no separation between brain and body. Healing arts require a combination of physical and mental interventions. Telepathy and mind melding are essential tools. Harmony and Strong gained a worldwide reputation as healers.

The Call

The communications entity floats into Harmony and Strong's sleeping chamber. It is obvious from their dimmed and slowly pulsating body lights that the couple is still deep in sleep. The communications entity says in a trembling voice, "You have a call."

There is a slight flicker in Strong's countenance, but he does not awaken.

"You have a call." This time, a little louder.

Harmony's lights brighten reluctantly to half consciousness. There's a slight agitation in their rhythms. "Go away. It's too early."

"It's from the university provost and the Ministry of Defense," the entity says.

"What?" Strong's lights have suddenly brightened, all of them blinking in alarm. "Why the hell is the ministry calling me at this hour?"

"And why is the provost calling me?" Harmony asks, now fully awake.

The communications entity, being of very limited intelligence, floats without comment.

Harmony and Strong contemplate each other for a moment. "Okay, okay," Strong says, his body membranes taut but compliant. "Put them on."

Immediately, General Ikabar's voice is replicated through the communications entity. "Hello, Strong. Hope we didn't get you out of your sleep cycle."

"No, sir. Is anything wrong?"

"Why, no, no, my boy. Something is very right. Very right, as a matter of fact."

"What do you mean?" Harmony asks. "Isn't everyone asleep at this hour?"

"I'm sorry, Professor Harmony–Lights," the provost's voice comes through. "But you see, this is a very important matter, and we needed to be sure to catch you and Strong–Presence before you started your day."

"Why? What's so all–fired important that you had to invade our privacy?" Harmony is amused to hear the irritation in her own voice. Usually, it would have been Strong expressing himself. But she knows he doesn't have that option in front of the General, so she's doing it for both of them.

The General takes command again. "Have you heard of the Other Worlds Contact Project?"

"I've heard of it," Strong answers, "but I don't know much about it."

"Well, you're about to find out all about it, all about it. You and your wife have the honor of being invited to join the Project. It's about the most important research project going on today. It has absolutely historical proportions. Historical proportions."

"We're honored," Harmony interrupted, "but I don't think we're interested." Harmony is still acting as her husband's alter ego.

"Don't jump to a position so quickly, Dr. Harmony–Lights," her provost says, a slight edge creeping into his voice. "You haven't had a chance to find out enough about it to have an opinion, if you'll pardon my saying so."

"Nevertheless, I'm quite satisfied with my career and my life as it is."

"Dr. Lights, your husband does not have the luxury of that decision. He works for the department, and I am his superior officer, after all. His superior officer," the general reprimands.

"He can resign his commission."

She realizes that she's overplaying her part when she feels Strong's pseudo limb on her membrane.

"Uh, sir, am I being ordered to join the project?" he asks.

"Why, no, my boy. Not to join, but merely to go for an orientation. You can make up your mind after that. You wouldn't be much use if you didn't enter into the project willingly. Willingly, I say."

"Am *I* being ordered?" Harmony asks.

The provost protests, "We don't have the power to order you, but your continued employment at the university depends upon your going to the orientation."

"You know I don't need the university to further my career, don't you?"

"Yes, of course, Dr. Harmony–Lights, but we do want to convince you to at least consider the project. It's a wonderful opportunity for you. If you will attend the orientation, the military establishment will be satisfied. No further persuasion will be attempted. We will be satisfied."

"Persuasion? You mean coercion, I think. Why are you so interested in us? Why are we so special?"

"Dr. Lights, as a telepathic team, you're the most powerful couple we know of, and that's perfect for the project," the provost says.

Project Fundamentals

Three cycles later, Harmony and Strong are picked up and delivered via military transport entity. Its body membrane is typically thick, stiff, and impervious to its inner lights. No visual hints of its occupants show through its dull exterior. No whispers of the vehicle's emotional or mental state can be detected, even to Harmony's keen perceptions. Even the passengers' emanations cannot penetrate its mental shields.

"Strong, do all military vehicles have so much mental armor?"

"It is a military entity, after all, Harmony. It wouldn't do to have its inner workings open to enemy scrutiny, would it?"

"But does it have any intelligence?"

"As little as possible. We want it following orders, not making decisions."

"Oh. I guess that makes sense. Sort of."

When the couple floats through the vehicle's expanding entrance, they are not surprised to find General Ikabar waiting for them.

"Good cycle. Good cycle, I say. Are you looking forward to the orientation? I tell you, it will be fascinating, just fascinating."

"I'm sure, sir," Strong says in a clipped voice, his lights steady and unrevealing.

"Humph," is Harmony's only response.

Except for a few minor devil swirls, the trip to the Other Worlds Project facility is uneventful. It is a large building made up of extremely strong building block entities.

"That enclave looks solid, sir. I'll bet it would take quite a blow to disturb it."

"Quite so, Commander. Yet it was only a short time ago that the building had to disassemble itself to escape a devastating downdraft. Devastating, I say. But these building block entities are good issue, very good issue. Reassembled itself faster than a methane browser can run away. Faster, I say."

Inside the building, there is little evidence of a military presence. Harmony is surprised. They are ushered to an office somewhere in the heart of the building by a young female Gazeon who shoots the usual sidelong glances at Strong.

Inside, a middle-aged Gazeon male hovers over some technical entities that Harmony has little notion of.

"Ahem, Doctor." The General tries to get the Gazeon's attention.

"Just a minute," the doctor says impatiently. "I'm busy."

Strong is surprised to see General Ikabar float patiently, apparently willing to wait for as long as it takes for the doctor to bestow his attention on them. After an uncomfortably long time, the Gazeon finally does turn his senses on his guests.

"Dr. Mind-Storm, this is Commander Strong-Presence and Dr. Harmony-Lights."

"Yes, yes, of course. Who else would they be?"

"Quite so."

Mind-Storm surveys his guests suspiciously. "Well, what do you already know about the Other Worlds Contact Project?"

"Just pretend we don't know anything," Strong replies.

Harmony chuckles. "That's no exaggeration."

"That bad, huh? You do know that there are other worlds besides this one, don't you?" Mind-Storm asks accusingly.

"I never thought about it," Strong answers defiantly.

Mind-Storm gives the equivalent of a Gazeon sigh. "Well, there are. Didn't you study any mathematics?"

"Of course we did. What has that got to do with other worlds?"

"Everything. Look." He points to a globe entity assuming the shape of a nearly perfect globe. Its surface is made of gases held together by something other than a membrane. These gases swirl, change colors, and otherwise mimic Gazeon's atmosphere.

"Everybody knows that Gazeon is a globe made mostly of gas," Dr. Mind-Storm says. "It has a core where the gas is congealed into a form called liquid by a force we call gravity. Gravity, in turn, seems to have something to do with mass. In fact, a lot of the matter suspended in our bodies and in our environment clump together to form a variety of matter called solids. The higher we go in our atmosphere, the more rarified the gas becomes. Have you ever wondered where that process ends?"

"No. Why don't you tell us?" Strong suggests, not trying to hide his sarcasm.

Mind-Storm ignores Strong's disparagement. "It gets so rare at a certain altitude that it might as well not exist."

"Okay. So, what has that got to do with other worlds?" Strong pushes.

"Look here, son. There is no reason to believe that ours is the only little bubble that exists. We have developed creatures that have been able to float to the edge of our atmosphere, and they have sensed a fiery orb out there. By triangulation, we estimate that it is so far away that I'm sure you couldn't fathom it, so I won't bother telling you about it."

"Yeah, don't bother wasting your precious time on our feeble minds," Strong says derisively.

Harmony looks disappointedly at Storm. She wants to know.

Dr. Mind-Storm throws out a figure that makes Harmony and Strong just stare at him.

"I told you that you couldn't understand it. Anyway, there are other tiny points of light out there, and we think they are even farther away than that little dot I just told you about. We've been studying it for a long time, now, and it seems as though we are the only things moving."

"Where are we moving to?" Harmony asks, before her mate can put in another dig.

"Not to anywhere. Just around that dot of light."

Harmony and Strong stare at him again.

"Just around? Why?" Harmony's lights are blinking in a very disorganized way.

Strong interrupts. "Even if all that is true, and I'm not ready to buy it, the idea of there being other worlds is just theory, it seems to me."

"Yes, I must admit that. But that brings us to the crux of the matter. What do you know about how telepathy works?"

Harmony begins to feel more at home. This is her area of expertise. "Mind energy seems to travel through a dimension that we cannot perceive with our senses. Perhaps there are many dimensions. The mind dimension appears to not be under the influence of time. Thus, mental transmission is instantaneous, regardless of the distance between communicators."

"What would you say if I told you that we have been able to tap into that dimension, and that we have detected other minds? Minds that are so strange that they could not possibly be Gazeon."

Mind-Storm looks triumphant. Again, they stare at him, but this time with an edge of extreme interest.

"Well, well. It seems I've got your attention. That's why we want one of you to make contact, while the other makes sure you don't get lost in the process."

Harmony's lights go uncharacteristically discordant, while Strong's burn with interest and intensity.

"That sounds dangerous to me," Harmony says. "I think it's crazy, and I won't do it."

But Strong has quite a different attitude. "I'll do it. When do we start?"

"Wait a moment," Harmony protests. "You forget that there

are two members of this team. You can't do it if I don't anchor you. Besides, when was it decided that you would do the contacting and I would do the anchoring? Why shouldn't it be the other way around?"

"Because I'm less likely to be overwhelmed by another mind."

"You're likely to rely on brute force. How do we know that this mind we're trying to contact won't be even stronger? If anyone goes, it should be me, because I can find my way around that kind of force," Harmony counters.

"Stop quibbling about it. It's already decided that Strong-Presence goes," Storm says with finality. "We've done a lot of thinking about it, and that's what we've come up with."

"We are all agreed on that, all of us," says General Ikabar, who has been floating nearby.

"Well, it's not going to happen," Harmony says just as emphatically. "I don't care if we get kicked out of our jobs. We can make a good living as a healing team."

Storm is about to protest when Strong extends a bubble finger to indicate that the older Gazeon should hold his vibrations. "What are some of the reasons why this project is so important?" he asks.

"Use your imagination, Commander. We know so little about our existence. We now know there are other worlds. The entities on those other worlds may know things we do not. They may live in totally different kinds of environments. It's even conceivable that they may live in liquid worlds, or stranger yet, solid worlds. They can tell us what they know. Doesn't that pique your curiosity?"

Strong looks imploringly at Harmony. He sees that Storm's words have had an effect on her.

Harmony's lights become soft as she contemplates her mate.

"I see where this is going," she says. "I know I don't have a chance. It will be impossible to live with you if I nip this thing in the bud—as I should. So all right. I'm willing to find out more about the project."

The Chamber

A young female enters the room, apparently summoned by a telepathic signal from Mind-Storm.

"This is Miss Pleasant-Lights," Mind-Storm says. "She will show you around the facilities and answer any of your questions. You must excuse me now. I'm very busy." He turns his attention to a data entity and seems to lose all interest in his guests.

"Ah yes, my boy," the General says. "I must also be on my way. Things to do, you know. I'll send a vehicle to take you home when you're ready."

"Thank you, sir."

"Yes, well— Uh, goodbye. "

Strong and Harmony turn their attention to Pleasant-Lights. She introduces them to the other major staffers in the project. Harmony is impressed by their obvious enthusiasm and finds it infectious. They are, for the most part, more congenial than Dr. Mind-Storm.

Harmony and Strong are presented with the technology that the team has developed. Pleasant-Lights leads them to an entity in the form of a small chamber. "This entity," she explains, "can focus in on and magnify the dimension through which mind travels—or perhaps it would be more accurate to say in which mind exists. That's why we call it a focus chamber."

Harmony is impressed by Pleasant's professional demeanor. She's one of the few females who don't go all weak and fluttery in Strong's proximity.

"When inside this chamber," Pleasant tells them, "one is subjected to a flow of thought in all of its forms, including images, emotions, words, feelings, and other sensations. "

"May we enter?" Strong asks.

"Yes, that was anticipated. But be cautious. These entities are very fine-tuned and quite powerful. Just become familiar with it. Don't go any further than that."

"I think we can handle it. We'll be careful," Strong says, while Harmony looks at him severely.

"Yeah, as you always are," she says.

Harmony and Strong enter the mind-focusing chamber together, although they don't attempt to explore as a team. They just reach out and explore on their own.

As Harmony reaches out with her mind, she touches wayward wisps of thought in a kaleidoscope of forms. Most of them she recognizes as coming from people outside the facility. They are regular Gazeon people from unknown distances around the planet. The experience is mundane, no different than everyday telepathic contact. As usual, she's careful not to discern too much and thus intrude upon the privacy of others. From the expression on Strong's countenance, she can see that he's experiencing the same thing.

Then a thought comes to her from a technician. "Reach into the focus entity and tweak it."

She and Strong turn their attention to the entity itself rather than the thoughts it's amplifying. They explore its quality of mind and get a sense of its unique kind of intelligence. Things begin to change in the chamber. The entity directs them to feel a sense of dimension. It's a quality akin to directionality, but it's beyond any kind of direction they've ever felt before. Direction is a concept that can't really describe what they're experiencing. This new sense is more than three dimensional. It defies description.

Slowly, Harmony feels a thought presence in the same way that a sound passes the threshold of awareness as its volume slowly increases. It is totally alien. It is so alien that she recoils and backs her mind away from the focus chamber's mind.

Strong stays several moments longer. He has never backed away from anything, and he's not going to do so now. He's staying there just to prove that he can. When he does finally break his connection with the mind-focusing entity, his lights have gone pale. The technician is looking startled and upset.

Strong and Harmony propel themselves out of the focus chamber and out of the project building to absorb some fresh gases and to revitalize their lights. After a period of regeneration, Strong can see that Harmony's lights are becoming uncharacteristically harsh. He knows what's coming but doesn't act fast enough. Harmony is spinning her way back into the building, quicker than a spin sprinter and more resolute than a deep atmosphere diver. He tries to catch up with her to stop her, but she's too fast. She swoops into Mind-Storm's office and confronts him.

"Why didn't someone tell us what to expect? Do you get your jollies from scaring people half to death? I didn't think it was a good idea to begin with, and now I'm certain of it. Goodbye, Dr. Storm. It was not nice meeting you. Come on, Strong. Let's get out of here."

She extends a pseudo pod to urge Strong out of the room, but he isn't going anywhere.

"Now hold on, Harmony. We weren't hurt. I want an explanation too. I won't get that by running away."

"Is that what you call it? Well—well—I— You *stupid!*" her coherence breaks down in bursts of rage and disbelief.

Strong has never seen her quite this way before. There's nothing harmonious about Harmony right now.

"Calm down and give the guy a chance to talk," says Dr. Mind-Storm. Harmony floats there silently, throwing dagger perceptions at him.

"Thank you," Mind-Storm says. "I do apologize. If I had

known, I certainly would have told you. The problem is that we didn't understand just how good you two are. All our other telepaths took huge amounts of time to get as far as you did in just your first session. They had time to encounter the aliens' thought patterns gradually. It's the strangeness that you find so alarming. If you had encountered it gradually, it wouldn't have seemed as strange, and it wouldn't have been as frightening. You'll get used to it. You're out of our league, so you can set your own schedule. I don't care how long you take."

Harmony looks at both of them for a long time. Gradually, her patterns return to their normal pleasantness, and her lights are normal as well.

"I'm glad I had this experience," she says. "If I hadn't, I might have been lulled into complacency. There are some things that people should not interfere with, and this is one of them. All my instincts tell me that this is too dangerous. Whatever you're trying to do will end in disaster. Please don't try to talk me into it, Dr. Mind-Storm. I'm not coming from a logical place, but an intuitive one." She turns and propels herself out of the building.

She makes her way slowly toward her present home coordinates. A play of phosphorescent colors swirls all around her. The gases are fresh and free of foul odors. Tiny yellow and green whirl devils play above her. People float by in every direction. Some are touching membrane to membrane. She passes children playing with a pet gosser creature that contracts and expands spiritedly. There is the gentle sound of moving gases, along with the murmurs of voices that blend together so that only a few words are discernible. She stretches out her bruised telepathic awareness and lets it be soothed by images of people being kind to each other.

This world is so beautiful, she thinks. Why would we want to mess with anything that had the power to change it? Without me,

Strong won't be able to go on, and he'll be protected in spite of himself. I can handle his disappointment and anger as long as he's safe.

Home Alone

Harmony reaches her present abode coordinates and has a sense of appreciation as it comes within her sensory limits. The cubes sparkle with myriad gem-like points of light that shine within the permanent building-entities. There are sixty units in all. Harmony reaches out her telepathic sensors and touches the building-entities. Their thought is rudimentary, but they give a sense of permanence and security. Their main purpose is to hold fast to their neighboring building-entities, exactly as the construction workers had instructed them to do. They will hold those positions until they die. In addition to providing privacy and shelter, they absorb waste gases from the inhabitants and pass them through themselves to the outdoors. The only nutrition they need is supplied by ambient gases within their environment. If one gets sick, veterinarians can usually heal them. If one dies prematurely, it can be replaced. Strong and Harmony can afford to have the best building-entities credit can buy.

As Harmony approaches her home, she sends forth a telepathic recognition signal. In response, two building-entities separate enough to form an entrance, and she floats through it. The portal closes behind her. Their pet tog floats to her excitedly, the way it always does when either she or Strong comes home after a work period. To a human eye, it resembles a fluffy pillow that is hopping up and down in midair, emitting greeting sounds reminiscent of a canary's tweeting. After a short period of recognition, Harmony lets the tog outside, trusting that it will be safe. She floats to the upper resting area and tries to relax. However, her colors remain intense, and her undulations don't slow down. She instructs the entertainment-media-entity to broadcast a news channel.

"Entertainment, play the news," she commands.

"Wasn't it just last deci-cycle when we had to change city coordinates?" comes the broadcast. "Well, guess what? Get ready for a new location. Owe that to a level six—yes, that's right, a level six cyclone—that's on its way. We seem to be its target. If things don't change in the next deca-cycle, we'll be on the move again. So stay tuned and don't get confused when your neighbor's dwelling seems to be a little off its mark. You should be used to this by now. Hey, don't blame me! I'm just the Weather Man."

"Entertainment, shut up," Harmony commands.

Strong should have been home by now, she thinks. What's keeping him?

She flits nervously around the building, looking for wayward pieces of flotsam that the housekeeping entities might have missed. But it doesn't help her anxiety.

Finally, Strong comes into the home with the tog. He fusses with some of the home utility-entities in the middle chamber while Harmony is dying of curiosity and fear. Eventually, he comes up to their resting chamber. He dims his inner glowings, slows down their fluctuations, dampens his sensors, and puts his mind at idle. In short, he falls asleep.

Harmony is wretched with disappointment and confusion.

How dare he just go to sleep? she thinks. Doesn't he know how anxious I am? Why won't he talk to me? But I'll be damned if I let him know how upset I am. I'll let the bastard sleep.

After a long period of sleep, Strong floats out of his sleeping place and stretches his membranes. He floats to the lowest level and then outside with the tog. There he spins to a slightly higher altitude and expels waste gases, which float away on gaseous breezes. He comes back down and expands and deflates himself as rapidly as possible, which is a part of his wake-up exercises. He distorts his shape in a variety of ways to his fullest capacity. He is satisfied with his suppleness and strength.

When he goes back inside, he finds Harmony floating listlessly in a corner.

"Well? Aren't you going to say anything?" she asks. Her lights have taken on a muddy red complexion.

"There's nothing to say. You've said it all."

"Good. I'll let the therapeutic community know that we're back in business and drum up some patients."

"You'll be doing that for yourself. I won't have time. I have a job to do," Strong tells her evenly but in a firm tone.

"What do you mean? You can't do that job by yourself. You'll need an anchor, or you'll be swept away in that horrid box."

The tog spins away furtively to another room.

"I won't be doing it without an anchor. We may be the best team, but we're not the only powerful mind mechanics. They'll find someone I can work with," he says matter-of-factly.

He swivels around and leaves through a portal, leaving his wife stunned and speechless.

Strong comes home on his regular schedule, but they have nothing to say to each other. Harmony's curiosity and anxiety are driving her mad, but she won't give Strong the satisfaction of seeing that. Strong exchanges pleasantries and asks her about her day. Harmony has little to tell him because she's done nothing that day to pursue her career. She's limited her activities to floats to neighborhood stores for the staples of civilized life, which consist of basic gases contained in returnable container-entities. She's been paralyzed with fear and uncertainty.

In the cycles that pass, one major community displacement is necessary to avoid annihilation by the weather. All entities have the power of locomotion. An orientation signal is broadcast by an appropriate entity that holds a central topological position in the community. That signal acts as a homing device and as a command to all non-sentient entities to maintain their same relative geographic placements. For those people engaged in business within buildings, no efforts need to be made, since the buildings themselves transport them. There are transport-entities for the infirm, rich, or lazy.

Harmony is barely aware of the maneuvers that are going on around her. Fifteen cycles later, she can no longer contain herself and inquires as nonchalantly as possible, "So how is the project going?"

"It's going as well as can be expected," Strong replies. "Storm was right. I'm getting used to the alienness of the creatures' thought qualities. I'm able to stay with them longer each contact."

Harmony's lights suddenly flare red. "That's not what I mean, and you know it. Who is your partner?"

Harmony is feeling left out. She no longer believes that she has pursued the correct line of action. Those actions have not succeeded in protecting Strong. In fact, she has endangered him, because no one else could anchor him as well as she can after having spent so much time with him in telepathic and mind-melding endeavors. Now she has only succeeded in isolating herself from him and making herself feel miserable.

"Her name is Dark-Lights. She's very young but amazingly powerful. She's at least as powerful as either of us," Strong answers with brutal honesty.

Harmony feels a cold shiver run through her and fights the desire to either spin out of the abode or attack him. Instead, she gathers her inner resources and brings her body into its customary balance.

At the next wake-up period, she's ready to leave her abode when Strong floats toward the exit entity.

"What are you doing?" he asks.

"I'm going to work."

"What? What do you mean? You gave up your job, remember?"

"At the same place as you, remember?" she says with a combination of humor and acidity.

"You quit, remember?"

"I did, but I don't remember anyone accepting my resignation."

Strong's lights actually light up. "I'm delighted to hear that." He hesitates for a moment, and his brightness dims. "But Dark-Lights has taken your position, and I doubt the staff will be willing to pull her out of it."

"And what do *you* want, Strong?" Harmony asks with an edge to her voice.

"There's only one answer to that. You know I'd rather work with you than anyone else. But I don't want to impose my will in this case."

"Don't worry. I understand. I'm sure I can make myself useful. If nothing else, I can be backup."

There's only a twinge of her bitter disappointment in her voice and countenance, but Strong isn't fooled. He admires her ability to mask her true feelings.

Harmony enters the project building self-consciously, but she's prepared herself to meet the inquisitive, intrusive glances of the staff. The people she meets are obviously both curious and trying hard not to gawk. She enters Dr. Mind-Storm's office sheepishly yet defiantly.

His attention slowly shifts in her direction.

"I believe it's Dr. Harmony-Lights, isn't it?" he says with sarcasm and amusement.

"Cut the crap, Storm. I want back into the program."

"As I recall, you spent less than one cycle in the program. Saying you want to come back hardly seems appropriate. We've already gotten somebody to do the job you were offered." He returns his attention to his previous interest.

All of Harmony's lights begin to flutter slightly before she gets herself back under control. "I can be backup to Dark-Light's abilities. I can monitor both of them from a distance, to make sure they remain in competent working order."

Storm surveys her again. "Why do we need that?"

"Obviously, if you need to ask the question, you need what I'm proposing. No matter how good your contact people are, the constant exposure to an alien thought form has the potential to disorient and distort their judgment."

"Why should it?" he asks dismissively.

Harmony just floats there without taking the unspoken invitation to leave. After a while, Storm turns his attention to her again. His membranes swell and then deflate, as though in a human sigh.

"Oh, all right," he says grudgingly. "I suppose you psych people are all a little unbalanced." Harmony suspects that he's making special reference to her. "Okay, you can stay. You'll keep constant surveillance not only on Strong and Dark, but also on everyone else who works on the project—except me, of course. Pay special attention to anyone who enters the focus chamber. You will be answerable to no one but me. You will have no power to make any decisions. Is that acceptable to you?"

"Yes, it is," she says in her most professional voice.

Storm relaxes further, seeing his complete victory. His lights soften, and the internal phosphorescent patterns become friendlier and more pleasant.

"Welcome aboard. It will be an honor to work with you, Dr. Harmony–Lights."

She's disarmed and a bit confused. She actually feels a touch of friendliness toward this crusty despot.

Dr. Mind–Storm returns his attention to his previous endeavor, and she's left on her own. During the remainder of the cycle, she re-introduces herself to the rest of the staff in her new capacity, which she has to explain to them. It isn't until the end of the work period that she gets to meet Dark–Lights.

Harmony has never had any doubts about Strong's fidelity to

her, but if anyone could sway him, it would be Dark–Lights.

There's a dusky veil over all her illuminations, yet somehow the light that shines through seems to have a deep intensity, giving her an exotic beauty and allure. Her membrane undulations are sexy and suggestive. They seem to be a matter of habit or basic nature.

Harmony notices that Dark's demeanor does not vary according to her company. In contrast to her physical appearance, her voice and statements are professional and clinical. Harmony does not dare to eavesdrop on her thoughts, because she knows Dark–Lights to be a most powerful telepath who would be sensitive enough to pick up on anything like that.

Thus passes her first work cycle.

First Contact

"Stay in contact, Dark," Strong–Presence thinks to her. "I'm not going to meld. I'm only going to get a peek. Just one little tendril in one little part of its mind."

Dark–Lights is too busy anchoring Storm to waste energy arguing with him.

Harmony can do nothing except float and witness. Strong has already started the process, and she doesn't dare distract him. Her membrane stiffens, and there are no undulating movements of her shape. Her phosphorescence gleams unnaturally steady and bright, like human eyes staring and wide when anticipating disaster.

Strong lets a thin chord of his awareness slink out and touch the alien presence. There is now a small part of Strong that is intertwined with the unworldly creature's mind. Strong expects a reaction on the part of the creature, albeit a small reaction, of knowing that there is something strange going on. But all Strong feels is his own confusion at the lack of response. The creature seems not to notice anything at all.

How can this be? Strong wonders. It's almost as though the creature is deaf and blind to thought and mind, he thinks. Yet it obviously has a mind, or else I couldn't detect thought patterns. What's really weird is that I can detect thought patterns telepathically, but not with that little bit of mind meld I've just accomplished. If I were to meld to this degree with a Gazeon, we would have holistic impressions of each other. They would be dim with such a low degree of mind infusion, but definitely there. With this creature, I don't get anything, no impressions. And it doesn't show any signs of getting anything from me.

All of Strong's experiences and thoughts are being conveyed to Dark, who has established a very powerful telepathic link with him.

"I wish you guys could experience this. It's really weird," Strong thinks to Dark.

"You know that multiple mind melds are impossible except in extremely intimate relationships, such as those between parents and children," Dark thinks back.

"Yeah, I know. But I can't get a pseudopod around this thing."

"It's time to let go," Dark shouts mentally.

"Don't worry. I'm in control."

"Good. You can be in control on a different day, when we've all had more practice," Dark urges.

"You know we'll never find the same thought stream again, and this is the most promising one I've come across thus far," Strong insists.

Harmony adds her urgent thoughts. "There'll be others. Let it go!"

Instead of responding, Strong lets a little more of himself slide into the alien mind. There's still no recognition on the part of the creature. However, there's a kind of fragmentary impression that Strong is able to glean. He experiments further, withdrawing almost his entire mind meld. There's a dimming of the melding impressions, but he manages to maintain some of them. The telepathic aspects remain intact but indecipherable.

Finally, Strong withdraws completely from the mind meld while maintaining the telepathic link. Dark and Harmony let their membrane tensions relax.

"Any theories?" Strong asks.

"You've got to be kidding," Harmony says caustically. "Your little escapade almost blew my lights. I'm not sure when I'll be able to think about theories."

"How about you, Dark?" he asks.

"I hate to admit it, but I think we need Mind–Storm to figure this one out. Let's call a conference. Come on, let's see if he's in his office."

"Nice try, Dark, but I'm not leaving this connection. Let Mind–Storm come here."

Dark–Lights answers, "I'll maintain the connection. You need the rest if you're to keep a safe level of alertness and judgment. Then you and Harmony can fetch Storm."

"Do I have it on your word that you'll hold onto that contact and not try anything foolish while we're gone?" Strong asks.

"I promise. But where do you get off telling me not to do anything foolish?"

It's impossible to lie when in telepathic contact, as Dark and Strong are. The holistic mind of a Gazeon cannot hide an intention. So Strong lets go of his telepathic contact with the alien mind while Dark takes over. A backup telepath is brought in to anchor Dark, and Strong and Harmony go off to find Mind–Storm.

Strong and Harmony torpedo into Dr. Mind–Storm's office. Storm is studiously floating around a strange-looking device-entity with many surface facets. The doctor seems to be compulsively finding every three-dimensional axis around which he can float. The duo's mad rush does not deter him from his task. They bob up and down impatiently, seeking his attention like two schoolchildren vigorously waving their hands for the teacher's notice. Finally, he sighs as he comes to a halt, once more floating in a normal horizontal attitude. He turns his attention to the impatient pair.

"All right. What's so all–fired urgent?"

Strong and Harmony both start to vocalize at the same time. Storm forms a protective membrane on the side facing the two of them, as though protecting himself from their barrage of sound. Then he extends a small pseudopod that points toward Harmony.

She understands that to be a signal that she has the court and tries to give a cogent description of the recent events.

"Well, why didn't you say so in the first place?" Storm says. "We shouldn't be wasting time here blabbing. Let's get down to the focus chambers." He spins out of his office, with Harmony and Strong following him.

When they arrive at the focus chamber, Dark-Lights is dutifully keeping the creature's mind flow in her telepathic consciousness.

"It seems we have some excitement," Mind-Storm says to Dark-Lights.

"What I don't understand," she answers, "is why we get a sense of a whole coherent thought pattern while in telepathic mode, but only bits and pieces of that pattern when beginning the mind meld. Normally when we meld with each other, the sense of wholeness is enhanced. Telepathy can't match the sense of oneness of the mind meld, in the same way that telepathic contact can't be matched by sensory or verbal communication. Why is it different when trying to contact this alien?"

"Have you made any progress in trying to communicate with the creature telepathically?" Storm asks.

"None. That makes no sense either. Even the most primitive organisms on Gazeon have at least rudimentary telepathic capacities. The complexity of the creature's thought patterns indicates something compatible with our own complexity, even if we can't make any sense out of them. Yet they seem to be telepathically deaf, dumb, and blind."

"Maybe that's just an interface problem," Harmony offers. "When we try to get some of our device-entities to communicate with each other, it's often difficult because they're so incompatible in their awareness of their environments. Our own minds need to set up an interface protocol with them to have any meaningful communication."

"That's good thinking," Storm compliments. "The creature

makes no efforts at all to respond to our attempts to communicate. Why is this?" he asks rhetorically. "Maybe its life experience is so vastly different from ours that there is little that we have in common, even to the point that a thought is not recognized as a thought. We need to create some sort of interface, and the only mechanism I can think of is the mind meld."

Harmony shows her displeasure at that last statement by dipping her ovoid shape slightly downwards. "Dark, what do you think?" she asks.

"I'm using all my think energy just to stay with this monster. But I did catch that last comment about mind melding being our best possibility. Frankly, that scares me to death. I'm not going to do it. I'm not sure I even want to be anchoring for someone who does!"

"Doctor, what about the lack of coherence in the mind meld perception?"

"Is it really so difficult to come up with a theoretical construct for that?" Storm answers with an air of superiority.

"Yes," Storm and Harmony say simultaneously.

Mind-Storm makes a buzzing sound, which is the Gazeon way of clearing its analogous throat before a lecture.

"When a video-projection-entity projects a moving visual image of what it has observed in accordance with the instructions you've given it, you see the entire image from the outside. You're not part of the picture, and therefore you're not seeing the image from the inside, so you see the whole thing. You may choose to focus your attention on one aspect of that moving picture, but you can also choose to take in the presentation as a whole.

"Now try to imagine that you find yourself to be part of the image itself. It's no longer something that's viewed from the outside as a whole. Now, inside the entity, you may notice a particular organ with a lot of blinking lights. You focus your mind on that single object, and thus you're not perceiving the wholeness of the image. That organ may actually block your line of sight, so that even if you make the effort, you can't see what lies behind it. Every time you pay attention to one object instead of another, you're choosing to see only parts. From that limiting perspective, the experience might lose its coherence and overall meaning, which is easy to perceive when being viewed from the outside," Storm concludes with a sense of self-satisfaction.

"Would that mean the creature has a mind that is compartmentalized and therefore not totally self-aware, like different parts of a community that are coordinated, but only to a certain extent?" Strong asks.

"Very good. Think of the possibilities. It's a creature at cross purposes with itself—just like our people who are often at cross purposes with each other, even to the point of war. A creature at war with itself that wants to come and go at the same time," Mind–Storm says dreamily, as though thinking about his favorite gas dessert.

"But why would such a system evolve?" Harmony asks. "The nature of gas is that it's fluid. It compiles a holistic fluidity. At a given moment, a molecule in one part of my anatomy will be split moments later in another part. To evolve a compartmentalized system makes no sense, given that factor. Such a system would have to work against the dynamics of fluidity."

"Yes, but there are other possibilities," Mind–Storm responds. "The only kind of matter we have experience with is gas. Yet we know that there are other forms of matter. For example, suspended in our atmosphere, as well as within our own bodies, are tiny particles of a class of matter known as solids. They're essential to our lives. They carry electric characteristics essential to our biochemistry. We're also aware of a form of matter called liquid. It's fluid, like a gas, but not *as* fluid. Unbound, it doesn't fly off in different directions and expand to the point where it loses its integrity of form. Our bodies, in fact, have a great deal of liquid content. Now suppose that the solid state of matter could be found in lumps that are bigger than these tiny particles. Suppose our creature is made of lumps of solid matter. Or maybe it's made of a combination of solids, liquids, and gases."

"But solids fall down," Harmony protests. "They can't float."

"Why do life forms have to float?" Mind-Storm challenges.

"You mean these creatures would just keep falling?" Harmony complains incredulously.

"That's not likely. We know that the farther down you go in our world, the thicker the gas becomes. If this trend were to continue indefinitely, eventually you would get to a place where the gas would not be a gas anymore. Eventually, the conditions would be more likely to hold great globs of liquids and solids. Our liquid and solid creature could alight on such globs and use pseudopods to drag itself around."

"But wouldn't all those globs be falling forever?" Strong asks unbelievingly.

"Maybe so. Maybe the solids and the liquids *are* falling forever. But if they are, then so are we."

"How is that?" Strong asks.

"What is the shape of Gazeon?"

Strong hesitates. "I never thought about it," he then says. "I never even thought of Gazeon as having *any* shape. But everything else is ovoid. Even if it's got angled surfaces, it comes back upon itself," he reasons. Then the light of awareness shines in his vision spots. "When we relocate away from a storm, the coordinates always reference a central point, and all the coordinates together would form a globe."

"Good," Storm says approvingly. "Now take that thinking a little further. So, solids and liquids, if they fall forever, could not be falling through our gases forever, because at some point, they would be going up rather than down. Therefore, this material would have to be in the center of our world. And if the whole world is falling, where is it falling to, and through what kind of medium?" Mind-Storm asks gleefully. "Look what that alien mind has done for our understanding already, and we haven't even made real contact. Think of what it can do when we successfully mind meld with it."

Strong's body tenses with the eager anticipation of an athlete facing a coveted trial.

Harmony sees his reaction and realizes there's no way she's going to be able to stop the inevitable. Her lights grow gloomily dull.

The shadows over Dark's lights become unattractive.

Luster–Shine

Dr. Mind–Storm is pensive as he rides in his personal transit entity. Things are moving along well in the Other Worlds Contact Program.

True, he thinks, Strong's encounter with the alien mind was a little unexpected. I found it a little startling. But isn't that the whole nature and purpose of exploration? If you knew the answers in advance, there would be no need for exploring. Just having new questions makes all the work and all the risks worthwhile.

I've put my whole life into conceiving this project and doing the personal research, and here we are on the brink of a culture-changing adventure. Gazeons' understanding of their universe and their place within it is on the cusp of a glorious evolution, and I, Dr. Mind–Storm, am the captain. All the sacrifices made and all the ones yet to come are the smallest price to pay. Insignificant. That means any sacrifice, mine or anyone else's. A thousand cycles from now, our names will still be remembered, and maybe not just on Gazeon.

I love Strong's enthusiasm. It's just what the program needs. It's backed up by tremendous abilities. New territories demand pioneers who are willing to take risks.

Storm chuckles and thinks, On the other hand, he *is* a little foolhardy. He could get himself into a lot of trouble. But I guess you've got to be a little crazy to be a vortex rider. Especially the champ. I was counting on Dr. Harmony–Lights to keep him out of trouble. After today's experience, I'm not so sure she'll stay onboard. But even if she doesn't, we've got to go forward. If I read Strong correctly, there's no power on Gazeon that will dissuade him—not even Harmony. She has good reason to be scared, but I'll have to keep that fact to myself. Strong doesn't respect the power of the unknown aspects of these new worlds we're encountering. If Strong were to make a self-endangering decision that could pay off big time, I won't stop him. I don't think his wife trusts me, and she's right not to. The interests of the project are more important than Dr. Strong-Presence's safety.

The transit entity reaches the home abode, and Storm floats out, carrying information bubbles in a number of pseudopods. The abode portals open, and when Mind-Storm floats in, he sees Luster-Shine emanating very attractive colors from within. Briefly, he notes her radiance. He says nothing, but quickly turns his attention to the translucent part of her body that harbors the developing fetal embryo bubble. A protective opaqueness hides it from direct scrutiny and outer radiation.

"And how is my little embryonic professor bubble getting along?" he asks Luster.

"She feels just fine. I think she's beginning to undulate just a little."

"Did you see the obstetrician today?"

"Oh, Storm! I can't see her every day, now, can I?"

"It seems to me that the last time you saw her was twenty cycles ago. Are you trying to avoid her?"

"Of course not, silly. It's just that I have other things to do. Would you like to know what I did today?"

"Yes. Yes, of course, but not just now. There are some things that have come up in the lab that I've got to work on. You can bring me dinner in my study."

"Storm, you never have time."

"Don't be ridiculous. We'll talk about it later."

"Sure."

Storm pats Luster-Shine over the fetal spot and spins into his study. Luster watches him leave, her posture and lights indicative of resented rejection. As he approaches his study, the wall entity senses his approach and opens a portal, which closes automatically behind him. Luster-Shine floats to the exit portal and spins away to a destination unknown and not cared about, as far as Storm is concerned. That dinnertime, Storm doesn't receive dinner, as he's done innumerable times in the past. He barely notices—if he notices at all.

Later, Luster-Shine can be seen wandering aimlessly past the abodes of the rich and influential. Those structures align themselves in a fixed pattern, which they maintain during stable weather periods. When weather and geopolitical events require relocation of the entire metropolitan community, they reconstruct their original patterns when they reach the new coordinates.

In a planet as large and as far away from its parent star as Gazeon is, there is no night or day in an Earthly sense. Even the knowledge of that far-off star, Earth's sun, is absent to all Gazeons except for the very few privileged scientists who have peered telepathically through far-seeing entities. These creatures float so high and through such great distances of the planet's upper atmosphere that they actually reach realms where the light of the stars can be physically seen through visual sensors.

All luminosity available to creatures dwelling at Luster-Shine's altitude level is provided by bioluminescence and other chemical sources of light. Nevertheless, the planet's biosphere does have its cycles of relatively quiescent and active periods that are created by a complex interplay of planetary tidal movements. These tidal influences are caused by unseen moons that orbit the huge gas giant.

So as time moves on, Luster finds the world around her dimming noticeably into evening.

The well-organized, three-storied dwellings eventually give

way to an area of vegetative structures of various sizes, shapes, and colors. These survive by feeding off nutrients from the gases and particles of the atmosphere that flows constantly about them. They, too, have their place and purpose in the Gazeon community.

Luster has been floating along a highway kept clear of houses and other obstacles. This is the equivalent of a roadway on Earth. As she spins along, lost in her thoughts and feelings, she is unaware of the other citizens who pass her in both directions. Neither does she notice the various kinds of transport entities and utility entities that move more quickly and more centrally to the throughway. Her mind is dulled by misery and loneliness. A deep rage burns in her inner core, dampened there by heaviness.

Now the throughway meanders past huge commercial and utility entities that form business and infrastructure aspects of her city. They were created as the need arose and thus not thought out in advance. They maintain their original juxtaposition as the city moves about, but those positions hold no obvious aesthetic appeal.

The natural bioluminescent lights dim further as evening darkens into night.

"Well, if it isn't Luster–Shine," a hated, familiar voice says behind her.

Luster does not respond.

"Oh, come on. Is that any way to treat an old friend?" A male Gazeon leers out at her through the aperture of a private transport entity as it draws abreast of her.

"You're not a friend."

"What do you mean I'm not a friend? Who else gets you pure xenon when you need a fix? Just like you need it now."

"Get away from me," she says as she picks up her pace.

"Yeah, you really do need it. I can tell. Your colors are pretty shabby."

Luster turns toward him, her dampened rage exploding into full flame. "Get away, you filthy piece of scum. Can't you see I'm pregnant?"

She turns off the throughway and starts to spin rapidly down narrow, unpatterned spaces. The male Gazeon pops out of the vehicle and gives chase. Ugly brownish red plasma runs amoeba-like through his inner body glow. He catches Luster and spins her around with an elongated pseudopod.

"Leave me alone! Leave me *alone*!" she shouts.

"Listen, little blister. If you didn't want the stuff, you wouldn't be wandering around these parts, so far away from your loving master mate. You're lucky I don't just slip you off my membrane and forget about making you happy."

"But I'll hurt my baby."

"It's not going to hurt anyone. It's just going to make you feel better. Did you bring credits?"

"No!"

"Then what's that bubble pouch you're sporting?"

"Nothing."

He grabs a purse entity off her body and examines it.

"Just enough to buy you three bubbles. I'll tell you what. I'm going to forget that you've been lying to me and give the xenon to you anyway. Or would you rather I just take the credit? Either way, you're still going to have to pay me in other ways as well."

"Oh, no!" She looks at him, the colors and rhythms of fear pulsating in her.

She turns to flee, but he blocks her way and forces her into the transport. Once inside, he orders the apertures closed and gives travel instructions to the vehicle.

The commercial/industrial section gives way to another area of free vegetation and then to a modest residential neighborhood. The abodes here are one- and two-story structures of modest but wholesome quality. The homes are closer together than in Luster's section, and there are occasional utility and commercial establishments. Then the buildings become increasingly unhealthy in appearance, more randomly spaced, and with little aesthetic order.

After a brief struggle, Luster cowers as far as she can against the vehicle's walls, a shuddering vibration emanating along her membrane. She notices little of the environment outside.

The transport floats to a stop next to a blotchy-colored building entity whose outer walls ooze a slight smell of escaping vital gases. The vehicle's port opens, and Luster is pulled out. She makes a half-hearted attempt to jet away, but her captor is ready for her move and barrels into her hard. The stunned Luster has little resistance left as she's dragged into the noxious building entity.

Once inside, her captor, Plasma-Swirl, pulls a container bubble off one of the fetid walls and slaps it over a particular spot on Luster's body. Then he floats to the top of the ceiling and looks lewdly down at her. At first, Luster makes an attempt to leave the enclosure, but the portals are not open to her. Gradually, her inner pulsations slow and dim. They become tranquil as her mind slips into a numbing fog.

"Okay, Luster. You know what's next."

She says nothing while Plasma-Swirl violates her. When he's finished, she is stuffed, stupefied, back into the transport and pushed out the portal at the edge of her neighborhood. Attached to her body are two more bubbles of xenon. She floats slowly, in an intoxicated state, to her abode. When she enters, she knows that Storm is asleep at his work. The luminescent walls have dimmed automatically, as they always do when they recognize his sleeping status.

She floats to the sleeping chamber, remembers to hide the xenon bubbles in a wardrobe entity, and slips into a deeper stupor for the sleeping period. She has no fear that Storm will find the contraband—nor any hope of that.

Taking Chances

Back at the project, Strong has made a particularly promising contact with an alien mind. While maintaining his hold on the contact, he talks to his monitor.

"I think this is the one, Dark. Get Mind–Storm down here. I vote we isolate and focus the chamber on this alien mind."

"Why this one, Strong?" Dark–Lights asks.

"I seem to be really tuned into it. It's the right one because it's the one we can get the best fix on."

"Okay. I'll send out a message for Dr. Storm."

Dark sends out a telepathic message to Storm's office, and he comes relatively quickly.

"Strong, are you sure you want us to put our resources into this one?" Storm asks. "You know that once we've made the decision, we're stuck with it. We don't have resources to squander on false alarms."

"Look, Dr. Storm, all I can tell you is that it's the best one that's come along. There might be better ones down the line, but we'll never be able to tune into this creature's mind again once we've tuned it out. Why don't you connect up with it and make your own conclusion?"

"Are you trying to be funny? You're the telepath and mind-melding specialist, not me. If you say this is a good bet, then we'll go with it. I just want to be sure you understand the importance of this decision."

"I do, but it's only a best bet. Do you understand that,

Storm?"

Storm chuckles. "Touché. I guess we'll have to live with this decision." He turns to Harmony, who has also come to the focus chamber. "Dr. Harmony-Lights, set it up. Make sure we don't lose our connection with the alien subject."

Schedules and procedures now have to change. This particular alien's mind must be kept in focus. This means that telepathic contact should never be broken. Telepathic specialists have to work in tandem so that there's always someone to take the place of the previous worker. It's always the anchor of the previous contact telepath who becomes the next contact telepath. Hopefully, that procedure minimizes the possibility of a broken connection. In that way, Dark-Lights takes over from Strong, she's anchored by someone else, and so on. Strong is the only team member who takes the process to the level of mind-melding. He increases the percentage of mind infusion very gradually.

Harmony continues her overall monitoring of that part of the program. She's given more management decision powers and responsibilities. She does, on occasion, fill in for another telepath, but only when absolutely necessary. She now shares her responsibilities with two other Gazeons who are there for two additional work shifts, although she maintains supervisory superiority over them.

"I've been working on this for three Deca-cycles," Strong says dispiritedly to Harmony as they spin their way to the project building. They live close enough to the project facilities to get there by non-assistive means. They find the trip to their jobs at the facility to be an opportunity to spend a pleasant time together.

"Watch out!" Harmony yells as a mass-transit entity careens out of control and heads for the two of them.

Strong reflexively uses his ram-jet bio-mechanism to spurt away from danger. As he does so, he extends pseudopods around Harmony to pull her with him. Their lights flicker frantically in the fright of the moment. Then gradually, the usual gentle rhythm of the lights returns.

"It's been a long time since I've had to use my jets. What kept you from using yours?" Strong asks.

"I haven't jetted since I was a teenager. I'm afraid I'd blow myself up. It's been known to happen, you know," Harmony answers in a shaky voice.

The mass-transit entity has come to a halt slightly off to the side and below them. The entity's master is looking sheepishly out a transparency.

"Either your creature needs a good puncturing or you do, you foul gas nincompoop," Strong screams as he approaches them with breakneck speed.

Harmony hastens after Strong, fearing the worst.

"Why don't you look where you're going, you son of a thistle slug?" the entity master screams back at him, waving a hammer-shaped pseudopod.

"If you had the lights to get out of that membrane-less transit thing, we could have a more definitive discussion," Strong says evilly.

Harmony puts a soft pseudopod on Strong to soothe him. "We have more important things to do than to beat up on stupid people," she says. "Don't you think?"

Strong's lights, which are burning a fiery red, begin to soften to a more soothing color.

"Yeah. But he could have killed us."

"But he didn't. Let's get on our way and let him bang into someone else. We're behind schedule."

Strong abandons his confrontation and spins onward toward the project building. "As I was saying, it's been a long time, and we haven't made much progress."

"That's not completely true," Harmony contradicts. "You've put forty percent of your consciousness into the entity's mind without mishap. That allows us to go a little further without undue risks."

"At this rate, the cyclone season will have come and gone, and we still won't really know anything," Storm complains.

"That's the only reasonable way to proceed. This is too important a project for us to become foolhardy."

"With that kind of attitude," he counters, "we wouldn't have gotten even as far as we have. We have to take some chances."

Harmony doesn't like the trend of the conversation. "Did you notice that I've changed my shape a little this cycle?"

Strong, who has not noticed, observes quickly. "Of course I did. It's very becoming. Kind of swept back. Very sexy."

"I'm so glad you noticed," she says with the merest hint of sarcasm.

Several cycles later, in the focus chamber, Strong reaches out with the tendrils of his mind. He enters what is, by now, a well-known pathway. The idea of a pathway had been foreign to the practice of mind melding and telepathy, but now it's commonplace in the focus lab. The path wanders through what is like a complex of building-entities. Strong allows ten percent of his mind to flow into that space that something tells him is the right place, the spot where the creature will become aware of him when there is enough of Strong to make himself known. Another ten percent fills the alien's mind. Ordered thought forms are loud and just on the other side of coherence, but still on the other side. Thirty percent more of Strong's mind flows, and as in the past, the thoughts are even louder. But there's no recognition of Strong's presence on the part of the alien.

Forty percent.

Forty-five percent.

"We're at the outer limits now," Dark says to him. "You're allowed another five percent."

Strong seeps in.

Suddenly, there's a very subtle difference, a kind of pre-recognition in the alien's mind.

Strong feels a surge of his own excitement. He tries to hold it down so as not to alarm the entity.

"Whoa, what was that?"

Strong creeps in a little more, cautiously. Recognition still remains unmanifested.

"Stay calm, Strong," Dark cautions. "Stay where you are and get used to the new feeling. We'll keep the creature here for you on the next cycle."

Reluctantly, Strong stays at forty-six percent. Dark continues to anchor him with words of restraint.

On the next work cycle, Strong moves in with fifty-five percent of himself as he penetrates the alien mind. Yet awareness from the creature remains below the level of consciousness. Strong feels both excitement and disappointment.

On the following cycle, Strong is sharing sixty-five percent of his consciousness with the creature. But there are still no further results.

Strong and Harmony are in Dr. Mind-Storm's office. "I don't understand it," Strong complains. "What's going on? I keep becoming a more significant presence, and the creature doesn't seem to react to it at all."

"I have a theory," Storm says. "Were you ever floating along, minding your own business, and then suddenly you noticed that it was really hot?"

Strong and Harmony give gestures of confirmation.

"Did it actually get hot suddenly?" Storm asks.

"Well, no," Harmony answers.

Then their lights brighten. "The temperature changed so slowly that I didn't recognize it till it got to a certain uncomfortable point," Strong says.

"Exactly," Storm declares.

"Are you saying that all I need to do is keep putting more and more of my mind in the creature's mind, and sooner or later, it will notice me?"

"Not necessarily," Storm responds. "With temperature, there's a danger point. There's a threshold that we must recognize or suffer physical damage. That may not be the case here."

"You mean Strong could be 100 percent mind-melded with the creature and it still wouldn't notice his presence?"

"Yes. After all, when healing gases are injected into a sick Gazeon, he may feel nothing at all, even though there's a substantial amount of that gas within him."

"Then all this effort may be doomed to failure," Strong says dejectedly.

"No, no. Even if we never get the alien's recognition, there will probably come a point where you'll be able to perceive its world through its senses. That isn't failure. That's success. But there's a way that we haven't tried that might get its attention."

Mind-Storm floats around the room in circles as he expounds. "What would happen if you experienced the same change of temperature that we were just talking about, with one difference? That difference being that the temperature changes rapidly."

Harmony understands immediately. She hopes she's wrong, and for once, she hopes that Strong is stupid.

However, Strong brightens and says, "I would have noticed the change in temperature way before it got as extreme as it did in the first example."

"Exactly."

"So, since we don't know the alien's tolerance, I don't dare waste any more of my mind by introducing it slowly into the creature. I have to go in quickly with the rest of myself," Strong concludes.

"That's too dangerous!" Harmony protests. Her lights begin to show a growing alarm.

"I agree there's an element of danger," says Storm. "To do this risks Strong's welfare and also the project's interests. But there are high stakes here. There's so much more we could learn with the open cooperation of this being."

Harmony wants to protest further, but she knows better. Once again, she feels deep foreboding.

"Strong," Dr. Mind–Storm says, "you're going to have to make the decision. Whatever you come up with, and for whatever reason, I'll go along with it."

Harmony floats motionlessly, knowing the only decision Strong is capable of making.

Trapped

As Harmony and Strong leave his office, Storm looks fixedly at both of them. He feels genuine concern for Strong's safety, but he's also clear that honesty was maintained. Perhaps he downplayed the degree of danger, but after all, Harmony certainly pushed the point. Not supporting her point of view was not the same as pushing Strong into taking chances. This was the time when faint lights would lose the moment of opportunity that would forward Gazeonkind to new heights. If anything bad were to happen, his conscience would be clear.

Storm's mind roams to his yet-to-be-born child. When was the last time Luster went to the obstetrician?

Well, he thinks, I'm sure she's doing what's necessary to assure her health and the health of my child. I've got my hands full dealing with my job. I just need to trust that she's doing hers.

Yet in the back of his mind, he feels something amiss. Something in the way she looks. Her lights are dull. The colors are muted, and the patterns are erratic.

That's probably just what happens to pregnant females, he thinks. After all, a lot of their energy must go into the growth and nourishment of the bubbling. I always thought that pregnancy caused a female to glow more brightly. But then again, what do I know? I'm not a biologist. It's Luster's job to look after her health. She has plenty of credits to buy the best medical care and the best consultations.

Storm becomes aware of an irritating sensation on a mid-underside point of his ovoid body. Automatically, he forms a pseudopod with a brush-shaped tip, which he reflexively uses to brush away a tiny creature.

Damn bug-entities! They get into everything.

His brush pseudopod morphs into one with a pincer-like tip. Suddenly, it elongates and catches the tiny creature and squeezes it until it bursts. A miniscule amount of foul-colored gas explodes out of the puncture.

Ugh, what a smell!

His mind returns to his mate and her pregnancy.

She does seem less attentive, he thinks. But there's a good side to that. She isn't bothered by all the times I end up sleeping in my study. I guess she's becoming more independent, and that's what I need right now. These conditions won't last forever. Things should start to get very interesting around the focus chamber very soon. The dull, patient work is about to pay off.

Back at the Focus Chamber

To Strong-Presence, melding with the creature is like floating along a well-known path within a complex of utility-entities, except that the functions of these alien structures are a mystery. He prepares himself to take that dangerous leap into the unknown. He takes the equivalent of one final breath and flows quickly, like quicksilver, into that promising area of the creature's consciousness. There is no longer any reason not to move rapidly. He gets all the way to the seventy-percent infusion level before he begins to feel the faint beginnings of recognition from the consciousness he's invading. Strong's vital signs quicken in anticipation of a great and dangerous transition. There remains only one thin strand of consciousness, reminiscent of a silver cord, that connects him to his corporeal body.

So here I am, he thinks. What happens next?

Little happens at first. Then there seems to be a slight distraction. Strong tries to communicate an image of knowing. He tries to broadcast an abstract concept of "I want you to know that I'm here." Since there is no material commonality between them, Strong is left only with abstractions as an option. But there is a sense of heightened awareness coming from the alien. Strong feels a surge of encouragement and continues to broadcast the *knowing* abstraction.

Suddenly there comes a totally unexpected reaction. The being is rejecting Strong's presence.

Why is it doing this? he wonders. I don't understand.

At first, Strong feels only confusion. He's not threatened. He has always considered the creature to be mentally inferior, having little mental capacity with which to harm the obviously more highly-developed minds of Strong's own species. It is with growing shock that he realizes that there is intensifying mental pressure.

Hey! That's beginning to hurt!

The sensation is similar to the pressure he felt when diving as deeply as he could into lower recesses of the Gazeon atmosphere.

I don't understand how a creature with such underdeveloped telepathic abilities can generate so much mental pressure, he thinks. It's getting pretty bad. I think I'd better get out of here. I'll worry about how it does what it does when I'm back in the safety of my own body. It sure is surprising.

"Get out of there now, Strong!"

Strong hears Dark's thoughts as though in the distance.

"Don't worry. I'm on my way."

Strong starts to flow back down through the thin, still-present silver cord. Suddenly, he feels his way blocked. This is an experience no Gazeon has ever had before. At first, Strong is puzzled. He's too surprised to feel fear.

"Come on, Strong. Get out of there," Dark urges.

"I'm trying. Something's wrong. There's a force holding me back or blocking my way."

"That's impossible," Dark says.

The pressure is still building, and it's becoming very uncomfortable. For the first time, there's a dawning sense of meaning emanating from the creature's thought forms.

"Kill!" the thought forms say.

Storm realizes abruptly that creature intends to kill *him*.

"Get out of there! Get out of there! You are Strong-Presence. You can do it. Do it now!" Dark screams at him.

Strong tries. He tries harder than he's ever tried to do

anything else in his life, but the crushing, squeezing force bearing down on him robs him of his power. In the focus chamber, his vital lights are beginning to dim. Dark-Lights holds onto his consciousness telepathically. She's refusing to let go. She feels his psychic vitality waning. Strong loses whatever strength he has left and panics. He feels the restrictive, suffocating world about him becoming faint. The fire of his self-awareness dies like an oxygen-deprived candle flame in a closed jar, until there's just the faintest hint of a glowing ember.

Dark-Lights holds onto the dying ember that is Strong-Presence. She sustains that ember with all her telepathic ability. When that fails, she does what she's never done before. She allows a little of her own consciousness to flow into Strong's remaining consciousness, fanning the flame of life. It's only the slightest amount of herself, just enough. It's far too little for the creature to notice. In the meantime, she screams for help with her physical voice. Harmony shoots back a telepathic message that she's jetting to Storm's office for assistance. She had started in that direction the moment she perceived the situation.

Moments later, Mind-Storm comes rushing back with Harmony. She briefs him in scant words as they come. There's an ashen texture to his usually bright, crisp lights. His staff has never seen him in such a state. That adds a deepening level of foreboding to Harmony's troubled emotional state.

"How long can you sustain him, Dark?" Storm asks.

"I'm not certain," Dark says with her physical voice—which has a distracted quality to it since so much of her attention is focused on Strong. "Probably for at least to the end of my shift. More, if I have to," she says reassuringly.

Harmony and Storm relax slightly. They have time to think.

"So the problem is not keeping him alive for now," Mind-Storm says, "but what to do to bring him back? Do you think you'll have any trouble reviving his body?"

"I don't think so," says Dark. "I could energize his body now.

After all, he *is* Strong. But if we revive him before he escapes, the alien might be threatened somehow and just crush Strong's consciousness again. Won't he?"

"Very possibly," Storm answers.

Harmony asks, "Then how will he escape?" Her lights are blinking at three times their normal rate, and their hues have shifted toward the red end of the spectrum. But coherence and rhythm are intact.

"Perhaps escape is unrealistic," Storm says.

"I don't believe that. I won't believe that," Harmony says, her lights and voice quavering.

"I mean, not immediate escape. Eventual escape, yes. For the moment, hiding may be more feasible."

Harmony waits nervously for elucidation.

"We've already determined that the alien's mind is broken into pieces that come together to make a whole," says Storm. "Strong is only in one part of that mind. It's the part of the mind that's probably most capable of being aware of another's presence. If Strong tries to escape and the alien becomes aware of it, that escape route might be cut off, and Strong's consciousness will be crushed to death. But suppose he hides in another part of the alien's mind, a place where the creature can't find him or even know of his existence. Strong could stay there indefinitely until he or we could find a way out of this. During that time, Strong could be fulfilling the mission of gaining knowledge about the creature's world and mode of existence."

Harmony glares at Storm. "Who the hell cares about that now?"

"Strong would agree with me, Harmony," says Storm. "You know that."

Harmony doesn't say what she wants to say. Instead, she suggests, "Why can't we just draw Strong down the silver cord? We could fully revive him when we got him back."

"You know as well as I do that we're pushing the limits of

mind-meld capability just to use it to keep him alive while he's joined with the creature's mind. We'll have to revive his awareness and somehow implant a plan that Strong will have to execute on his own. It will depend on Strong himself. He'll have to grasp it and carry it out. I can't tell you what his chances will be, but I believe it will be his only chance. He'll be on his own."

Another telepath is summoned to support Dark as she maintains her contact with Strong. Then Storm and Harmony retreat to Storm's office to work out a plan. Shortly afterwards, they return with their plan and instruct Dark, who will have to implement it.

Dark-Lights implants words that are expressed over and over again, as if to a sleeping Gazeon, in the hopes that the message is getting through to the sleeping consciousness. The message is simply, "Hide. Don't go back. Hide." They don't know enough of the creature's mind structure to make any suggestions concerning where or how to hide.

After what seems a long time, Storm instructs Dark to go on with the next step. With trepidation, she gathers her strength and allows that little bit of her that has been melded to the tiny ember of life to swell into her full mental stature. With all her power, she pours every bit of her mental vitality into the enfeebled Strong-Presence. Then, when she feels his self-awareness beginning to rally, she quickly withdraws and slides back down the double silver cord to her own body, before the effects of her efforts can be recognized by the creature. She lets go of her telepathic link at that point, too exhausted to hold on. Harmony, who is expecting that, establishes her own contact with Strong.

Strong, who is unaware of the fact that he's been unconscious, wonders why the pressure has suddenly ceased. He feels himself gaining strength, and then the pressure begins again.

This time he knows what to expect. He has time now to dread. The fear of death overwhelms him. He must escape. He tries desperately to slide down the cord to safety, but again, the creature squeezes his escape route shut. Panic overtakes Strong once more.

Harmony screams the message, "Hide, Strong! Hide!"

"Harmony? There's no place to hide. Help me!"

"Listen," Harmony commands. "You have to hide!"

Suddenly, Storm understands. Were it not for the messages impressed on his mind earlier, more precious moments would have been lost, and it would have been too late to hide. Was it already too late? Strong sends out probes of his consciousness into the area around him, like a gas looking for openings in which to dissipate. He finds one surprisingly quickly and seeps into it.

Immediately, the agonizing pressure ceases. Strong is relieved to the point of exuberance. He is alive—and for the moment, safe. He begins to take stock. All he's aware of is himself. There's no thought from the creature. Then, abruptly, he realizes that there's nothing else with him. Harmony's thoughts are gone.

He reaches down telepathically through the silver cord, trying to contact someone back in the focus chamber, but his thoughts are disorganized by some sort of force. Again, Strong feels a pang of terror, the terror of abandonment. But he manages to control it. He tries to decipher how his thought transmissions are being blocked. His growing experience with the creature intuitively leads him to the concept of denial. The creature is denying its experience with Strong. Strong's thoughts would not be allowed to exist in that awareness section of the creature's mind. The silver cord remains intact, but for all intents and purposes, he's cut off from his world.

Harmony has followed Strong's thoughts as he's wrestled with his panic. She witnesses the dawning of his intent to hide. Her own membranes are so tight with her anxiety that he might not make it that she fears they'll tear. She follows him into the dark crevasse, afraid to interfere with his thoughts. She doesn't want to distract him in any way.

Then she begins to feel a strange sensation, like a buzzing that becomes increasingly disruptive. She can't maintain the coherence of her own thought patterns. Suddenly, she's no longer connected to Strong. Nor is she, any longer, connected to the creature. Her vital organs whirl in a sea of despair and dread. She tries desperately, defiantly, to push through the static to reconnect with Strong. For a moment, she can sense the echoes of her beloved's waning thoughts trying to reach out to her. She's trying too hard to hold onto them to say goodbye.

The Earth Boy

Thirty days earlier, Zeke, a seven-year-old farm boy from Missouri, has his penknife out and is scraping some partially dried resin out of a wound in an old pine tree.

Zeke talks to himself as he works. "This here old pine sap oughta work pretty good. Nice and sticky. I'll just stuff it in the mast hole of my boat and then jam the mast into the hole. That sap oughta keep the stick glued there pretty tight."

Suddenly, he stops his work. The whites of his eyes show as he tries to look inside his head.

"What's that tickle inside my head? I don't like it. I never had a tickle inside my head before. Sure is a funny kind of tickle. Wonder how long it's been there. Oh my gosh, maybe a bug is in my noodle. It feels more like a buzz than a tickle."

Zeke stands there transfixed.

"You trying to say something, bug? Seems like you're trying to say something. I can't understand a word. What? You want to know something? What do you want to know? *Everything?* I don't understand. How do I know what you're saying when you aren't even speaking English?"

Abruptly, Zeke's curiosity turns to fear.

"Hey! You're not supposed to be in my head. You shouldn't be there. How did you get in there? Did you bore holes in my nose and ears? You better not be eating holes in my brain, like wormy apples. *Get out!*"

Zeke panics and drops his knife. He starts to run home.

"Papa will help me get the bug out of my brain," he says as he runs.

Abruptly, he stops.

"Bugs don't talk, and they don't make any kind of sense even if they *are* in your brain. What will Papa say if I tell him I have a bug in my head that's trying to talk to me and find out everything? He'll laugh at me, or even worse, he might take me to the doctor. The doctor might cut my head open to find the bug. Maybe the doctor will make me go to the loony bin that Tommy's always joking about. Nobody will be able to see my bug, and they'll think I'm crazy. I can't tell Papa. I can't tell anyone. What am I gonna do?"

Zeke stands there, scrunches his eyes closed, and frowns as hard as he can.

"I'll squeeze you out of my brain, bug. That's what I'll do."

The bug starts to buzz frantically. Zeke squeezes harder.

"I'm gonna scrunch you dead. I don't like having a dead bug in my head, but that's gotta be better than one eating up my brain and everything it knows."

Zeke squeezes his eyes shut as hard as he can. His forehead wrinkles in exaggerated concentration.

"Take that you, damn bug. I'm gonna kill you dead!"

The buzzing gets quieter and weaker, to the point that the boy can no longer hear or feel it. The effort has made Zeke very tired, and his head muscles ache. Although exhausted, he's not too tired to play. He finds his pocket knife, goes back to the pine tree, and finishes gouging out the resin. He stuffs the resin into the hole for the mast of his little boat and then forces a straight stick in there.

"Sure am glad that bug is dead. I hope he stays dead forever. He better not try coming back."

Unexpectedly, the bug begins to stir again.

"Oh, no, I thought you were dead! I even almost forgot about you. You sound like you're scared. Oh, I'm sorry. I'm really, really sorry. But I can't have you eating holes in my brain. I can tell you're just trying to get out of my head now that you know I've got to kill you for good. But you may eat a hole just to get out. Besides, how do I know you won't bring back your friends? I'm sorry, but I gotta kill you for good this time so you won't never come back again. Mmmmmm," Zeke grunts as he squeezes with all his physical and mental energy.

"Hey, where you going? That's not the way out. Are you hiding on me? How am I gonna scrunch you if I can't find you? I can't hear you anymore. Where are you? I know you ain't dead. Where'd you go to?"

As the buzz of the Gazeon invader's presence vanishes from the boy's experience, so does his memory of it. The only remnant of the experience is a vague sense of Strong-Presence's intent—*the desire to know everything*.

Zeke threads a big maple leaf onto his stick mast and watches the breeze blow the boat to the opposite side of a little pond.

How does the wind make the boat go? he wonders.

He runs around the pond to intercept his toy and reaches down to pick it up.

It feels wet, he says to himself. Why does it feel wet? Why does the breeze blowing on my wet hand make it feel cooler? I never thought about those things before. I really want to know. I want to find out about stuff like that. Didn't the radio last night say that college was a good place to find out about all kinds of stuff? I gotta get home and tell Papa I'm going to college.

Zeke finds his father with a huge lug wrench and a mallet, trying to bang a bolt loose on their tractor wheel. For a split second, he looks to Zeke like the print on the living room wall of a farmer engaged in chores, but when he hears the solid clank of steel on steel, the illusion is broken.

I'm gonna be as big and strong as Papa when I grow up, he thinks.

Tom Isacks pauses to regard his youngest son for a moment. Then, slamming the mallet down on the end of the lug wrench once again, he returns his attention to the task at hand.

"I need a bigger lever or a bigger hammer." His voice isn't perturbed. There's a trace of humor in it that comes from a lifetime of facing stubborn, sometimes seemingly impossible problems presented by everyday farm life.

"Stubborn nut. One way or another, you're gonna loosen. May take a while, but gol darn it, you're gonna turn sooner or later." He swings the big hammer again. The nut does not budge.

"Papa, I want to go to college."

His father stands up from a half-kneeling position with a slight creaking of joints and an appropriate moan and walks off toward the adjacent tool shed. Inside, there are enough tools to supply a hardware store. They're all neatly stacked, hung, or enclosed in their proper places. Tom finds a four-foot cast iron pipe about an inch in diameter, hefts it, and walks back to the tractor.

"Papa, I want to go to college."
"I heard you, son. Why?"
"Because I want to learn about things."
"What things?"
"Everything."
"That's a mighty tall order. How come?"
"I don't know. I just do."
"Since when?"

Zeke pauses to think about it.

Yeah, since when? he asks himself.

"Well, since just a while ago."

Tom sighs. "You know, Zeke, there's a lot to learn about on this farm. And what you learn on a farm will always stand you in good stead. If you know what you're doing, it'll feed you and take care of you. If you don't, it'll break your heart and you'll lose it— if it doesn't kill you first."

"But I want to learn about things out *there*."

"Look, Zeke, one summer's afternoon of wanting don't amount to much. Probably by this evening, if I let you alone, you'll forget all about it."

"I don't think so, Papa."

"Well, we'll see, won't we? In the meantime, I'm sure your mother has something she needs you to do."

Zeke puts his head down, slightly disappointed by his father's reaction. But actually, it wasn't so bad, he says to himself. At least he didn't say no. He didn't make fun of me. He just doesn't think I mean it. He thinks I'm gonna forget about it. Well, I'm not gonna forget about it. I'll show him.

As Zeke trudges toward the large family house, he passes the varied edifices that testify to the diversified nature of the family enterprise. But he barely notices the everyday structures. His mind is somewhere else as he passes the tall silage steeple, the red hay barn, and the stanchioned milking building.

When Zeke approaches the main house, the free-ranging chickens scratching in the back yard make way in cackling protest as he plows through them. He mounts the wooden stairs to the veranda, plunks himself on the wooden bench, and begins to take off his shoes, which have accrued helpings of chicken manure.

"Don't bother to take them off. I've got something that we need to do in the milking barn," his mother says as she comes to the door.

"Aw, gee whiz. I'm tired. How did you know I was out here?"

"Zeke, you don't exactly tiptoe up the stairs, and you seem to revel in exciting the chickens. It probably cuts down on their egg laying."

Isa Isacks steps out on the porch wearing a clean, flower-print apron and holds out another for Zeke. She's just an inch shorter than her husband. At thirty-seven years of age, she maintains an enviably flat stomach, although her unadorned features are on the plain side. Under her sunbonnet, her hair is pulled back into a bun. But a wisp of dark hair that has a strand or two of grey in it has fallen out in a curl along her left temple. She strides out with a calm urgency down the stairs and through the hens, her body straight and farm-wife strong. Somehow, the fowl do not bluster as they did with Zeke, who follows closely behind with a dragging quality to his gait.

"I found something that looked like dirt on the bottom of the family milk bucket before I put it in the ice cooler," his mother tells him. "So we're going out there and scouring every last milk bucket we have. This evening, I'll have a talk with the family. It won't be my fault if everyone takes ill and dies in a hospital filled with bad bugs."

"But Mama, that's only one dirty pail. The rest of them are probably fine!"

"If you have one bad one, you can't take a chance on the rest of them. Now quit arguing with me. You'll need your strength for cleaning all of them, and that includes the coolers."

"Aw, gee whiz." That's all Zeke says, because he knows he's reached his allotment of protests.

Somewhere in the middle of scrubbing, Zeke remembers what he wants to tell his mother.

"Mama, I want to go to college."

Isa straightens up and looks with keen interest at her little boy.

"Do you even know what college is, Zeke?"

"I know it's a place where you learn about things, and I want to learn everything.

"Since when?"

"That's what Papa asked me."

"Well?"

"It's kind of funny. I kind of always wanted to know about things, but I just now found out that I did."

"Like what, Zeke?"

"I don't rightly know, Mama. Just about everything, I guess."

"Well, son, every day you wake up in the morning, you can start learning about things. College is a place where only the best learners get to go. The first thing you have to do is learn how to learn and get really good at it."

"How long will that take, Mama?"

"No telling, really. But most people who go to college don't go until they're about seventeen or eighteen years old."

"Wow! That's a long time."

"Not really, when you think about it. Because you'll be in school until then—if you even go to high school."

"Do I have to go to high school?"

"As far as I know, college is just a continuation of high school, only you get to learn more things."

"You mean college is just like high school?"

"I've never been, but that's my idea of it. Zeke, you've never liked school. Maybe college is not for you."

"I don't know why, Mama, but something got into me today. It's like I don't know nothing. I don't know what makes rocks, or what water is, or stuff like that. All of a sudden, I gotta know. But it's also like I always wanted to know. It's got me all mixed up."

"Well, about college, one thing is for sure. You have to be a good student in grade school and high school, or they won't let you in."

"So if I start right now being good in school, will they let me into college?"

"There'll have to be a way to pay for it, Zeke. Rich folk usually go to college. But I've always believed that where there's a will, there's going to be a way."

Human Gazeon

Meanwhile, back on Gazeon, despite several tries over many cycles, none of Dr. Mind-Storm's staff are able to pass through the static created by the alien. As far as they can tell, the silver cord remains intact and is viable. That in itself is a clear indication that Strong is alive. If he weren't, the cord would have dissolved into nothingness. Without Strong's immediate presence, the vitality of his body will diminish, but it will not die. As long as the silver cord remains in contact with his disembodied consciousness, the body will survive. However, the corporeal body will have to be nourished artificially.

The proper life-support entities are set up in and about the focus chamber, along with uninterrupted vigilance. Teams of telepaths monitor the silver cord. As long as it remains intact, the connection with the creature will be maintained.

Strong huddles in his crevasse, feeling the despair of isolation and abandonment. Slowly, reason begins to take hold again. He begins to evaluate his status objectively.

What's happening on the other side?" he asks himself. What would I do if I were in charge in the focus chamber, where my body is?

His reasoning takes him to the same conclusions that they are coming to back at the project.

As long as the silver cord remains intact and attached to my body, they'll keep my body alive and maintain surveillance. They'll do that forever if necessary. They'll try to get to me. Looks like I have all the time in the world to figure out a way to get back to them. However, right now, I have no chance at all. I need knowledge. Then perhaps I might find a way.

This place is just like when I was a mere bubbling and my parents took me to an amusement park maze entity. All these different rooms, in every shape and size and at multiple levels! They're all put together in a crazy bunch of patterns. It's impossible to make sense of it. There's no way to get a sense of direction. Now I don't know when I'm going up, down, or sideways. You'd better go slowly, old bubble, or you'll be hopelessly lost. Note every feature, every color, every everything. Go slowly and be patient. Humph, when did I ever have any use for patience? Well, you'd better learn how to be patient if you want to be alive.

At some point, Strong realizes that the silver cord is not trailing directly behind him but is going around corners and through corridors.

How and why, by the great gods of Gazeon, is it doing that? I didn't know that was possible. It's always gone the most direct route, disregarding any kind of materiality. Maybe it has something to do with the denser quality of this alien's thinking apparatus. Dr. Mind–Storm might be able to explain it to me when I get back—*if* I get back. In the meantime, I can use that aberration to my benefit. If I get lost, I can simply follow it back to my beginning point.

This alien entity is the weirdest thing I've ever encountered. Not in all my university training in mind–melding have I ever seen the likes of it. Some entities are self–aware to one degree or another. Others are without any kind of meaningful consciousness, just automatons. But this one is fully aware of itself in some ways, fully unaware in other ways, and in between in still others. That's not the worst of it. You can't count on which part is going to be aware or not aware at any time. It changes. How do they function at all? Well, maybe I should just be thankful for the unaware aspect of the creature's consciousness. How else would I hide from that vicious, primitive will to kill me?

As Strong continues his meticulous exploration of the environment in which he's trapped, he continues to make interesting and sometimes startling discoveries. At one point, he slides unexpectedly into a barrage of raw emotion. He pulls back as though he's touched the core of a hot whirlwind.

Whoa! You don't want any part of that, old bubble. Well, maybe just a little bit. I think I understand what that was. Finally, something I can relate to. This alien is angry. Definitely angry. I hope it's not something I said. Maybe I can stick just a little part of me into it—just enough to know what's going on emotionally with this creature but not enough to get overwhelmed.

Strong projects a small percentage of his consciousness into the emotional area.

That anger is mixed with fear, he concludes. The anger and the fear are fueling each other. I can certainly relate to that, Strong thinks. Maybe we have some things in common after all. Just the same, I'm glad I got out so quickly. Hmm, I hope the alien isn't always in such a foul mood. If I hang around awhile, perhaps it'll cool off. Then who knows how I might use this new fact?

As Strong hopes and expects, the emotions gradually dissipate into a relatively calm state.

I wonder what would happen if I projected an emotion of my own into that maelstrom? he thinks. Hold on, Strong. You'd better know a lot more about this creature before you risk your presence being detected again.

Strong wanders for many cycles without coming across anything else he understands. He's despairing about ever finding anything more when he hears something new.

That sound! It's different. Those aren't just the strange

noises coming from its thinking apparatus. It's real noise coming from outside this contraption. My god! It's speech. Not telepathy, but spoken language. Real, honest-to-god vibrating gas. Can't understand a word of it. But it sure sounds good. I've got access to the creature's hearing organs. So now I know it can hear. And not only that, it speaks. I wonder what else it does.

Strong gradually discovers the centers of the creature's other senses. He's dumbfounded when he sees what the creature sees. It's a world of visual impressions that at first make no sense to him. But eventually, as a baby learns to understand what it's seeing, Strong learns as well.

Mind-Storm was right, he says to himself. These creatures live in a world of solids, liquids, and even gases. It's incredible. I'm flabbergasted by how similar the alien's senses are to my own. They're close enough that I can understand what I'm experiencing. There are touch, smell, temperature, pressure, texture—almost the whole works. It doesn't seem to have any sense of more than just four dimensions. It's bound to lack perspective. I don't think it has practical telepathy, let alone mind-melding capabilities. Its chemical perception is also weak. I don't think we see colors in the same part of the spectrum. On the other hand, it probably has some senses I wouldn't know if they poked me. I don't have a clue as to how they manage to get around. They don't appear to float. They can't jet. They have no propellers. Their body shapes are bizarre. But it's wonderful. I'll never be able to explain this back on Gazeon—that is, if I ever get back home.

There's something missing, though. I'm still just an observer, watching what someone else is experiencing. I'm experiencing what the creature is seeing. I'm not seeing it firsthand. I'm looking at a projection. I can't understand those projections. I get visual sensations, but I have no idea what's being seen. This being's surroundings and culture are so different from my own that I have no reference points. It's chaos for me. I can recognize some repetitive patterns, but that's all.

I need more. There must be some separate mechanism that enables the creature to integrate all these disparate inputs.

On the other side, maybe there *is* no separate mechanism. Maybe the alien's mind is a holistic phenomenon, where the whole is greater than its parts. Its consciousness could be an emergent quality. The mechanism I'm looking for may simply be the entire mind functioning in all its parts, without any one separate coordinating device.

What would happen if I spread my consciousness throughout the entire mind? After all, that's what I do when I mind–meld with a Gazeon. But with a Gazeon, you're not dealing with this kind of divisional mind, but rather with a holistic mind.

Hey, slow down, old bubble. Remember the magic word? Patience. Remember how you got into trouble in the first place. Learn more. Take it slowly.

So Strong continues his slow, methodical exploration of the creature's mind. He hasn't given up on the idea of a mind–meld with the creature. As his knowledge and experience accumulate, he comes closer to taking the risk of a mind–meld, which he now refers to as a matrix–meld when applied to this alien and its strange mental qualities.

Eventually, the sheer need to make something change, to make something happen, overcomes his caution, and he prepares to do the matrix–meld.

Strong begins to infiltrate all the areas of the creature's mind.

It's like filling the holes of a sponge entity, he tells himself. Stay sharp, old bubble. Be meticulous. Be in control of every slight change.

He feels his consciousness taking on the quality of shape. The sensation of mind taking on shape is not as foreign to him as it once was. The time spent in the focus chamber exploring different parts of the creature's mind has prepared Strong somewhat for mind being related to topology.

All this disjointedness of separate compartments! he thinks. It's still too foreign. Too strange. Go slow, pal. Hey, wait a moment. That's a strange feeling. It feels like I'm becoming... what? It's...it's like I'm changing in some strange way. I'm...I don't have a word for it. There's something Mind–Storm said. Something about gas, liquid...solid. Solid! I'm becoming solid! I'm becoming one with the creature's mind. Liquid, solid, slow. Everything's going more slowly. I'm slower. No, not just slower: integrated. I'm becoming integrated into its matrix. I'm getting a sense of wholeness, a sense of everything coming together. I should back out. No, no... I'm in control. I can let a little more of myself become absorbed, integrated. I'll be okay. I can't stop now. I'm on the brink of a breakthrough. This is a completely new way of being. A new sense of wholeness.

But as the human brain absorbs the mental energy of the Gazeon, it claims it as its own. Strong is only vaguely aware of his loss of self–determination. Suddenly, the realization hits the small part of him that has not been incorporated.

Oh, no! It's pulling me in. I've got to fight it. Pull back. I'm Strong–Presence, a Gazeon. *I am a Gazeon!* I am... I am... I... I am...

I am Zeke, a small human boy.

Strong has been overpowered by the host's mind to the point of complete identification with the human. Yet all that he was, he still is. The Gazeon remains as part of a new symbiotic entity. The little boy Zeke is as changed by this relationship as Strong is. The qualities of both organisms have been enhanced.

Thus, Strong continues his mission, even if he's not aware of it. The mission is to learn all that he can about the creature's world.

Heart–Break's Birth

In the cycles immediately following Strong's capture, Dr. Mind-Storm holds fast to his resolve not to feel remorse if such a disaster were to occur.

At the end of a work cycle, after having dictated notes into his recording entities, he stops to reflect.

It's not that my gases are cold and that I have no feeling for Harmony and Strong, although I'm sure I must seem unsympathetic. On the contrary, I feel deeply for their plight. But the project must come first. Nothing can stand in its way.

As he says these words to himself, a metallic, silvery sheen permeates his membranes, as though they have become solid and impermeable.

I can't permit those emotions to dampen my resolve to keep this Other Worlds Project prominent in Gazeon purpose, he thinks.

In fact, there are potential benefits to the disaster. Strong is now totally involved with the alien. He will be so for an unknown period, perhaps forever. During that time, if he survives, Strong will have knowledge of the aliens and their world that will be monumental. Retrieving him would promote our species' evolution in ways we cannot begin to imagine. Even if Strong is never saved, the effort to bring him back will safeguard the program. Our society will never abandon a citizen to the kind of fate threatening Strong.

In the meantime, we have enough funding to broaden our

research to other related areas. Strong's situation assures that this funding will remain and even be increased. We'll be able to develop new facilities. So, all in all, progress is being made toward my goals.

The one consideration that can distract Storm's attention from his scientific dynasty is his anticipated parenthood. Uncharacteristically, his thoughts turn to the impending birth of his new little bubble. The metallic, silvery sheen fades and leaves in its place a pink skin, which allows soft, pastel-colored lights to twinkle through.

"What a scientist she'll make!" he says aloud. "She will carry on my work and bring it to heights not even I can foresee."

He daydreams wonderful pictures of the future as he's barely aware of having left his offices. His transport entity takes him toward his home. When he reaches his habitat, he floats distractedly through the opening aperture.

Abruptly, his thoughts are torn away from his reveries to the immediate world around him by the pungent, distinct smell of a birthing. He jets excitedly into Luster-Shine's sleeping compartment, his lights flickering with anticipation. But what he encounters turns him stiff.

The baby floats in a corner while Luster floats beside it. Fear emanates from every vital sign in her body. The baby's color is dull and grayish-green. Its pulsations are slow and lack crispness. The symptoms are unmistakable and undeniable. The baby's processes are permanently dimmed. Luster-Shine, her newly erupted birth membrane still in the process of closing, floats there with terror oozing from her tortured body, staring at Storm and waiting for him to react.

"Xenon deficiency!" he rages. "There's only one way for that to have happened, you damned drug pervert. You've ruined my child!"

An awful pause of dead silence ensues as Luster watches Storm's lights turn into a dark swarm of chaos.

"Storm, no! Please!"

"You fucking stream of putrid gases! You—you—"

"I'm sorry. I'm sorry. Please don't hurt me. Please—"

But Storm is deaf to her pleas. He rams into her as hard as he can, all reason blotted out by his mindless fury.

Luster's body distorts grotesquely before slowly returning to its normal ovoid shape, although her birth rupture threatens to seep internal gases.

The horror of what he has just done brings back some small semblance of awareness to Storm's raging mind. Realizing that he cannot contain his murderous impulses, he attacks the wall entities, not stopping until gases are leaking out of them.

Storm's own membranes are dangerously stretched, bloated and discolored. But he is oblivious to the pain. Finally, the angry intensity of his lights dims, and he cannot continue his raging. He stops, floating, waiting for some energy to return to him.

"How long have you been addicted? Why didn't you tell me you were having a problem? Didn't you know the risks you were subjecting my baby to? Who is your supplier? Why— What— How— Where—?"

Luster, having caught her breath, is filled with her own rage, which has been accumulating for many cycles. "Tell you? How the hell was I supposed to tell you anything? You're never home. We're not really married. You're married to that goddamned research. I can't even talk to you when you're at home. Home! That's a laugh. It's just another laboratory. We never do anything together."

Luster wants to ram the walls of her abode like Strong, but she feels the pain in her body, especially around the birthing rupture. Eventually, overwhelmed by guilt, with her anger spent, Luster breaks down and begs for forgiveness. But her pleas fall on deaf sensors.

"Don't try to lay the guilt on me, you stupid drug pervert," Storm tell her. "Your selfish hedonism has destroyed your daughter. You'll have to live with that, not me."

Storm turns away from her and floats into his study, ordering the walls to close. But in his innermost being, he knows that every accusation she has thrown at him is absolutely, undeniably, devastatingly true.

After a sleepless sleep cycle, Storm sets out to locate a wet nurse without informing Luster-Shine. Three days later, when the wet nurse is scheduled to come, Storm approaches Luster-Shine as she tends to the baby.

"Get out," he tells her.

"What? This is my home."

"Not anymore."

"I won't leave my baby."

"If you cared about your baby, you wouldn't have destroyed her with drugs."

"She needs me. I have to make it up to her."

"The best thing for her is to never have to see you again. The same goes for me. I've got a wet nurse who will do a better job than you ever could. She's not an addict. Now get out before I throw you out."

"No, please!"

Storm wraps pseudopods around her and drags her to the exit opening. She fights, but in the end, she loses. She is cut off from her baby and her life. Storm hires thugs to see that she doesn't return. When she tries, he watches from a window aperture as she's roughed up. Eventually, she's dragged off in a vehicle entity, screaming for her baby and for mercy. Three times she tries to return, and three times Storm watches coldly from within his abode.

By the time the wet nurse surmises what is going on, she realizes that to leave would be to endanger the damaged infant by exposing it to the rages of an out-of-control male.

Three days after Heart-Break's birth, Storm goes to work as usual. He wears an emotional straitjacket that makes him even more impervious to others than before. With his great powers of concentration and compartmentalization, he's actually able to function effectively in the technical aspects of his work.

But others do notice that there's something wrong. They perceive a coldness that warns others to stay away. His usual fiery passion for the work is gone. What remains is an automaton, pre-programmed, and therefore relentless in its mission.

Even after her failures to physically gain access to her baby, Luster-Shine tries to gain custody of the child through the legal system. But with the combination of Storm's financial power and the irrefutable fact that she had consciously endangered the welfare of her unborn child, the court not only awards Storm full custody, but also forbids Luster-Shine to ever see her offspring again.

After the success of his vendetta, Storm continues his cold, harsh administration of the project. The soul has gone out of him, though, and only the devotion of Dark-Lights, Harmony, and some of the other staff members with very personal connections to him gives real life to the rescue mission. Storm's scientific insights never fail him, and although reluctant, others go to him for help.

Storm's Breakdown

Half a season later, Luster–Shine's body is found dead of an overdose. Her bloated body had begun to float almost out of sight in the atmosphere.

"Dr. Mind–Storm, there are two constables requesting to see you," a clerical assistant says, floating apprehensively at his office aperture.

"Tell them to go away. I have no time for them."

The assistant leaves dutifully but reappears a short time later.

"I told you to tell them to go away. Why are you back here?"

"I'm sorry, sir, but they gave me this for you." She hands him a preserved membrane with writing on it.

"Damn it. Okay, send them back here."

Two bulky law enforcement Gazeons are brought to his office. Their inner lights are nearly monochromatic. They seem bored and unimpressed.

"What is it, officers? I'm very busy."

One of the officers, who has a scar on the upper forepart of his body, says, "We need you to identify a body."

"Why me? What's it got to do with me?" His voice is sharp and impatient.

"We think it's your wife." His lights show no modulation. His voice is matter-of-fact.

"I don't live with my so-called wife anymore. We're in the process of divorce."

"We know. But you still need to come down to the morgue to identify her."

"Why do you think it's Luster-Shine?"

"Please, sir, we haven't got all day. I have a court order here if I need to serve it."

"Oh, never mind. I suppose you want me to come down right now."

"Yes, sir. We do. If we wait any longer, the membranes will burst, and then there will be little way for you to recognize her."

Storm grabs a communication entity and begins to spin hastily out of the building.

They arrive at the morgue. Storm has never been in one before. They bring out the body, enclosed in a transparent net of membrane. At the sight of Luster-Shine's bloated, decaying body, something breaks in Storm. He suddenly remembers how beautiful she once was.

"Oh my God! Oh my God! What have I done?"

He remembers what they were like together at the beginning. All the denial, the guilt, and the self-loathing regarding his negligence and cruelty overwhelm him. His brittle self-discipline shatters. He starts spinning erratically out of control while crying hysterically.

"I'm sorry! I'm so sorry! Please forgive me! Please... Oh, God... Please..." As his voice loses coherence, his lights turn dark and chaotic. Bursts of dark red and spikes of brilliant additional colors flash randomly, the way a tempest swirls and discharges electrical impulses.

Outside the morgue, in the ancillary part of the building entity, Storm's wailing and the accompanying turmoil of the others attempting to restrain him startle the staffers.

"What the hell? What is all that noise in the morgue?" attendant Milky-Glow asks of her lab technician coworkers.

"I don't know. Do you think we need to go see?" Hesi-Pod ventures timidly.

Jump-Squirt is already on his way to investigate. The others follow, with Hesi bringing up the rear.

As they approach the morgue portal, it fails to open at their approach.

"Damn, they've blocked access. I sure hope that's what they intended," Jump says.

He jets to an observation port, where a transparent membrane allows visual access.

"Oh boy, this is crazy!" Jump says.

The others squeeze around his viewport, trying to see. In the meantime, other personnel from other departments rush in and make a clamor almost as loud as the violent ones within the morgue.

Jump sees two detectives and the coroner trying to contain a Gazeon gone mad. The berserk Gazeon rams into one wall and then another. As the others try to contain him, he spins into them with his jets so that they're bounced around like deflection game balls. All the while, the crazy fool is screaming gibberish mixed in with vile curses. As far as the astonished onlookers can understand, the halfway intelligible words are directed against himself.

"That idiot is going to bust himself," Sergeant Taught grumbles as he feels his own outer membranes still vibrating from his last encounter with Storm's maniacal rushes. "Peidball, will you please tell me you brought your net?"

Peidball, the other officer, is jarred into sudden understanding. "Oh, yeah." He forces his body to momentarily take on the shape of a corrugated surface, which reveals a web-like structure made of bubble skin that is all but invisible against his smooth body. With pain born of multiple impacts against walls, ceilings, and bodies, he manages to extract himself from the webbing.

"Where should I put it?" he asks Taught.

"Anywhere. Just make it fast."

Peidball casts the netting across a portion of the room. In a matter of seconds, Storm's blind, hurtling body ensnares itself. Before he can bounce out of the netting, Peidball and his comrade grab the open ends and expertly maneuver the contrivance into the shape of a net bag. Still, Storm's jets pull them all over the room, banging their hanging-on bodies as though they're tied onto a runaway riding-beast entity.

"Green, will you kindly get out of that corner and help?" the sergeant manages to say between bruising bounces.

Green, the coroner, narrowly dodges the onrushing net-enmeshed Storm and somehow succeeds in grabbing onto one of the officers. With the added weight to drag around, eventually the exhausted Storm lies still, pulsating in a spent stupor.

Luster-Shine's remains have been battered about the examining room of the morgue. Gazeon bodies, when they die, usually become bloated as gases change and expand, causing them to rise higher than the relevant biosphere. Eventually they burst, and the congealed elements sift back down to the biosphere and beyond. Consequently, many Gazeons disappear without a trace. Luster-Shine's remains now lie on the floor of the morgue. She is a limp membrane, bearing only the most limited likeness to the living being she once was.

"Doc, are you all right?" the sergeant asks the coroner.

"I think so," Green answers tentatively. "I'll call the mental hospital. This guy is going to need a long rest."

"Yeah," the sergeant responds. "If he ever gets out, let me know. I'll leave town."

The next work cycle, Dark and Harmony are astonished to find that Storm has not shown up. Time passes, and they become concerned. A call to his home by Dark, when she is alone in her office, brings the voice of a strange woman.

"This is Dr. Mind-Storm's residence. Can I help you?"

"This is Dark-Lights from the project. Is Dr. Mind-Storm there?"

"I'm sorry, but Dr. Mind-Storm is ill."

"What? What's wrong with him?"

"He's in Mercy Mind Hospital. You'll have to talk to them. They won't tell me what's wrong."

"Excuse me, but with whom am I talking?"

"I'm the wet nurse and nanny for Dr. Storm's child."

"But—but—I didn't know Storm had a child," Dark says, astonished.

"I ain't supposed to talk to anyone about it, but things being the way they are, I ain't gonna keep me voice shut up any more."

"Of course. Where is Luster-Shine?"

"Dead, I'm told."

"Good heavens! When did that happen?"

"All I know is that Dr. Mind-Storm was asked to go down to the morgue and point out her remains. The next thing I know, they're calling me and telling me he's in the hospital. Do you know how I'm gonna get paid?"

"Don't worry about that. We'll get that all straightened out. Just take care of the infant. I'll get back to you as soon as I can."

"Okay, but if you ask me, he as good as killed her himself. I wouldna took the job if I known what he planned. Threw her out in the wild gases to fend for herself, he did. Got bangers to keep her from coming back to gets her baby. Wasn't nothin' I could do. Couldn't let the poor little retard die of starvation now, could I?"

"Of course not. You did the right thing. We'll take care of things for you. Just give us a few cycles. Do you need any credits right now?"

"No. Dr. Mind-Storm let me have rights to the bank. Someone with that much money can take chances with it, I guess. I won't be packing it away. Lord knows I couldn't carry it anyway. I'm a good, honest citizen. He as good as punctured her himself, I says."

Dark–Lights terminates the connection. Then she slowly and dazedly floats out of her office to join Harmony in the focus chamber to share the news and make plans.

"Dark, what's wrong? You look like you've seen a ghost," Harmony says with concern.

"Worse. Did you know that Storm's baby had been born?"

"I knew it was due sometime soon. I was wondering why he wasn't talking about it. Why? Has anything happened to Luster–Shine and the baby?"

"Luster–Shine is dead."

"What? Oh, no! That's awful. No wonder he isn't here. Was she sick? Storm has been acting funny lately. Is the baby okay?"

"I don't know, Harmony. But I just finished talking to the wet nurse. She accused Storm of killing Luster–Shine."

Harmony stares at her, stunned into immobility. "I don't understand. I didn't even know they weren't getting along. How did he kill her?"

"Oh, I didn't get the impression that he committed murder directly. Hell, Harmony, I don't know. All I know is that Storm is currently in a mental hospital."

All the sensory organs in Harmony's body widen to three times their normal size. "In a *mental* hospital? What have you been sniffing, Dark? This isn't making any sense."

"No, it isn't. I'm going to have to get more information," Dark says. "What are you doing now?"

"I'm about to monitor a new team who are in contact with a new creature in focus chamber two."

"Don't let any of this get out. Get someone to cover you, and get down to my office right away."

"Of course," Harmony answers.

Later, in Dark's office, the two Gazeons face each other.

"Harmony, you and I can run the operation—at least for the short run," says Dark. "The first thing I think we need to do is call the hospital. I didn't want to do that without you. Besides, you outrank me."

"We can't afford to stand on ceremony here," says Harmony. "Neither one of us can get through this crisis without the other. But I appreciate your bringing me in before you made the call."

"Isn't Mercy a psychiatric hospital?" Dark asks.

"Yes."

"You ought to make the call, then, because that's your field of expertise."

"You're right, of course. I'll find out what I can, and we'll have to proceed on the basis of that. But there's a good chance they won't tell me anything."

"Why not?"

"Because a Gazeon's health is considered a confidential matter, particularly where mental health is concerned. They're probably going to be very hesitant to give me that kind of information because I'm not part of the therapeutic team. But I'll do my best to pull strings. This project is a top government priority, and scruples often go out the window in this kind of matter. I know, because the government was not very ethical in getting Strong and me into this program to begin with. I'll make the call, and if they get tight-lipped, I'll sic the military on them."

Harmony summons the communication entity floating in its spot within Dark's office. As it comes to her and she's about to give it instructions to connect her with Mercy Hospital, it suddenly gives an alarm, indicating that someone is trying to get in touch with her via the same device. Somewhat startled, she opens the communication channel and sets it on speaker mode so that Dark can hear and be a participant in the contact.

"Hello, this is Dr. Harmony-Lights. Can I help you?"

"Oh, Dr. Lights, this is Dr. Mind-Bender. I'm the hospital administrator at Mercy, and you're exactly the person I wanted to speak to. I've been trying to chase you down all cycle. I didn't realize that you and Dr. Strong-Presence were not actively involved in providing therapy at this time, but there's a case of utmost importance, and we need the very best team to work on it. I was hoping that you and Dr. Presence would consider working on it, or at least advising."

Harmony and Dark look at each other in astonishment.

After an uncomfortable pause, Harmony says, "The patient involved wouldn't be Dr. Storm, would it?"

"Why, yes. How did you know?"

"Dr. Bender, I work in the government project that Mind-Storm is heading. In other words, he's my boss, and we were just informed by his child's wet nurse that he was hospitalized at Mercy. In fact, I was just going to call you."

"Oh, my. Then I suppose you can't take on the case."

"No. It would be a conflict of interest, of course. But Dr. Bender, it is of utmost importance to the project that I know what his status is."

"Ah...this is highly awkward. You know we can't give that information to anyone who isn't part of the treatment team."

"Yes, I know it's irregular and involves container-entity loads of ethical issues. But this project is top government priority stuff. They will definitely lean on you, and I'll get the information anyway. In fact, because of my knowledge of this man, I think I should be in a consultant role."

"Dr. Lights, even if the government does force me to divulge confidential information in the interest of national security, how can you personally aid and abet such goings on? You have your own professional ethics and oaths to deal with."

"Because, Dr. Bender, my husband's life could well depend upon what happens to this agency and its leader. At the moment, I don't have the luxury of fine ethics."

There is another uncomfortable pause before Bender continues. "I can sympathize with your position. It would protect my membrane if you did actually get the government to put me in a situation where I was not given a choice about the confidential issues. Do you understand me?"

"Perfectly. I'll get back to you."

Once again, Harmony and Dark are left alone, staring at each other.

Finally, Dark says, "I think getting the power people on this is my job."

"No question about it."

Dark engages the communication entity, and within a fifth of a cycle, Harmony finds herself at Mercy Hospital with the best assemblage of mental health people that can be roused in that short a period.

Coming Back

At the mental hospital, Dr. Mind–Bender watches the catatonic figure through the observation portal. Harmony floats alongside him as they both gaze at Mind–Storm. A fine mesh net prevents the protrusion of any pseudopods that he might use to hurt himself or anyone else.

Harmony feels a mixture of conflicting emotions. There is shock at seeing her unassailable and masterful boss reduced to this insane feebleness. The rage she has always harbored at his encouragement of Strong to take chances competes with the fear that her one hope of getting Strong back now lies deep in the unreachable depths of Storm's hidden psyche. As ruthless as he was, Storm always projected hope and confidence.

"Harmony, you mean no one in the whole operation ever even knew he had a child on the way?" Bender asks.

"That's right, Bender."

"That amazes me. You and I go back a long way, and I know just how perspicacious you are. How did you let that one get by you?"

"Bender, you have to understand the project, the circumstances I find myself in—and most of all, Mind–Storm. That Gazeon is of demonic or heroic proportions, whichever way you want to see him. He didn't invite you into his private life, and you didn't dare trespass there. The idea that there was any vulnerability just didn't fit him."

"But Harmony, those characteristics are themselves signs of

a brittle psyche."

"I know, I know. But believe me, when you work for him, you simply don't see those things. Besides, my clinical perceptions were focused purely on Strong's dilemma and getting him back. Very personal stuff. I *needed* Storm to be invulnerable, invincible. We all did. In fact, we all still do."

Bender shakes his head in disbelief. "Well, that's not the version of Mind–Storm that you're apt to get back—if you get him back at all."

"We don't know what we'll get back," Harmony says. "You're talking theory. You don't know that Gazeon yet. But I know there's no one else able to do a better job than you. I'll cooperate all I can. I also need to work on getting Strong back."

"Fair enough."

Storm feels the anguish of one of the seven Gazeon Hells. His membranes are stiff to the point of absolute rigidity. His internal gases are stagnant and barely able to move at all.

This is like the world of the alien, he thinks.

He is totally alone. There is no one to reach out to. No one to complain to. No one to offer him solace.

I am here for eternity, he thinks.

Suddenly, he is aware of another being.

"Who the hell are you?" Storm asks. "Are you my tormentor?"

"You mean tormentor as in Hell?" Mind–Bender asks.

"Yeah. That one."

"Do you think you're in Hell?"

"Where else would I be?"

"Why not Heaven?"

"Why not go fuck yourself?"

"Why so hostile?"

"Look, if I have to spend the rest of eternity with you answering every question with a question, I don't have to be polite."

"Why do you believe yourself to be in Hell, Dr. Storm?"

"I'd tell you to get lost, but that isn't an option in this Hell, is it?"

"Storm, I know you won't believe this. At least not yet. But you're not in Hell. You're not even dead."

"So why can't I move, and why is my body like a solid?"

"That's what I hope you'll tell me eventually."

"I asked you a question. Who the hell are you?"

"I'm Dr. Mind–Bender. I'm a mind healer."

"I don't need any stupid mind healer."

"You're in a catatonic fit, imagining that you're in Hell, and you're telling me that you don't need your mind healed. That's pretty crazy."

"I know what the inside of a hospital looks like, and this isn't it."

"I know what you see, Storm. I'm in your mind, and I'm looking at things with your senses. You think you're in a world where gases don't move and flames stick up rigidly, like hard scalpel entities. But it's a world you've conceived for yourself. I have to know why."

"You don't have to know anything. You're my tormentor, and part of your job is to confuse me, to give me false hope. You know damned well why I deserve to be here."

"I admit I have some idea. After all, I did do a social investigation. But it's important for you to tell me."

Storm fixes his visual receptors on a dagger of blue–green flame and refuses to say any more. Bender fades out of his perception.

Bender finds himself back in Storm's confinement room. He gives the coded command to the door entity and floats to the special office the government has made available to him for this special assignment. He summons his communicator entity and makes a call to Harmony. Within the cycle, Harmony calls him back.

"Have you made any progress yet?" Harmony asks.

"I think so. This is the first time he acknowledged my presence. He actually communicated with me."

"That's wonderful. Did you get anything out of him?"

"Yes. He admitted that he deserved to be in Hell."

"So he's punishing himself."

"Of course. His conception is of eternal damnation. He won't speak of his reasons, though."

"I wouldn't expect so. When he does, that will be a large part of the battle that's won."

Storm feels his membranes splitting open. He feels the tearing agony cascade through his entire being. He waits for the final burst of searing pain when his gases will explode into the Stygian darkness surrounding him. But the tearing doesn't stop. The tearing never completes itself, and it never ends. His gases remain confined. It is the second Gazeon Hell.

Mind-Bender feels some of the agony within himself as he perceives it through Storm's senses. Despite cycles of training and practice at isolating the patient's experience in order to protect himself from it, the power of the agony is so great that Bender must concentrate just to maintain his focus on his patient. He begins to understand what Harmony was trying to tell him about this Gazeon's power.

"Why are you here, Storm?"

"You know why I'm here," Storm grits out through screaming senses.

"It doesn't matter whether I know or not. You have to say it."

"Can't you see I'm busy, you imbecilic demon?"

"Busy doing what, Storm?"

"Oh, for God's sake. Are you that stupid?"

"That would be the greatest crime of all. The crime of stupidity, wouldn't it?" Bender shoots back.

"No, there are worse crimes."

"Are you guilty of worse crimes?"

"Go spin yourself into a fan entity, you nincompoop."

"Your daughter is stupid. Isn't she?"

Storm's imagined self turns into blind rage. He attacks Bender with such ferocity and quickness that even though Bender expected such a response to his last prod, he is caught off guard, momentarily paralyzed. He wills himself out of harm's way only after receiving an initial psychic blow.

"What's worse than being stupid, Storm? Stupid people don't deserve to live. They should be punished for it. They should suffer all the Gazeon Hells," he taunts.

Suddenly, Dr. Mind-Bender is back in the restraining room. The transition is abrupt. Bender shakes his head in wonderment at his patient's strength. He leaves the catatonic Storm floating almost lifelessly in his restraining net.

Storm's body is bloated to twice its normal size. Putrefying internal gases extend his outer membranes to almost, but not quite, bursting pressure, as Storm suffers another Gazeon Hell.

"You ought to just let your membranes split. It might end the agony," Bender says. "Oh, but that's not really the point, is it?"

Storm does not reply. Neither does he utter a sound, although it's quite obvious, by the chaotic bursts of energy and twisted internal patterns, that he's in extreme agony.

"When will you have suffered enough?" Bender asks him. "Watching you like this cycle after cycle is getting rather tiresome."

"How terrible for you, demon," Storm strains out.

"You may condemn yourself to eternal damnation, but it isn't fair to the others that need you. In fact, it's the most selfish act I've ever witnessed. And I've seen more than my share."

"Nobody needs me."

"Do you want to tell me about it?"

Storm bursts out laughing. "Why would I want to do that?"

"Oh, I just thought that you might have found some courage somewhere in all this self-indulgent masochism."

"Courage? I don't know what you're talking about."

"Let me tell you, then. All this self-flagellating is simply to distract you from facing what you did. It's a coward's move, a retreat against the real battle."

"And just what would that battle be, demon?"

"Facing yourself. Instead, you wallow in self-pity and pain. You can face your indulgent, self-inflicted agony, but you can't face yourself."

Bender has thought out this approach for some time. In a way, he feels defeated, because it would have been much better if Storm had given some opening and thus taken the lead. But obviously, the Gazeon is able to hold out indefinitely, and Bender is under pressure to make something happen. If this direct approach doesn't work, Bender has no idea where to go next. What's worse, if he tries to lead Storm, the effect could instead be cutting off a possibility that Storm might have eventually discovered for himself.

But Storm doesn't reject or accept the notions that Bender has presented. He remains silent and pensive.

"If you want to do real penance, Storm, you're going to have to do that which is most frightening and most punishing to you," Bender tells him.

At this point, Bender chooses to make a strategic retreat. He doesn't want to risk an oppositional standoff with Storm. *Especially* not Storm. Better to let the suggestions assimilate themselves into his patient's psyche.

He leaves the ward and spins to his office.

When Bender returns to the safe room, Storm's body is floating there as usual, deaf and blind to the real world. With some trepidation, Bender initiates his mind meld. He thinks he's prepared for anything. But despite that, he's taken totally by surprise and is almost overwhelmed by a sense of panic. There's nothing, just a total blank, a void. Bender feels himself a disembodied spirit with no bounds. He desperately reminds himself that he is in a maximum security hospital room.

Pulling himself together, he manages to say, "You can flee, Storm, but you cannot hide. All you're doing is proving how colossal your ego is. It encompasses the whole universe."

A booming voice emanates from the very essence of existence. "My evil encompasses the whole universe. I am King of Hell."

Bender is terrified. The non-beingness that has become Storm's universe, the universe within himself, actually exudes a feeling of evil. But Bender still manages to say, "You're just a coward, afraid to face your own reality. You're a megalomaniac who probably never had the courage to face the rejection of his own parents."

Bender is fishing, but the words he speaks are well founded in clinical experience.

Suddenly, the nothingness is split by a kaleidoscope of multicolored lightning bolts crisscrossing the universe with blinding intensity and mind-numbing thunder.

"Shut up! My parents were proud of me. I earned their respect and pride. I was the best. I *am* the best!" His voice expresses absolute authority housed in a citadel of rage. Yet Bender detects the underlying bluster.

"Yes, you were the brightest. They were proud of your mind. But without your brilliance, they would have given you to a wet nurse and pretended you didn't exist. Stupid people do not deserve to live. They do not deserve to be loved. They are to be reviled for their ultimate sin of retardation. Storm, it doesn't matter how smart you are or how much you accomplish. It will never be enough. And now you have sired an imbecile. You deserve to rot in all the Gazeon Hells. You and your feebleminded child. Since she has no father, she will be committed to an institution, where she will receive no love, as is deserved. Then she can join you in your Hells when she reaches her long overdue death. I'm leaving. I can see that you are where you belong."

Bender has put all his cards on the table. It is now or never. Storm either breaks now or remains in his self-torment for the rest of his life and probably beyond. Bender wills himself out of Storm's mind and finds himself in the hospital room with the lifeless body.

But that body begins to stir. A voice starts to rumble out of it—soft at first, then culminating in a desperate, "No!"

Then the body is shaking with sobs.

Bender sends out a telepathic message to a hospital aide. "Send in my lunch. I'm going to be here for a while."

The journey back has begun.

New Beginning

Mind–Storm remains in the safe room for the next twenty sessions. Mind–Bender becomes convinced, early on, that Storm poses no danger to himself or others. Still, he deems it preferable for Storm to request an end to his isolation. When the patient desires fellowship, it will mark readiness for the next therapeutic milestone, the desire for social involvement.

"Dr. Bender, I don't know whether to ram you or embrace you."

"Tell me about it, Storm."

"I hate it when you do that, Bender. It's such a cliché."

"And we definitely don't want the great physicist to be accosted by a cliché," Bender says.

Storm chuckles, then dips to acknowledge a point for the psychiatrist. "There's absolutely no doubt that you saved my life, but I'm not sure I'm better off for it."

"Oh?"

"Those monosyllabic words are driving me crazy." After a long pause, "My whole *raison d'être* was to be the smartest guy in my neighborhood. Then to be the smartest guy on Gazeon. Now I'm not sure who or what I am."

"I guess you're going to have to find more basic purposes, Storm. Isn't there anything else in your life that's worth doing, anything besides being smart?"

Storm's lights dim as he focuses his attention inward. After an interval, they brighten again. "When I first met Luster–Shine, my overwhelming purpose was to make her my wife. That was the only thing that mattered."

"How did you win her?"

Storm's lights begin to blink on and off in accompaniment to his sudden, spontaneous laughter. "The way I've won everything. With my brilliant intellect."

"So what you're saying is that your intellect served a purpose greater than itself?"

Storm's lights freeze where they were, as though stunned into immobility. "By Gazeon, you're right." Another long moment of silence ensues. Then he lets out a plaintive sigh.

"What's going on, Storm?"

"Once I won her, she ceased to be so important. My intellect took over proprietary status. I became detached."

"How do you feel about that?"

"Damn, there you go again."

Bender remains quiet and does the equivalent of a Gazeon stare.

"I didn't feel anything about it while it was going on. Now I'm mortified. Get the hell out of here, Bender. I need to be alone."

Dr. Mind-Bender does not challenge this. He turns around and spins out of the chamber. He immediately goes to the one-way observation portal to watch his patient. All his lights smile as he watches Storm crying his heart out.

The following session, Bender directs attention to the material of the previous encounter.

"Are you ready to continue where we left off, Storm?"

"Aren't you being a little directive, Bender?"

"Non-directiveness is way overvalued, Storm. Besides, I'm the therapist here. Don't tell me how to do my job."

"Sounds like you're getting caught in a little counter

transference, Doc."

"That's right. You see me as someone else to get an advantage over, and I'm putting you in your place. But I'm not the patient, Storm. You're approaching your therapy the way you've approached everything in life. You dominate everyone with your superiority. Is that where you want to stay?"

"No! But humility is hard for me."

"What else is going on, Storm?"

"Self-loathing. I can't get beyond it. Don't worry. I'm not on the verge of slipping back into psychosis. But every time I recognize how all my behavior led to Luster-Shine's death, I just can't stand it. I retreat to being Super Brain."

"Why are you reading all those psychology books, Storm?"

Storm laughs the equivalent of a spontaneous guffaw. "I was wondering when you'd ask me that. And I've got the answers. One, to play that one-upmanship game we just played. The other is to really understand myself."

"Is it helping?"

"No, it's just a head game."

"Well, it's been fun sparring with you again. But I've got to get on with seeing some other patients."

"You mean you have other patients?"

"See you next time, Patient." Bender exits, leaving Storm dissatisfied on purpose.

A later session:

"I want to see my daughter, Bender."

"Oh?"

"Yeah. I figure the best way I can atone for what I did to my wife is to take good care of my daughter."

"So your motives are to atone for your sins?"

"Damn you, I didn't see that."

"Let me know when you come up with a better reason. See you later."

The session has only lasted moments before Bender is spinning out of the isolation ward.

As soon as Bender settles himself in the next session, Storm fixes him with his gaze. "I know what the better reason is for wanting to see my daughter, but I'm not there yet."

"What is the better reason?"

"Not one reason, actually. Many reasons. The first one is that I love her. But I can't feel that yet."

"The second reason?"

"I'm her father. Whether I'm a whole person or not, I owe her what fathers owe their children. She needs a parent, not just a housekeeper."

"So you're saying you can't see her before you can love her?"

"You know that's not what I'm saying."

"What are you saying, Storm?"

"I have to see her as soon as possible. She needs my love, and I'll have to learn about love from her."

"Does that seem logical to you, Storm?"

"Not logical, just true."

"Good job, Dr. Storm."

"I can't undo the evil I've done to Luster-Shine. But if I can learn to love Heart-Break, I'll feel better, even if I don't deserve to. So I'm still being selfish."

"There's nothing wrong with a little bit of selfishness. You're not competing for sainthood. A certain amount of egocentrism helps everyone. Besides, you can't claim all the blame. Luster-Shine was still responsible for her actions, and her behavior has played havoc with her family. She knew what kind of chances she was playing with her child's life."

"She wouldn't have done it if I had been any kind of mate. Hell, even if I had just been a good friend!"

Mind-Bender gives a dismissive blink of his lights. "Regardless, what do you think should happen next to get you closer to being able to see your daughter?"

"Are you asking me to direct my own therapy, Doc?"

"Yes, at least for right now."

"I think I need to get out of this God-forsaken isolation room."

"I agree. By the way, Heart-Break isn't the only person who can teach you how to love."

It's not long after that when Storm is taken out of the maximum security safe room. He is offered his own private hospital quarters but elects to stay in an open ward.

"Still self-flagellating, Storm?" Bender asks.

"No. At least I don't think so. There's been an area of my education that is sadly lacking. I've never really been around average people. I've always been among the elite. I don't know what gives common people their sense of self-worth."

"But Storm, these are hardly ordinary people. They're all crazy."

"Yes, I know. But that merely scrapes away a lot of the façade. If I can learn to relate to them on their level, maybe I'll have an easier time of relating to myself."

"Very well, but the private room is available to you whenever you feel you want it. Tell me, Storm, what do you want as your most immediate goal?"

"I want to start visiting my child."

"Out of penance?"

"No. As you pointed out to me, that would just be self-indulgence. Outside of her needing a father, I need to love that part of myself that I guess I was always afraid my parents would reject. As you said, I was always brilliant, and I never dared be any other way."

And so it goes. Storm goes from being a callous, ruthless, single-minded tower of strength to someone whose sharp edges are softened by a new dimension of sensitivity.

Within the cycle of a season, he's ready to take his private room, but not to live in. He's come to understand that the project he had devoted his life to really is as important as he had always assumed it to be. He needs to get back up to speed concerning the project's status. Eventually, he regularly devotes a full work cycle to studying reports and recording recommendations. So his influence is gradually reintroduced to the project personnel. However, he does not yet have direct contact with those people.

Storm and Dr. Mind-Bender float facing each other in Bender's office.

"Bender, I'm having a problem."

"Mmm."

"It's time I faced the personnel. I need to do that as a step before I move back into my position. Assuming, of course, that I still have my position."

"Let me assure you of that. When you're ready, the government will split its membranes to get you back in the saddle. So, what's this fear all about?"

"You're right. It is a fear. But I'm not sure what it's about."

"I've got a hunch. Tell you what. Make a list of all the people you know in the project. I'll monitor your vitals, and we'll see which ones cause the greatest internal reactions."

"Okay."

Storm begins reciting all the names he knows. His recall, as always, is 100 percent. Bender, who has the capacity through training and Gazeon nature to monitor Storm's vital signs, observes closely. When Storm mentions Strong, the vitals peak. When he mentions Harmony, they go off the scale. At the end of the brief recitation, Bender just looks at Storm and waits.

"'It's so obvious, isn't it?' Storm says. "I could have prevented Strong's situation. I could have saved Harmony from unbelievable grief, grief that never has the opportunity for closure. I don't know how to face her. I don't know if I ever will."

"And if you don't?"

"The most important thing is that Strong and Harmony won't have 100 percent of my resources to resolve this unthinkable horror. Secondarily, I will continue to live as a moral coward the rest of my life. But how do I face Harmony?"

"I don't know, Storm. There are no good answers. I do know, though, that you'd better be clear as to what kind of reaction you're looking for from Harmony and what reactions you're willing to accept."

Gradually, Storm spends more and more time at his abode, building a relationship with Heart-Break and her caretaker. He increases his communication with the project personnel via communicator entity. Then there's an occasional appearance at a board meeting, which is chaired by Harmony or sometimes Dark-Lights, who is subsidiary to Harmony. But he's there in the role of a consultant, not as a boss.

Storm and Bender, as is their habit, once again float facing each other in Bender's office.

"I think I'm ready to start taking over command again," says Storm.

"Oh?"

"You don't seem to be too encouraging about it."

"I have a concern."

"What is it?"

"I'll talk to you about it after a while."

"So you're just going to throw me into the monster's lair and tell me you'll talk to me after it's eaten me."

"Something like that."

Storm is puzzled and bothered. It's with less than supreme confidence that he leaves Bender's office.

Many cycles later, Storm and Bender are facing each other once again.

"It's not working," Storm says.

"Oh?"

"Something's missing."

"Where?"

"Good question. Somehow, I feel it's with me. But I don't know why. I have more compassion and more understanding of how the staff thinks, what the personnel issues are, and nothing is wrong with my mind."

"What do they need from you that you're not giving them, Storm?"

"What do you mean? I'm giving them more of myself than I ever did before."

"What did you give them before?"

"I gave them ruthlessness. I gave them a will that didn't know how to bend. I gave them contempt for what they didn't know or couldn't figure out on their own."

"How would you evaluate their morale, Storm?"

"It's not bad. Except that they're understandably discouraged about their progress with Strong's dilemma. There's a lack of spark, somehow."

"What about their efficiency? Their work ethic? Their focus?"

"By my old standards, I would consider those things wanting. But that's when I had little concern for their feelings."

Bender sighs.

"I don't understand," Storm complains. "I just spent all this time getting in touch with my compassion, and you seem to be disappointed in my expression of it."

"Storm, what do they need? Not what do *you* need."

Storm floats in silence for a very long time. Bender feels no discomfort in the vacuum because he can sense it is a pregnant one, in which a new insight is dawning in Storm.

"So that's the way it is," Storm finally says. There's a sound in his voice that Bender hasn't heard for a very long time.

"Yes," says Bender. "You've hidden your hard edge. They need that from you. I've met all the key participants in the project. No, *your* project. They'll never admit it, but they need the crusty ruthlessness from you. They depend on that image, that unswerving sense of direction without compromise. They even need you to manipulate them against their will. Oh, they'll do all right without it. Hell, they'll do all right without *you* if you can't give it to them. But the ambitions of your project need these qualities from you. And I know that if Strong is ever to get back, it will take the kind of single-minded high-handedness that only you can give the program."

"That means I'll have to hide my feelings almost all the time."

"Are you strong enough to do that? Are you willing to make that sacrifice?"

Storm smiles. "It's strange. I have to go back to the way I was on the outside, but changed on the inside. Before, I was unaware of my weaknesses. Now I'm pitifully aware of them. Yet to act the way I was once will take more strength than I've ever shown before. Life is a mystery."

"Yes. Isn't it wonderful?"

"Bender, after I've received a clean bill of health from you, are you going to leave the area?"

"It's an uncertainty. I know what you're getting at. You'll need someone to consult with about your thoughts and feelings while you battle in this new world. I'll be there for you as much as I possibly can. But there are no guarantees."

At the end of that work cycle, Storm carries out his first new ruthless act. He calls the military.

"General, this is Mind-Storm."

"Well, hello, Dr. Storm. It's good to hear your voice. What can I do for you?"

"I'll make it short, General. If you want this project to stay on a good footing, you'll have to guarantee that Dr. Mind-Bender is always available to me whenever I need him."

"But Doctor, that means he has to stay around here. He won't even be able to go on vacation."

"I'm glad you understand. And General, I don't give a damn if he knows who pulled the strings on him."

Harmony, Widow?

Sometime later (Earth equivalence: one year) in Mind–Storm's office.

"We've been working on this problem for ten seasons (Earth equivalence: thirty years)," Harmony says to Mind–Storm. "We've made no progress in saving my husband. I don't know whether to give up and go on with my life, or whether I should keep trying until I get old and develop leaks in my membrane."

Mind–Storm remembers when her lights were lighter and brighter. "I can't imagine what you must be going through," he says with uncharacteristic sympathy. "I've been wrestling with this whole thing, trying to come to some conclusions. All I can do is look at all the possibilities."

"Have you come up with anything new?"

"Maybe not new, exactly. But we haven't sat down and talked about it. I think we should before you make any decisions."

Harmony sighs. "Why not? I don't see how it can make things worse. Tell me your thoughts."

"Well, first of all, we know that the block is caused by the alien. We know that it's a rather young specimen. At least it was at the beginning of Strong's entrapment. I think it still has most of its lifetime ahead of it. But eventually, it's got to die."

Harmony interrupts. "Do we know that for sure?"

"Yes, we know that because of the work we've done in the other focusing chambers built since Strong's mishap."

Harmony's lights respond to his choice of the word "mishap"

with a static electricity quality on the edges of some of her lights.

Storm notices her reaction but ignores it. "We've been able to determine that the alien was young by the relatively unstructured quality of its mind. We kept pretty good records in those early times. Quite a lot of information was gleaned in those few moments before the barrier went up. So we can compare the organizational qualities of Strong's alien with our more complete and longitudinal records of the new aliens we've contacted since."

"Yes, yes, I know all that, Storm. Their minds become more structured and more organized as they mature. Get to the point."

"Please, Harmony. Be patient and let me develop my line of reasoning."

"There was a time, Doctor, when you didn't have enough patience to explain anything. Now you're trying my patience with your endless prattling."

Storm recognizes her allusion to his mental breakdown. Prattling is not a kind or accurate description, but he knows that Harmony holds a longstanding and growing resentment regarding the part he played in her husband's disaster. He understands and does not respond to the half-hidden barb.

"Some of the older minds are in the process of disorganizing."

There's silence as that information is absorbed by Harmony.

"Are you sure?"

"I'm positive about my analysis."

Harmony turns away from Storm and floats into a corner of his office. She stays silent for many moments while she integrates the new information. Then she turns back to her boss.

"I guess that does support the idea that the creatures age and die."

"In fact, Harmony, their life span appears to be much shorter than ours. Strong will still be a young Gazeon when his captor disintegrates," Storm says with a note of triumph.

"Do you think that damn static that keeps us from reaching

my husband will break down as the alien's mind breaks down?"

"That's what I'm hoping."

"Then he can come back home?"

Storm knows that Harmony is now talking out of hope, not an objective scientific perspective. She's looking to him for confirmation. He wishes he could give it to her.

"There's a good chance of that, but I can't be certain."

Harmony's lights become hard and opaque. "So we have to sit around waiting for that monster to grow old in the hopes that maybe, just maybe, it'll let my husband out of prison. We don't really know for sure."

"I can't deny that. On the other hand, it could die from causes other than old age. It could happen just a few cycles from now. We have accidents here, so it stands to reason that they have accidents in their world as well. There's also illness."

"So what the hell happens if the damn thing dies? Does he take Strong along with him, or does Strong find his way home?"

Storm doesn't say anything. He waits.

Harmony continues. "I wish I knew what condition Strong is in. If the creature dies of illness, he might take Strong with him into death. Strong might be incapable of taking any kind of action on his own by this time."

"We have the silver cord under constant surveillance. The moment we detect the slightest weakening in the barrier, a telepath will try to contact Strong and attempt to bring him back. And Harmony, try to have a little faith in Strong. He is, after all, Strong–Presence. If anyone can come through this, he can."

"Okay, Storm. I'll stay around, but I don't know how long I can do this."

Harmony stays with the project for the equivalent of three more Earth years.

Then there is a time when she finds herself supposedly monitoring two telepaths who are working in tandem to keep watchful consciousness on Strong's body and the silver cord. The cord is barely perceptible to the naked eye. It goes only a very short distance before it disappears into nothingness. But the telepathic eyes can trace it into another dimension, where it connects to the alien and then Strong, beyond the creature's mind barrier. But Harmony is not really watching the telepaths; her attention is fixated on the awareness–empty body.

Suddenly, she turns and jets desperately out of the focus chamber. She heads directly for her office.

Dark-Lights is passing by and sees that something is very wrong. Her colleague's lights are chaotic and pale. She spins after her.

"Harmony! Harmony, wait! What's wrong?"

Harmony doesn't seem to hear her. Dark-Lights follows her into the office. She waits for some semblance of order to return to Harmony's light patterns. She moves in closer as that begins to happen.

"I can't do it anymore, Dark. I just can't. I'm worn down. If I stay here, I'll die. Every time I have to be near him, I just see a lifeless, unaware body. It's waiting there, just like the rest of us, for the master to come home. But I don't think he's ever going to come home."

"You don't know that."

"It doesn't matter. I'm feeling so out of balance that I'm no good to anyone. I've lost all perspective. I'm no good for the project. I'm no good to Strong, and I'm no good for myself. I've got to get out of here."

Dark drapes a pseudopod across Harmony's now quivering orb. "Maybe you're right. Maybe you need to get back some sort of life. I'll be here looking after Strong's welfare. I promise."

"I know you will, Dark. I couldn't have made it this far without you. You've been more than a colleague. You've been a friend." She reaches out with a pseudopod and entwines it with Dark's.

She leaves the project and tries to get on with her life, but she never feels free. Strong is always there, haunting her. How can she find another mate when Strong is not dead? So, although she goes through life's motions and even learns to laugh again from time to time, she's always waiting for Strong to come home.

Five Earth years later:

"Doctor, as callous as this sounds, it doesn't make any sense for me to continue to anchor Storm's mind," Dark–Lights says as she floats into Storm's office. "He seems quite connected to his body. It doesn't make any difference what we do. We can't establish communication with him or with the creature."

"You can't be suggesting that we abandon Strong, are you?"

"Of course not. But it's not a job for one of your best telepaths and mind–melders. Any apprentice or graduate student could do it. In fact, babysitting is more challenging," she says.

"Strong isn't dead, and eventually he can be saved. I'm confident of that," Storm affirms. "We don't know when the opportunity will present itself. Won't you be disappointed if you're not there to take advantage of such an opportunity?"

"Of course. But waiting around for it is like waiting for your goldank to win a race. I don't enjoy waiting around for that sort of thing to happen."

"You're not just waiting around, Dark. You're second in command in this entire project."

"What that boils down to, Doctor, is that when I'm not babysitting, I'm doing paperwork."

"That paperwork involves making important decisions every work cycle."

"With all due respect, you make all the really important

decisions. Being a bureaucrat was never my first choice."

"Well, what do you have in mind? As if I didn't know," he replies.

"The newest focus chamber is just about ready to be assembled. I believe in the work, and I want to be on the newest team."

Storm looks at her, a slight twinkling in his lights. "What part do you want to play?"

"I have more experience now than anyone else in the program. I'm not just a promising operative any more. I want to direct that part of the program. I want to be membrane-deep in the moment-to-moment action."

"I have Steady-Course in mind for that job," Storms says.

"Have you spoken to him yet?"

"Ah, no."

Dark-Lights floats, waiting for him to give a more complete response. Her inner clouds are fluctuating in intensity and rhythm, like a human swinging its foot with impatience.

"Dark, there will come a time when a change happens in Strong's mind, a time that will offer an opportunity for him to return. When that takes place, I want you at my disposal to be the point Gazeon. I want the best one in that situation, even more than I want the best in the newest focus chamber."

"You can make Steady-Course my backup. He can take over my responsibilities at a moment's notice," she says emphatically.

"Yes, but what if you're in the middle of a breakthrough with a new alien contact?"

"What if I'm on vacation? Or what if I'm too sick to get out of my sleeping chamber? You can't rely on me alone to be there at the critical time. Actually, Harmony would be better than me in those circumstances."

"I'm not so sure about that. Harmony is unreliably emotionally involved. We need a cool mind for that situation. Besides, you know Harmony has not been associated with the program for some time. She would need time to get back in the groove."

"Harmony is a quick study," Dark argues.

"We don't even know if she would accept getting re-involved."

"Storm, if she thought there was a real change, a real chance, she couldn't refuse."

"You're probably right about that. There's no sense in talking about it at this point. Anyway, I'm not against giving you the position. In fact, I anticipated it. I had to make sure that you had thought about the possibilities."

"Then I've got the job?"

"Did you ever doubt it, Dark?"

Twelve-Year-Old Zeke

Twelve-year-old Zeke sits in the rural Missouri classroom. Mrs. Fitzsimmons is in front of the math class, standing as straight and rigid as a fence post, all five feet one inch of her. Stiff as a spike and thin as a rail. There are no curves, no bends, no give, and no weakness. The students that had terrorized Mrs. Kerner in geography class just fifteen minutes earlier are quiet and attentive to Fitzsimmons' slightest moves. Her hazel eyes dart from one end of the room to the other, like the eyes of a hungry cat watching mice trying to make a run for it. Every member of the class fears her. She carries a ruler in her right hand and slaps it lightly against her left palm. Never has she even threatened to use it on a student, but the warning is there. This is one force of nature that not even Mishi Capp will challenge.

Her eyes suddenly stop and fix on Billy McMann. Billy feels a cold chill run down his spine, and he stiffens, waiting for her words to descend upon him.

"Billy, go to the blackboard."

Billy wonders, Why me? But he also realizes that all in her class are game, and all are chosen from time to time. Besides, why should I be worried? he thinks. I know my math very well.

"Billy, divide 21 by 2,926.05."

Billy proceeds in a half-confident manner to do the fractional division. He is careful to show all the steps in neat and orderly numbers. All the numbers show in their proper places, just as Fitzsimmons desires. Billy knows the procedures and follows them precisely. He arrives at the correct number and in reasonable time.

"That's very good, Billy," Fitzsimmons says. "You may sit down now."

Billy walks carefully to his seat. He must be careful not to show any pleasure in his success. There are others in the class who would make him pay for any pleasure he might show in pleasing this nemesis of weisenheimer twelve-year-old males who are beginning to taste puberty. Also, no one really wants to please Fitzsimmons. They just want to survive her. He sits down in his desk chair, his right thumb and forefinger powdered with white chalk.

Again, her eyes scan the rows of students like an executioner choosing her next victim. Her eyes alight on Jackie Dornham.

"Mr. Dornham, please go to the blackboard."

Jackie's blood freezes, and he finds himself unable to move.

"Mr. Dornham, did you not hear what I said?" Her voice is as tight as her ramrod body. The words are forced through a tiny slit in ultra-thin lips that look as though they would twang if bumped by a fork or spoon. The words seem to be further tortured by their journey past clenched teeth.

Jackie finds his body suddenly moving, as though shot out of a catapult. His upper thigh grazes the bottom of the desk with an audible sound. There is a snicker from the back of the room. Fitzsimmons' eyes lurch immediately to focus on the offender, who tries to pretend the snicker did not come from him.

"Roger, come here."

Roger Dulow slides carefully out of his chair. He is used to getting the whip from his father, but this woman is not to be trifled with. He comes dutifully to face her, like a condemned man looking fatalistically at the hangman's noose.

"Stand over there by my desk. If anyone laughs at you, both—or all of you, for that matter—will be sent to Mr. Dissendanner."

Roger obediently does as he's told. He doesn't take advantage of the situation to gain attention and status by disrupting the class, as he would in any other period. Thus does Fitzsimmons demonstrate her awesome, almost supernatural, powers to petrify her students into obeisance.

Jackie stands with chalk in hand, ready to be thrown into a vat of humiliation.

"Mr. Dornam, before you do a problem on the blackboard, it will be necessary for you to erase what is already there."

Jackie drops the chalk on the floor in his jerky attempt to grab the felt eraser and release the chalk at the same time and with the same hand. He hastily bends down to pick up the stub of chalk with his free hand and deposit it in the trough at the base of the blackboard. Then he rubs vigorously to remove the previous writing. The eraser catches and turns unexpectedly under his hand and flops violently out of his grasp to the floor. A twiddle of snickering escapes multiple mouths but is quickly squelched.

"Now, Mr. Dornam. If you are ready, here is your problem."

Fitzsimmons gives him a lengthy long division problem that Jackie writes down with shaking hands. He has difficulty concentrating, but somehow manages to work through the task with proper written protocol. He finishes and waits nervously for the teacher to respond.

"Mr. Dornam, how much is eight times eight?"

Jackie's eyes roll up to the top of his head, as though the answer is written somewhere between the ceiling and his upper eyelids.

"Ah, sixty-four?"

"Are you sure?"

Again, Jackie searches the heavens for the answer, until he reluctantly and hesitatingly says, "Yes, ma'am."

"Good. That is correct. I was just wondering, because in your problem, you seem to think it's seventy-two. That may be the reason why you got the wrong answer."

Jackie looks quickly to his writing and hastily erases it to the point where he made his mistake. Carefully, now beyond fear, since the worst has happened, he works the problem through again.

"Thank you, Mr. Dornam. Everything looks just fine. You may be seated."

Jackie returns to his desk, feeling relief that he's walked through the lion's den without being eaten. At the same time, he's wrung out like a dish rag from being sent through a terrible ordeal.

Fitzsimmons' eyes are again on the prowl. Her head does not move, but Zeke knows, in a strange way, that they are becoming fixed on him. Even before she speaks, he tenses his muscles to slide out of his seat.

"Mr. Isacks, are you going somewhere?"

"Yes, ma'am. I was going to the blackboard to do the next problem."

"Did you hear me ask you to?"

Zeke is dumbfounded for a moment. In fact, he had not heard any such demand from her. But he knew that was her intention. How he knew, he can't say. This is not an unusual occurrence for him.

"No, ma'am."

She looks at him quizzically for a moment. "Since you seem so anxious to go to the blackboard, please do so."

Zeke is confident about his ability to solve any problem she gives him. With a relaxed stride, he goes to the board and calmly erases the previous work.

Fitzsimmons gives him an unusually long series of digits. Zeke copies them, and without further ado, he writes down the answer. There's a hush from the classroom. Fitzsimmons goes to her desk, writes down the problem on a piece of paper, and works it out. She sees that the number she gets perfectly matches Zeke's figure.

"Mr. Isacks, you did not work out the problem. You simply gave me an answer."

"Isn't that what you wanted?"

"Yes, I wanted an answer, but I also want the procedure followed. Please do so," she says in a tortured voice.

Zeke tries laboriously to work out the step-by-step approach. He misses steps and botches the procedure. In the end, he comes out with an incorrect answer.

"Now, step by step, let's work it out right."

For the next ten minutes, Fitzsimmons pushes and pulls in an attempt to get Zeke to follow protocol. Just as he seems to be achieving it, the bell rings.

"Mr. Isacks, I want to see you after this class. I'll write you a note to excuse your tardiness for your next period."

Zeke is horrified. A time alone with this teacher from the torture dungeon could not be a good thing. The rest of the class files out the door, with many giving furtive sidelong glances as they leave. They're stealing a last glance at a condemned prisoner. Alas, poor Zeke, they knew him well.

"Come to my desk," Fitzsimmons says. "I don't have a class this period, and I want to talk to you."

It's very strange, because her voice is not threatening. In fact, there actually seems to be softness there. Zeke feels himself to be in a new unreality. He walks to her desk.

"Please, Zeke, pull up a chair."

Zeke does so, with questions racing through his mind.

"Zeke, how did you know the answer to that problem? I know you didn't cheat, because I made the problem up as I went."

"I don't really know, Mrs. Fitzsimmons. There seems to be a part of my brain that just knows certain things. Not just in math. Like I knew you wanted me to go to the blackboard, even though you hadn't asked me. Honest, I wasn't trying to be a smart-aleck."

"I believe you, Zeke. I'm going to give you another problem. I want to see if you know the answer right off. Okay?"

"Okay."

She gives him a five-numerator figure and a three-digit denominator. Immediately, Zeke gives her the answer.

"Wait a minute while I work it out," she says.

She does so and then looks up at him quizzically.

"That's correct. Now let me give you a longer problem."

She adds an extra digit to both the denominator and the numerator. Again, he gives her an immediate correct response. She keeps adding digits to the problems submitted, and Zeke continues to give quick, accurate responses.

"How long have you been able to do this, Zeke?" Fitzsimmons asks in a congenial voice.

"I don't really know. I never used to have much use for numbers before."

"I've been looking at your school records. In the fourth and fifth grades, your grades weren't very good. Then suddenly, you became an "A" student. I've looked at some of your older brothers' school records, and none of them were good academic performers. What happened to you, Zeke?"

"I don't know. All of a sudden I got real interested in learning about things. All kinds of things. I don't know why. I never used to have a good memory or anything. I didn't like reading. But all that changed about two years ago. I went to the swimming hole to sail a boat I made, and I came back all interested in things."

"I've never heard of anything like that before. But I think it's wonderful. Have you thought about going to college?"

"Yes, but I don't know too much about college. Mama and Papa say that it costs a lot of money, so I don't know whether I can go or not."

"There are ways to get to college without a lot of money if you're willing to work hard. Are you willing to work hard, Zeke?"

"Yes, ma'am."

"Then if I'm still around when you're in high school, I'll try to help you."

Zeke is bewildered. It's as though the boogie man just turned into his fairy godmother.

"In the meantime, Zeke, it's necessary for you to learn the proper procedures to get to those answers that come to you without working. I don't care that you don't need to do it to get the right answers. Following proper protocol is important in ways that I can't fully describe to you now. Do you understand me?"

And suddenly, the old fire-breathing Fitzsimmons is back.

"Yes, ma'am."

Doctor in Training

Toward the end of Zeke's second year at the University of Virginia, he receives an emergency telegram:

> Jerry in bad way. Accident. Coma. May not make it.
> Papa

Zeke gets permission from his professors and other authorities for a two-week leave. He'll be given an opportunity to catch up on his studies upon his return. If his brother doesn't recover, at least he'll have had a chance to say goodbye.

When Zeke arrives at the lonely Missouri train station, his father is there to meet him in a two-horse buckboard. His face is drawn, and his body is hunched in on itself. The pungent smell of the horses is somehow comforting as Zeke passes them to throw his suitcases into the back. With leather thongs, he ties the valises to the floor to keep them from bouncing out, then silently joins his father on the wide seat.

Mr. Isacks flicks the reins, and the horses start off at a walk. They ride in silence for some time. Zeke wants to ask questions, but he knows instinctively not to break in on his father's cocoon of quiet. Finally, his father breaks the somber isolation from his son.

"There are times when fiddling with harnesses and animals keeps your mind from stampeding," he says. "Letting the horses do the work and bumping along these old roads feels good somehow."

"How's Jerry, Papa?"

His father sighs. "Not good. Doc Pritchard says he can't really tell the extent of his injuries, but it don't look good."

"Why isn't Jerry in a hospital?"

"Doc Pritchard says he's afraid to move him. He doesn't know if his back is broken. When Jerry wakes up, Doc says he'll be able to tell if his nerves is cut. If they ain't, and he has a broken back, then moving him could cut them."

Zeke notices the blackened skeleton of an oak tree. "Papa, what happened to that oak? The last time I remember, it was full of life."

"Lightning. They say it happened on a perfectly clear day."

Zeke stares into empty space, nodding. They ride along in silence for a long time. He feels helpless. He hates that feeling.

What good is my education? he thinks. I can't do anything to help anyone, least of all Jerry.

They finally arrive at the homestead.

"Everything is just the way I remember it," Zeke says.

"Ain't been that long, son. Only two years."

"I don't know, Papa. It seems like a long time to me. I feel different. I'm not sure I belong here anymore."

His father drives the team to the side of the stables and sits quietly looking at the reins in his hands. "Things change, Zeke. Don't suspect you'd be off for two years at a university and not be changed by it. For one thing, your fingernails ain't dirty."

Zeke glances reflexively at his hands and chuckles. "It's true. It does change a body. I've learned a lot, but I think I'm losing something. I was hoping to take the summer off and work on the farm."

"Miss the dirt, huh?"

"Something like that."

Mr. Isacks turns and looks at Zeke. "You know, son, I suspect this going to college ain't just about gaining knowledge. It's probably got a lot to do with losing some of the stuff you went there with. Maybe you can't get all that back by taking a vacation back home. And maybe that ain't a bad thing."

"You mean you can't go home?"

"Suspect not. Maybe."

"Papa, if Jerry doesn't pull through this, I'm not sure there'll be a home for me to come back to. We just got so close in the end, there, that I'm not sure I could deal with his absence."

His father takes a deep, long breath and lets it out slowly, returning his gaze to his hands.

"Let me help you with the horses, Papa."

"No, Zeke. I think it helps me to do these things on my own right now."

Zeke pats his father on the shoulder and dismounts from the buckboard. Then he unties his suitcases from their moorings and makes his way to the farmhouse. With trepidation, he mounts the old porch steps and walks in through the front door, suitcases in hand. His mother is coming down the stairs from the bedrooms to meet him. He frees his arms to embrace her as she hugs him.

"He still hasn't opened his eyes. But he mumbles sometimes," she says as they walk back up the stairs. "Put your luggage in your room, and I'll get you something to eat. You must be starving."

"I am hungry, Mama, but I want to see Jerry first."

Zeke enters his old room—which, as the youngest, he'd had to himself in the last few years. He sees that it has remained unoccupied, and everything is just about the way he left it.

"We kept your room for you just the way you left it," his mother tells him, "so that when you come back home to live, you'll feel comfortable."

At her words, Zeke feels a sinking sensation in his gut. Even though he had intended to spend a summer here, he had no illusions that he could return for good. But it's not the time to confront his mother with that, not when she might be losing another son.

"Thanks, Mom."

Zeke turns out of his old room toward the one down the hall. Inside, one of his older sisters is sitting vigil next to Jerry's bed. Jerry lies motionless, his breathing barely perceptible.

Zeke bends over and says softly, "Hello, Jerry. How are you feeling?"

He imagines that his brother's eyelids flutter slightly.

"Where's the doctor?" Zeke asks of no one in particular.

"Dr. Pritchard said he'll be here this evening," his mother answers. "His office nurse will take a message if we need to contact him. She knows his schedule and where he is most of the time."

After Zeke has stood around uselessly and awkwardly for a while, his mother offers, "Why don't you let me fix you something to eat now, son?"

"All right. I guess I'm not doing much good here."

The afternoon passes into early evening. The sound of an automobile is heard coming down the Isacks' driveway. Zeke goes out the front door to greet Dr. Pritchard.

"Well, I'll be a son of a gun, if it isn't little Zeke."

The men exchange warm handshakes, but Pritchard knows better than to engage in any trivial conversation just now. Zeke knows not to ask any questions until the doctor has had a chance to examine Jerry.

Four of the family members crowd into the bedroom, trying to stay out of the way, while Dr. Pritchard lifts his patient's eyelids to peer into Jerry's eyes. He uses a stethoscope to listen to his heartbeat and other vital signs. He taps his knee and shoulder with a rubber mallet. He takes Jerry's temperature and looks into his mouth and ears before leaving the room. The family members follow Dr. Pritchard, like a crew of somber workers, into the living room. The doctor sits down.

"I don't think he's gotten any worse. That's a good sign, because if there were too much internal bleeding, it would have shown up in his vitals. Obviously, he's still in a coma."

"Well, do you know when he'll be coming out of it?" Mr. Isacks asks.

"There's no way of knowing. It could be in a couple of minutes, or it could be he'll never come out."

"Oh, no!" one of his sisters exclaims. "Of course he'll wake up!"

"You're probably right," Pritchard says. "One thing I do think would be wise, though. And that's to set splints on his arms and legs. It's been three days since the accident, and those bones that are broken are already beginning to do a substantial amount of healing, most likely. I don't want them healing crookedly."

"Why have you waited this long?" Zeke asks.

"Now you're putting your finger on the crux of a major problem. Without knowing the condition of his back, any twisting and pulling we do to straighten out those limbs increases the possibility that we could injure his spinal cord."

"Why don't you get him to an X-ray machine?" Zeke asks.

"The nearest one I would trust is in Kansas City. Seems to me that all the positioning of his limbs and body we would have to do could defeat the purpose of the X-rays. Tarnation, just moving him could injure the spinal cord. Jerry could help us out by moving his toes and hands and telling us what hurts. Since we don't have that option at this point, I opt to take a chance and set what bones I can tell are broken."

"Damn it! Why don't you know more than you do? Why are we so goddamned backward?" Zeke yells. He stands there with fists clenched, staring at the doctor. Then he spins around and storms out the front door, while everyone else is frozen in shock and disbelief at Zeke's behavior—all except Dr. Pritchard, who remains seated with his head bowed.

"I'm so sorry," Mrs. Isacks apologizes for Zeke. "I've never seen him that way. I don't know what's gotten into him."

"Please don't be concerned about it," Pritchard says. "Zeke feels exactly like I do. I'm just the nearest target. He and I are fine. I think maybe I'll try to have a talk with him after I eat the dinner you're going to be so kind as to invite me to."

Zeke walks, then runs, then walks, as the gnawing, angry frustration feeds his muscles. Eventually, he finds himself at the stream with his favorite sitting rock. He sits and remembers the day Jerry came to tell him about the hunting trip to the Ozarks. Before he can get deeper into his thoughts, he hears the clanging of the dinner bell. Remembering now, for the first time, his rude behavior, Zeke heads for the farmhouse as fast as possible, not wanting to add further to his family's pain and concern. When he arrives, he's surprised to see Dr. Pritchard's car still parked in front of the house. He walks in sheepishly.

"Oh, there you are, Zeke," Pritchard says. "I invited myself to dinner because I didn't want to miss the chance to talk with you."

"Look, doc, I'm sorry about what I said before. It's just that..."

"That you felt angry and helpless to do anything for Jerry, and not even the so-called expert has been much better," Pritchard interrupts, waving his hand dismissively.

"Yeah. How did you know?"

"Because, as I was telling your family, that's exactly how I feel, and I want to talk to you after dinner about that very thing," Pritchard continues amiably.

Although Zeke is a little late, the others slow down and try to make him feel at home again. The dinner proceeds with a certain kind of quiet grace. There are undertones of tension caused by the waiting and not knowing.

Following the dinner, Dr. Pritchard thanks his hosts and turns to Zeke. "Zeke, can I persuade you to go for a walk with me in the moonlight?"

Zeke smiles. "Sure."

The two of them head out the door into twilight. A gibbous moon hangs in the sky, while purple and red illuminate the western sky. The landscape, through its very simplicity, seems to reach to infinity, or just to be a painting on a flat canvas. Zeke wonders if Jerry will ever see this kind of magic again.

"What did you want to talk to me about, Doc?"

"Zeke, have you decided what you're going to major in?"

"Actually, no. I was planning to come home for the summer and let my minds give me a clue."

"Minds? I thought we had only one mind. But I guess when you really think about it, we're almost always conflicted somehow in our thoughts and desires."

"I don't know why I said that, Doc. Strange things come out of my pudding head all the time. I figure I must have a screw loose or something."

"Like the rest of us, you mean?"

"Maybe. I'm not sure. But anyway, to answer your question, I don't know. It's got to be in the sciences, though."

"Do you consider medicine a science?"

"I haven't thought about it much. I guess it involves the sciences and the scientific method. But I think doctors do a lot on hunches, as well."

"Right you are. How do you feel about that?"

"Making educated guesses about what's going on inside someone else does have a kind of appeal to me. But right now, not knowing what's wrong with Jerry and what's going to happen to him is not very pleasant. It's hell, actually."

"Yeah, it sure is. It's hell for me, and he's not my brother. Do you think you can live with that kind of hell, Zeke?"

"Are you asking me whether I would consider medicine as a profession?"

"Yes."

"Even if I did consider it, I don't have the money to pursue a medical career."

"I can help you."

"Why would you want to?"

"Because I've been following your progress ever since you showed interest in learning about academic things. And I've been talking to Mrs. Fitzsimmons."

A broad smile spreads across Zeke's face as he thinks, with fond gratitude, of his old teacher and guardian angel. "How is she?"

"Just as scary as ever. Zeke, medicine needs people like you. People who have your kind of brilliance and who aren't spoiled. Who know what it's like to have dirt under their fingernails and know what it's like to be loved."

Zeke is quiet. He feels embarrassed by what the doctor is saying, even though he knows it's all true. Suddenly, an owl's hoot wafts across the meadows.

"That's Gus," Zeke says. "I'm glad he's still around."

"Gus?"

"That owl. Jerry named him a long time ago. You know those birds can live for a long time."

"How do you know it isn't a different owl?"

"I can tell. Jerry wouldn't have any trouble knowing it was old Gus either."

"So what about becoming a doctor?"

"It's something to think about. I really appreciate what you're saying. But I have the summer to think about it."

"Not the whole summer. You're about to go into your junior year, and it's time to start specializing if you're going into medicine. It's a good thing that you've been taking a lot of biology and physical science courses."

"How do you know what I'm taking, Doc?"

"I said I've been following your career. I don't have a family, Zeke. I don't have a son to pass my profession on to. You're obviously not going to be a dirt farmer, so I'll get more than just a little bit of satisfaction if I sell you on this idea."

They continue on their walk as the western colors fade to deep indigo. Zeke relishes the occasional sound of a bellowing cow in pasture. Fence railings become luminescent in the moon glow. They walk for over an hour before they return.

Dr. Pritchard doesn't bother to come back into the house but leaves, asking Zeke to inform his family that he'll be back the next afternoon.

That night, Zeke sleeps fitfully. He dreams of strange voices speaking to him—not in audible sounds, but in mind sounds. Words come together in recognizable patterns, but somehow he knows that the words are not being transmitted via the tympanic membrane or other organs of hearing. Although the language is perfectly understandable to him, it's not English, Latin, German, or any other language he has studied or heard before. One part of him evaluates the experience and knows it to be a form of telepathy. When he awakens in the middle of the night, he understands it to be a dream, but it has a peculiar quality to it. It's a kind of inexplicable reality.

He closes his eyes and attempts to go back to sleep. As he slips into a hypnagogic level of pre-sleep, the dream picks up again. But there's something different. The voice is in English and has a different character. Suddenly he becomes aware that it's Jerry's voice.

"Zeke, pull me out. Help me back. Touch me. Speak to me."

The voice continues as Zeke lies there in a state of near disembodiment. Suddenly he jerks bolt upright with a sharp inhalation. He concentrates on leveling out and calming his breathing until his heart stops pounding like a rabbit fighting for its life.

As the adrenalin levels retreat, panic gives way to a strange sense of conviction. Zeke knows that it was not simply a dream. Jerry was asking for help. He was asking for it in Zeke's own mind. Zeke also feels that he can contact Jerry telepathically. The knowledge has the same feeling as when he knows what someone is about to say or what they're thinking. Although it's not an everyday occurrence, it's also not rare for him.

He gets out of bed and walks quietly in bare feet to Jerry's room. One of his sisters is sitting in vigil next to Jerry's bed. The family has taken night watch duty.

"Zeke," she says in surprise, "what are you doing here?"

"Shh. Please give me some quiet for a while. Please don't ask questions."

His sister is puzzled and concerned, but the way in which Zeke has requested her silence has made it very clear to her that this is what she must do.

Zeke stands looking at Jerry. He reaches down and picks up his hand with one of his own, then puts his other hand over Jerry's closed eyelids. He waits there for a while in that position, until a channel seems to open up. The passage through that channel is both totally alien and totally familiar to Zeke.

"Jerry, I'm here. How can I help you back?"

A thought that is Jerry's but somehow more than Jerry's answers.

"Keep the channel open. The touch of your hands will be my roadmap back."

Zeke maintains his body and mind posture and feels Jerry's mind becoming aware of sensations of touch, pressure, temperature, and pulsations. Then Zeke feels his brother's eyes moving under his hand. He moves his hand to Jerry's forehead as the eyes flicker open and eye-to-eye contact is established. There is a soul-to-soul connection in that mutual gaze.

Jerry croaks, "I think I must have fallen off the roof. How long have I been here?"

The second the sound comes, the deeper communication breaks off. The feeling of knowing leaves Zeke, and he can't imagine how he did what he just did—if indeed he did anything.

"Over three days, brother. How did you know to call for me?"

"What are you talking about? All I know is that one minute

I'm screaming at the top of my lungs like a little girl, and the next minute I wake up with my strange little brother holding my hand. What kinds of things are they teaching you in college, anyway?"

Zeke lets go of his brother's hand and jerks his other hand off Jerry's forehead as though he'd been touching live coals. He turns around in embarrassment to see his sister staring at them with eyes so wide they look like they're about to pop out. Her mouth is so open that he's concerned it might never close again.

She bolts out of her chair and runs down the hall calling, "Mama, Papa! Zeke woke Jerry up!"

On December 7, 1941, Zeke is halfway through medical school when his anatomy class is interrupted by a professor who announces to the students that Pearl Harbor has just been attacked by the Japanese. Like most of the students in his medical school, Zeke decides to enlist. He knows he will probably be drafted anyway, and he wants to be able to choose the branch that he'll serve in. Having been raised on a farm, he knows that he's experienced dirt and mud aplenty in his life, and it's time to concentrate on a different medium. He enlists in the Navy, but the Navy wants him to finish medical school. If accepted, he will do his internship in a hospital chosen by the armed services and then serve as a Navy doctor for a number of years.

Zeke has mixed feelings about the fact that by the time he sees active service, the war will probably be over. There's never any doubt in his mind as to the eventual outcome of the war.

How ironic, he thinks. Every time there's a boat in my life, my life changes. First there was that weird thing that happened to me when I was sailing that little homemade boat when I was a kid, and my whole perspective on life changed. Now I'm enlisting in the Navy because we're in a world war. What next?

It's 1943, and now it's not Zeke, but Dr. Isacks. It's December in the cold, wet university town of Charlottesville, Virginia. Somehow, many members of Zeke's family have managed to attend the graduation ceremony. Zeke spends the next day showing them around the historic sights of Thomas Jefferson's town.

"Well, little brother, are you going to set up an office with Doc Pritchard?" Jerry asks.

"Whoa. Slow down. Just because I have my medical degree doesn't mean I'm ready or allowed to practice medicine."

"What do you mean?"

"Well, first of all, I have to go through my internship. That'll take another two years. "

"You're kidding."

"Not on your life, big brother. Even after that, I owe at least four years to the U.S. Navy."

"Wow. I guess you won't be going overseas, then."

"Yeah. The war will be over by then."

"I sure wish I could have gone," says Jerry, "but all them broken bones from a few years back left me a little too busted up to slog through swamps for days at a time and keep up with the rest of them. I can't help it, but it sure makes me feel bad that I can't."

"I don't feel really good about being left out either," says Zeke. "But I'm not sorry you're stuck safe and sound here in the good old U. S. of A. Funny thing, but the accident that just about killed you will probably end up saving your life."

"Well, I got the aches and pains to pay for it, so I guess I shouldn't feel *too* guilty. Say, Papa, when are you going to give Zeke his graduation present?"

"Oh, look, folks. You being here is enough of a graduation present for me. I really don't want anything else."

"Sorry, son, but we already got it, and we can't give it back. It was part of the deal for getting it so cheap."

Zeke sighs, "Well, okay. What is it?"

"It's an all-prepaid trip to Miami. You get train tickets, and you get a room on the mainland for five days."

"Actually, it's more like a boarding house," his mother says. "That way you get free food, too. We checked with your commanding officer, and he says you're not scheduled to report until after the end date."

Zeke is not sure he likes this gift, but he shows great appreciation. After he sees his family off at the train station, he wonders what he's going to do with his graduation gift. Finally, he decides that a trip to sunny Florida might not be so bad.

When Zeke arrives at the train station on Flagler Street, he's met there by the proprietor and owner of the boarding house. From there, he's driven to his living quarters in a small complex of apartments on Southwest 17th Street, which is five miles from Coconut Grove and about eight miles from the ocean. There are no swank hotels here, just residences, some of which have been converted to boarding houses or bed and breakfasts. Instead of the ubiquitous red clay and rock he'd become used to in central Virginia, here he finds sand and some coral rock. Mostly, the lawns are covered by a kind of leguminous grass that leaves bare spots of sand here and there. The street is lined with tropical trees, with a healthy scattering of tall coconut palms. Coconuts are seen lying in their tough, brown-green husks along the street for anyone to gather.

Zeke's quarters are small and certainly not luxurious. But that suits him fine. The landlord supplies his guests with bicycles equipped with coaster brakes and wide balloon tires.

"These bicycles were hard to come by, Dr. Isacks," Marcus Peeling says. "They're not producing any bikes right now. The war effort, you know."

"I'll take good care of any bike I use. And please don't call me Doctor. I'm not really a doctor yet."

"Oh, I know that you still have a long way to go. My nephew is a doctor. He has a practice in New Jersey. But you do have a medical degree, and you might as well get used to the moniker. Or do you want me to call you by your rank?"

"No thanks. There'll be plenty of that. I guess I'll have to get used to titles. But right now, it makes me feel like a fraud."

Zeke talks further with Marcus about the physical layout of Miami. Early the next day, after breakfast, he takes a bike and heads towards Coconut Grove. There he walks around the marina. A small flotilla of various kinds of boats is anchored along the wharfs and against the seawall. Others are anchored farther out in the harbor. The larger boats are obviously the homes of their owners. Some are elaborate and beautiful in their design and with all their polished wood. Others are much simpler and more basic, but all are maintained with loving care. Bicycles and motorbikes are evident everywhere.

I wonder where the war is, Zeke thinks.

After a while, he gets on his bicycle again and heads farther south along the bay to a place Marcus called Matheson's Hammock. There he finds a small parking area with some cars, a horse, and a few bikes. Keeping his bike close to him, he finds a path through a line of mangrove trees. The path opens up to an area that forms a beach that's three-quarters of the way around an inlet of water, which is about seventy-five yards from one side to the other. The far end is blocked by a barrier of huge, bunker-sized rocks with one inlet for the water. Beyond is Biscayne Bay. Directly across the bay is the last string of the islands that make up the Miami area. It's called Key Biscayne.

Some people sunbathe and picnic on the beach area, while others swim and play in the protected waters. Many children frolic there, supposedly under the watchful eyes of their parents.

One particular young woman stands at a distance,

apparently enjoying the antics of some of the children. Something about her is intensely appealing. Zeke finds her beautiful with her blond hair and one-piece, skirted bathing suit. He can't take his eyes off her. Even at the substantial distance that separates them, he feels self-conscious as he steals long glances at her. She has an uninhibited way about her that allows her to laugh out loud at the children and engage them in conversation.

Zeke, basically a shy man, feels compelled to find a way to talk to her. Fear and desire battle somewhere deep inside him. From someplace that has often proven to be a place of unexplainable resources comes a voice that tells him he has faced far more dangerous situations. That inner voice chides him. How will he feel if he lets his timidity keep him from merely saying hello to this beautiful and charming woman?

He finds himself walking an oblique path in her direction that finally brings him, apparently by accident, to within hearing distance. She's focused on a group of children and laughs gleefully as one of them successfully sneaks up underwater on another one. Her eyes innocently encompass Zeke. She laughs as though to include him in the joke.

"Are those your children?" he hears himself ask.

"Oh, no," she says in surprise. "I'm much too young to have children like that. I mean I'm too young to have any children. No, what I mean to say is, I don't have any children and… I'm not married."

"That's all right. Neither am I."

They stand there in an embarrassing silence for a while.

"Uh, I'm Ezekiel Isacks. I'm here on a vacation."

"Well, I'm glad to meet you, Mr. Isacks. I'm Lila Globe. I live here with my sister and parents. But I'm going to nursing school at Johns Hopkins in the fall."

Zeke's mouth drops. "You probably won't believe me, but I'll be going to Johns Hopkins next month."

"Oh, I'm sorry. I hope it isn't very serious."

"No, no. There's nothing wrong with me. I'm doing my internship there."

"Are you a doctor?" she asks, her eyes wide with surprise.

"Well, yes, I suppose I am."

From that point on, everything flows. Zeke doesn't have to search for things to say. Lila leads him through the rigors of verbal communication like a sherpa guide in the Himalayan mountains. Those five days spark the beginning of Zeke and Lila's relationship. It's continued when they rendezvous in Baltimore, where Zeke meets her at the train station to take her to her dormitory.

Two years later, when Zeke stays on at Hopkins as a resident, they are married. By the time he begins serving in the Navy at Guantanamo Bay, their first of two daughters, Dee, is well on her way.

See the Creature

The years pass relatively quickly on Earth. Zeke has had a long, successful medical career. His life, with some of the glitches that are common to the lives of Earthling's families, has been a good one.

It's over, Zeke thinks. I've been a doctor for a long time. Funny, it doesn't seem long at all. Anyway, it's over. Am I sure I want to do this? What the hell am I going to do tomorrow? Lila's sure I want to quit. After all, I'm sixty-five. It's not easy, this retiring stuff. It's just like quitting. That's what it is. It's quitting, and since when have I ever been a quitter?

Lila and I have gone through a lot of hard times. No silver spoons in our mouths. I guess we did pretty well, though. I'm the head of my department in a pretty prestigious hospital in the Shenandoah Valley—even if I won't be tomorrow.

His mind is about to wander into his boyhood years spent on the family farm in Missouri when the man standing to his right makes a theatrical gesture toward the cloth-draped portrait of the retiring head of the X-ray department. Dr. Isacks' attention is jerked back into the Madison Hotel banquet hall. His wife is sitting to his left. The two young women to her left are Dee and Dodi, his daughters. Dr. Isacks recognizes all the heads of other hospital departments sitting at their dinner tables, their spouses in attendance. With a flourish, the man slips the cloth off the portrait frame. A chorus of "Oohs" and "Aahs" floats dutifully out of the mouths of some of the women.

Dr. Isacks stares at the portrait.

Is that supposed to be me?' Hmm, it bears a possible resemblance. I wonder whether anyone will really bother to look up at it when they hang it on a wall somewhere. I think I would have preferred a gold watch.

Why am I retiring? Because I deserve it? Because I'm tired of going to the hospital every morning and being called on to read film, when I would rather stay at home? Because I want to have more time to do other things like…what? Oh yeah, like woodworking. Isn't that why I bought a table saw? Or is it because Lila wants me to? Am I retiring because I want to leave my farm home and go to live on the beach? At least that's what Lila says I want. She wants me to spend more time with her. Isn't that what I want? She's tired of making all those fancy dinners for the lord high muckety-mucks. She'll be retiring too. I wonder what she'll do with her time. Oh, hell, I don't know what I want. Everything seems to be so confusing lately.

Dr. Isacks notices that Dr. Metcalf is speaking. He's a short, chubby man with a neatly trimmed, thin-line mustache that streaks across his upper lip as though it's been drawn there with a black Magic Marker.

He looks more like a caricature of a 1940s banker than a medical doctor to me, Dr. Isacks thinks. He sure is going to be a different sort of head of my department than I am. Was. He's not the best film reader I've ever met. I guess he's competent enough, though. Paperwork, administration—that's what's important these days. He sure is a damn sight better at those things than I am. He should do fine. Maybe that's the reason I'm getting out. The paperwork is getting worse all the time. I'm a doctor, not a file clerk. Maybe Metcalf wants the job so badly he's brainwashed me into quitting. Probably in cahoots with Lila. Maybe they've been drugging my coffee. Could be why my brain seems so fuzzy these days.

Isacks smiles at the image of Metcalf furtively slipping a

powder into his cup.

Coffee doesn't smell the way it used to. On the other hand, they say that when you're getting old and senile, olfactory sensitivity is the first to go. It's a sure sign of mental deterioration. I'm probably doing the patients a favor by getting out before I can do some real damage.

Metcalf's voice drones on, and Dr. Isacks' mind wanders back to his boyhood home in Missouri. His memories of that place are more vivid than the drabness that surrounds him at the banquet. He suddenly remembers being filled with a longing that seemed to come from nowhere, something suddenly foisted upon him from some unknown force that had alien qualities.

"Papa, Papa, I want to go to college."

His father just blinked and stared at his seven-year-old son who came running toward him, breathlessly uttering these strange words with the excitement he usually reserved for finding a bird's nest.

"Do you even know what that word means, Zeke?"

"It's a big school where you get to learn about everything."

His father blinked again.

"What's put that foolishness in your head?"

"I don't know. I just know that I gotta."

"Nobody in this family ever thought such things. We're honest, hard-working farmers. You'd do well to be a good farmer like your papa and your grandpapa. Now go wash up. It's almost dinnertime."

A burst of laughter jerks Dr. Isacks' senses back to the present. The abrupt change gives him a sense of vertigo and nausea.

"And so, following in Zeke's footsteps is not going to be an easy thing, as you can see," Metcalf is saying. "But I don't know who can speak better for Zeke than he himself. So I give you, finally, Dr. Isacks, alias Zeke."

Dr. Isacks takes his cue and rises to make his farewell

speech. He realizes that he harbors no ill will toward any of the people there—except maybe Lila—for pushing him to this inevitable point, perhaps earlier than he would have preferred. He's envious of those who will have a purpose tomorrow morning. That makes him a little disgruntled, but he manages to hide that behind his usual good humor.

The rest of the night is spent in the warm congeniality conferred by too many cocktails. Lila buzzes around among the guests in her usual butterfly manner.

I don't get it, he thinks. Why does she want to give all this up? She loves it. Nobody really knows us at Colonial Beach. Sure, we've vacationed there, and some people know our names, but we don't have any real friends. She'll never get to be queen bee again.

The glitter of the 17th-century chandeliers of the banquet hall blends into the smells of food and alcohol. The sounds become a meaningless din punctuated by islands of attention as people come up to him and offer their congratulations. He dances a few minutes with each of his daughters, hoping they don't notice that something is off with his coordination. Alcohol never used to have that effect on him. At an appropriate time, he allows Dee to drive them all to the farmhouse in his Jeep Wagoneer.

Later and mysteriously, he finds himself in bed in his pajamas with Lila at his side. There is a barely perceptible tremor in his left hand as he slips into sleep.

He finds himself in a dream. A thin and far-away voice, maybe more than one voice, calls to him pleadingly, "Come home. It's time. Come home. We need you."

They're not really voices. They're thoughts in his mind. He's intrigued by their quality. There's an essence there that is not quite human. As that thought floats through his awareness, Zeke recoils, as though his mind has touched a hot flame. The voices are Sirens luring him into oblivion.

"No!"

Zeke is sitting bolt upright in bed. He's soaked with sweat, and his left hand is quivering.

"What in the world is wrong with you?" Lila is braced on one forearm as she stares at him wide-eyed, in fear and resentment.

He takes long, slow, deep breaths, trying to calm himself. Gradually, his heart stops pounding so hard. His pulse and racking heartbeats become gentler. After succeeding in moistening his dry mouth with reluctant saliva, he manages to croak, "It's nothing, Lila. Just a bad dream."

"You scared the living daylights out of me, Zeke! I'll never get back to sleep now. What in the world were you dreaming about?"

"I, ah... Never mind. I can't remember," he lies. He doesn't want to have to explain himself. Besides, he doesn't think he can describe the dream.

Softening a little, Lila says, "You're just scared about retirement. It'll all seem better in the morning." Her voice takes on the quality of a mother talking to a baby or a pet.

But Zeke doesn't fall asleep again until 5 a.m.

Ten Years Later

Dr. Isacks sits at the head of the table. On either side of him sit his two daughters, two sons-in-law, and five grandchildren. The long table is loaded to capacity with food. Turkey, ham, stuffing, candied sweet potatoes, and other delicacies stretch so far down the table that he isn't quite sure what all of them are. Lila is sitting the closest to him on his right. Behind her is the wide picture window overlooking the Potomac. Everyone is sitting with their heads bowed.

They're expecting something, he thinks. Something from me.

There's a moment of anxiety as he searches his memory. What am I supposed to do?

Then, automatically, he begins. "Thank you, Lord, for our bountiful blessings, for bringing us together on this wonderful occasion to enjoy the gifts of your everlasting love. In Jesus' name, amen."

The others echo, "Amen."

Zeke wonders what the wonderful occasion is. He looks out the picture window and sees that the grass is green and there are lots of sailboats on the river.

It can't be Christmas, he reasons. It doesn't look cold outside. Have I been outside today? It must be Thanksgiving.

The feast progresses with the usual background hum of Lila's voice directing all the talk, which is based on topics of no interest to anyone except herself.

"Don't you remember that time when your sister Alva was

visiting us from Missouri and we were afraid that her water was going to break? Tell us about it, Zeke. Tell us how you went out to buy some white towels just in case you had to do the delivery. We didn't have the supplies to do it with. Go ahead, Zeke, tell us."

Zeke remembers and begins to describe it halfheartedly. It's an overworked story.

"Well, she was having intermittent abdominal pains. She wasn't due for another month, but you never know. So I took stock of the towels and sheets we had on hand. Wouldn't you know it? They were all dark colored."

"So I told her," Lila interrupts, "Zeke is not an obstetrician. I was trained as a nurse at a very good school, and I had enough training to get us by quite nicely."

Zeke thinks to himself, Well, that's a record. I don't think she's ever let me get that far into the story before.

Then he remembers that he's still hungry and continues his feasting. Miraculously, food appears on his plate even before he asks for it.

Time passes. He retires to the living room where the women are talking. He's very sleepy. He sits down in his easy chair. Soon his head is nodding, and he's back in Missouri, discussing things with the Navy recruiter. He wants to know how he can be guaranteed training as a doctor. Slowly, he realizes once again that he's in his Potomac living room. No one else is there except this strange woman.

"Zeke, why do you have to go to sleep when we have company? It's very rude. Don't you care about hurting your own family's feelings? I think you're awful," the glowering, angry woman scolds him.

He tries to get up and out of his easy chair. His arms and legs don't seem to have the strength, and he falls back down into the he chair.

"Oh, honestly!" the woman says disgustedly and grabs both of his hands. She pulls hard, putting all her weight into it. With that, Dr. Isacks is freed from the greedy grasp of his armchair.

He shuffles out into the breezeway, his left hand shaking almost violently. Leo, Dee's husband, is there.

"Leo, who is that woman in there?" Zeke asks seriously.

Leo smiles at him good-naturedly and answers, "That's Lila, your wife."

Dr. Isacks feels extremely embarrassed. He manages a little laugh and says, "Of course. My mind is a little broken, you know."

Leo doesn't seem to make much of the incident. Zeke notices then that his other son-in-law is working on the riding lawn mower that Zeke keeps in the shed. It's been a long time since he's been able to operate it. Apparently the automatic starter is not working, and Ralph is trying to pull-start it.

The damn fool, he's got the mower in pieces all over the yard. All he needs to do is put in gasoline, Zeke thinks to himself.

"Ralph, it needs gas," he says.

"It's not getting a spark. We've tried putting gas directly into the spark plug well," Ralph insists.

Leo goes and gives the starter cord a hefty pull. Nothing happens. As the two of them fiddle and toil away in vain, Dr. Isacks shuffles to the shed and finds a half-filled can of gasoline. With some difficulty, he lifts it and shuffles back to the carnage. Leo looks up in astonishment as he sees his father-in-law carrying the heavy can.

Zeke thinks to himself, What's the matter? Do you think I'm a complete invalid?

"Okay, Pops," Ralph says. "We'll try it your way."

Ralph pours in the gasoline, and Leo yanks on the starter rope. The engine roars into life.

Dr. Isacks shuffles away to the seawall and falls into a chair set back from its edge. The younger men stare at him as he goes. They never know how much of their father-in-law's mind is there at any given moment.

Zeke stares at a wild duck in the river. Its beak moves in a strange way. It seems to be staring at him. It forms words that are directed toward him.

"Wake up. It's time to come home. Remember. Be strong and remember," it says.

"Remember—remember what?" Zeke asks of the duck.

"Be strong and remember that you are Strong. Come home," it says.

Zeke remembers a buzzing bug in his head. There is something else. Something down so deep that he can't quite touch it. It's something frightening. Something alien. Yet something familiar.

"Papa, what's the matter?" Dee is kneeling in front of him. Tears are coming from his eyes.

On Gazeon

Dark-Lights looks around at the staff. Mind-Storm has asked her to chair the meeting, even though he holds rank on everyone.

I hate chairing meetings where Mind-Storm is present, she tells herself. It's like trying to run a wild entity show. Storm speaks whenever he wants to, regardless of protocol. All it does is point out how little control I actually have.

Assembled are as many of the staff as can be spared from all the shifts. They are arrayed in two concentric circles. The larger circle is above the other to form a floating, living amphitheater. In the middle are the chief proponents, who are arrayed in their own circle. Most of the discussion will be held in that small inner ring. Occasionally, the outsiders will be called upon for contributions, or the floor will be open for impromptu inputs.

"So what have we actually found out in these last ten seasons?" Storm asks academically. He continues, answering his own question. "The barrier imposed by Strong's alien is probably the product of its being shocked into an experience too difficult for it to bear, something so foreign to its world that it closed down the awareness through a process of denial. Our experience with the second alien creature, in which we did not try to be noticed, turned out to be a completely different matter. There was no resistance at all. No resistance, because there was no awareness."

Storm pauses for questions, as though he is delivering a lecture.

"What exactly is it, do you suppose, that the creature finds so horrible and threatening about our presence?" an outer circle member asks.

"An excellent question," Storm responds. "I am convinced that it is not the content of our minds but simply the idea that another mind can coexist in their own consciousness."

The outsider follows through with a second question. "Then how can a creature that has so little experience with mind-melding and other forms of direct mind-to-mind communication be so powerful as to be able not only to capture and kill the mind of a Gazeon, but also to keep all other Gazeon minds at bay?"

Storm looks toward his chairman. It is a meaningless gesture of recognition. Everyone knows that he will be the one who will respond to the question. Dark-Lights nods her body to indicate that she wishes him to continue.

"It is in the nature of matter."

That last statement sets up a hum of confusion from the audience.

"I'll explain what I mean," says Storm. "The Gazeon mind exists primarily in a matrix of gas molecules. There is a smattering of solids, but they are in the form of dust, rarely larger than tiny motes. Liquid molecules are also present in minuscule amounts. Yet the presence of this solid and liquid content is absolutely necessary for our life forms. Gas is mobile. So mobile, in fact, that life's challenge is to maintain and replicate patterns that must be forever in motion. It must work to provide structure. Our outer membranes are a prime example of how our gases, solids, and liquids create this structure. But the creature is made of solid and liquid matter. There is a significant quantity of gas as well, but compared to Gazeon physiology, it's a tiny amount. The majority of its substance is liquid, but there is a significant amount of solids. Consequently, the alien is faced with quite a different set of challenges."

Another outer circle member asks, "Forgive me, Dr. Mind-

Storm, but most of us are not physicists. Can you explain what solid matter is and how it is that we know about it? I don't remember much being said about it in my high school physics class."

"We know about it because of the focusing project. We have been able to feel and sense the same things that one of these aliens feels and senses. We have looked at their world through their own visual sensors and heard their world through their own auditory senses. So we know—actually know rather than just theorize—that they live in a world composed of gases, liquids, and solids."

There is a buzz of excitement throughout the auditorium. Dark allows the buzz to continue and then calls the assembly to order with a pucker-entity.

"It's not easy to describe solid matter. I'll try, but it will, of course, be an overly simplified explanation. We're all familiar with gas. We float in it, ingest it, smell it, taste it, and feel it. We know that it must be contained in gelatinous membranes for life to exist. Now, imagine a membrane so stiff that a large transport entity would be smashed if it were to run into it at full speed. Imagine that the membrane was so stiff that its own shape would not have been affected in the slightest manner by this impact. Next, try to visualize that this membrane was thick, as thick as you can imagine. For example, it might be as thick as a building, or perhaps even a whole city."

The audience makes a collective gasp, followed by startled cross talk amongst the staffers.

Dark-Lights waits for the hubbub to die down before calling the people to order.

"How big could it get?" another Gazeon asks.

"As big as the entire world, or even larger. In fact, there is reason to believe that our world is made of a solid core. Someday we'll have the ability to withstand pressures that exist below our bio level altitude to make first-hand observations."

Bedlam erupts again. When the commotion dies down, Mind-Storm continues.

"Solid matter cannot change shape. Most solids can, however, be changed into a liquid and even a gas if made hot enough. As a matter of fact, most gases can be made into liquids and solids either by cooling them down substantially or by subjecting them to extreme pressures—which, by the way, the creature's people are capable of doing."

This time the audience is too dumbfounded to say anything. They show confusion by the relative loss of rhythm in their inner light patterns. They wait for Mind-Storm to continue.

"Liquid states are between gaseous ones and solid states. Like gases, they will take on the shape of the vessel in which they are contained. But they don't automatically fill up the vessel and put it under uniform pressure, as do gases. They would form a surface that would be absolutely parallel to what we call bottom. Liquids cannot expand as easily as gases. Imagine a vessel-entity without a top. I know that is hard to conceive of, since all vessel-entities must have a membrane that completely contains them. If you were to tilt this impossible vessel, the liquid would maintain a surface that remains perfectly level. But if the vessel were tilted far enough, past the level of the water surface relative to the vessel's edge, it would flow out. And it would fall downward, never stopping until it ran into an obstacle, such as the theoretical core of the world that I have already made allusions to."

Storm looks around at his completely baffled audience.

"I anticipated that I might need help in explaining these things, so I've prepared a visual program in this projector-entity."

Mind-Storm telepathically summons the entity, which has been floating outside the meeting hall. He comments as the visual program runs.

After the presentation, the questioning continues. Another questioner comes to the fore. "At the risk of sounding insensitive, if we have already been able to use the creature's own senses to experience its world, why are we putting so much time and resources into keeping Strong-Presence's body alive? "

"There are very important reasons why we must pursue our interests concerning Strong-Presence's survival," Mind-Storm responds. "Although we can sense what the aliens sense, we can't do it with the same understanding that the aliens themselves have. We've been able to mind-meld with individual parts of the aliens' minds, but it's as though we have an array of individual, disconnected entity sensors. In this analogy, each entity is non-sentient and therefore unable to interpret or even to subjectively experience what it senses. So we're still limited to trying to deduce what these sensations mean."

The same questioner follows up. "So what happens next?"

"We have to find a way to do a true mind-meld, not just experience piecemeal, different aspects of the alien's perceptions. We need to meld with the whole organism at one time," Storm explains.

"That seems simple enough," the inquirer says. "What's stopping us?"

"I knew you were going to ask me that."

There is a slight titter of laughter throughout the auditorium.

"To do that," Storm continues, "unfortunately requires that the Gazeon mind infuse itself into the solid and liquid components of the alien mental machinery in total. The alien mind cannot be separated from the physical aspects of the creature's physical organizational components. It serves as an anchor point. When we try to do that, we get stuck. We forget our own identity and lose the power of self-determination. Were it not for the fact that our operatives had strong contacts with their anchors, we would have lost them. We dare not go any further. If we do, we will have other disasters just like Strong-Presence," he concludes.

"Does that have anything to do with why the creatures' minds seem to be so powerful?" another questioner offers.

"Precisely," Mind-Storm responds. "Their minds may be

slow, but they have the power of mass. Once a thought is set in motion, its direction cannot be altered by minds as light as our own. We know that heavy gases sink and light gases rise in our atmosphere. Imagine the heaviest of the heavy gases we know multiplied thousands of times. Imagine a Gazeon trapped in a downdraft of a huge cloud of that gas. That poor soul would not be able to fight his way out of that current and would eventually be crushed by the increasing pressure. Once our lighter minds are enclosed by an alien's denser mind, we are powerless," Dr. Mind-Storm says with finality.

"Why hasn't Strong-Presence been crushed in the density of the creature's mind?"

"Because Strong has found a way to become part of the alien. He is not separate. There's the potential to distill his Gazeon mind out of the alien's. We don't fully understand how Strong was able to do this. I must confess that these explanations I'm giving you are analogies at best. We don't really know why mind and substance are so interwoven. The borders between metaphysics and science are very blurred here. Ultimately, I should think that mind is independent of matter. But while it's in the physical universe, it seems to be ruled by material, at least to some degree."

"You mean you're not sure what you're talking about?"

There is a sudden hush in the auditorium. All senses become riveted on the source of the voice.

Storm has been very aware of Harmony-Lights' presence. Although she is not yet officially a staff member, he has little doubt that she soon will be. He made sure that she was given an invitation to attend this meeting.

"You are precisely correct, Dr. Harmony-Lights. Fellow Gazeons, for those of you who might not know her, let me introduce you to Strong-Presence's spouse."

Storm begins to make the Gazeon sound equivalent to human applause. It is created by the tensing and relaxation of their bodily membranes at the rate of several pulses per second. Dark–Lights takes up the applause, and the entire audience is soon engaged in the ovation. Harmony, who asked her question out of sarcasm, is not prepared for this reaction.

The old cuss is as wily as ever, she thinks. She feels a combination of embarrassment and admiration.

Dark–Lights permits the crosscurrents of communication that follow to continue until she feels the moment has passed. Then she brings the proceedings back to order. "Dr. Mind–Storm is still fielding questions. Please don't hesitate to ask yours."

"At the risk of sounding insensitive, what is it that we expect to achieve with this Strong–Presence aspect of the project?" someone asks.

"As I have already intimated," says Mind–Storm, "Strong may have made the journey into the solid and liquid state of the alien mind. If so, he is probably thinking of himself as the alien. In fact, he actually would be. When the physical organ of consciousness deteriorates, Strong will either die with the alien or he will be freed. If left alone and unaided, he will almost certainly die. With help from us, he might survive. If he survives, he might be rehabilitated. Then he will be able to talk to us, not just as a fellow Gazeon, but as the alien itself. He can give us understanding of things we probably haven't even thought about. Don't you think that possibility makes this project, with all the resources of energy and time invested in it, worthwhile?"

Murmurs fly around the auditorium. Again, Dark–Lights brings the assembly back to order. She notices a shy attempt to gain attention from another member of the outer circle.

"Did you have a question?" she asks of him.

There follow many questions that prolong the conference far beyond its allotted time.

Heart-Break

Mind-Storm is thankful that he manages to free himself of the conference with little more than an occasional meeting of glances between himself and Harmony.

His private travel-entity spots him as he leaves the building and dutifully comes to pick him up. Mind-Storm is one of the very few Gazeons who can afford to have a private travel-entity. Most people use the public travel-entities or just propel themselves from place to place. But Storm isn't able to travel very quickly under his own power these days. Most travel-entities require constant telepathic control to direct them, but Dr. Mind-Storm's entity is able to follow a route independently.

The private transporter opens its aperture at Storm's telepathic signal, allowing him to float into the operator's space. Mind-Storm enters and gives instructions for the vehicle to proceed to his home. He closes his visual perceptors to focus inward and go over his plans for the following day.

When they arrive at his huge house, which is made of eight building-entities, Storm is so engrossed in his thoughts that it's some time before he becomes aware that they've stopped.

Damned mindless thing, he thinks. No matter what I do, I can't get it to learn something as simple as giving me notice when we get someplace.

At his signal, the vehicle's door opens, which allows Storm to float out. At another telepathic signal, the home opens a portal to receive him. As he enters, he encounters the home caretaker, who is using a blower entity to blow out stale gases through a small aperture in the receiving room wall. She doesn't seem to notice his arrival, as her senses are trained on her present task. Suddenly, with a start, she becomes aware of his presence.

"Dr. Mind–Storm, I do wish you would make some kind of noise when you're sneaking about. You'll shock me into bursting one of these days."

"That would make quite a mess, Caretaker. All those bio gases and pieces of membrane fouling up my abode. For my sake, please don't burst."

"If you get any more crotchety, I might burst just to spite you."

Storm fixes her analytically in his visual gaze for several seconds. "Since I can't be sure that you're not joking, please accept my most sincere apologies for whatever I might have done to displease you."

"I'll take your apology under advisement."

"Where's Heart–Break?" Storm asks.

"Your daughter is asleep in her sleep chamber."

"Is she all right?"

"Yes. She's just fine."

Storm knows that Caretaker is not being totally honest. Heart has been in her sleep chamber more and more frequently lately. His daughter is getting weaker, and he knows that her illness will continue to worsen. The inevitable course of the disease is certain. All victims of it die an early death.

Heart–Break was born with an imperfect balance of gases in her system. The telltale greenish tinge to her inner glow was unmistakable at the moment of birth.

Storm floats through the abode to Heart's sleeping chamber. On the way, he encounters one of her doll entities floating aimlessly near the floor. He extends a pseudopod toward the almost mindless creature, and it instinctively clings to him. Thirty seasons old, Heart still plays with an infant's toys, as Storm knows she will for the rest of her life. He passes the small scar on the wall entity where he went berserk and attacked it rather than killing Luster-Shine, his mate, at that time. He purposely never had the wall replaced, in order to remind himself how vulnerable he could be to the rule of raging passion.

He hesitates there, almost involuntarily.

He remembers the day his child was born. Her color and the slow tempo and lack of crispness in her luminescence were too obvious to allow any kind of denial. Luster-Shine, her newly erupted birth membrane still in the process of closing, floated there with fright oozing from her body. She stared at Storm, waiting for him to react.

They both knew, as every Gazeon knows, that the only way to contract xenon deficiency syndrome was through the habitual use of certain narcotic gases by the mother.

There were no words spoken in those first few horrifying moments. Then Storm rammed her as hard as he could. Somehow, he managed not to extend sharp pseudopods into her weakened membrane. Even so, her body's shape was momentarily distorted. Realizing that he could not contain his rage, Storm vented it on the wall entity, not stopping until gases were seeping out of it. His own body was leaking.

Later, while he bled gases, came the inquisition.

"How long have you been taking drugs?"

She floated in silence, her bubble body shaking in fear and despair.

"Why didn't you tell me?" he screamed. "Why didn't you tell me you were having a problem? You knew it could hurt our baby. Who's your supplier?"

Finally, she found her voice and screamed back at him, "You're never home! You're not married to me; you're married to your damned job. I can't talk to you even when you're at home. We never do anything together. This little girl doesn't have a father. She has a fucking scientist."

The fact that her accusations were absolutely true only served to fuel his rage. Because he could not forgive himself, he could not forgive her.

More memories came. They would always come.

Luster-Shine eventually broke down and begged for forgiveness, but her pleas fell on deaf sensors. After a sleepless sleep cycle, Storm set out the next morning to locate a wet nurse without informing Luster-Shine. Three days later, when the wet nurse was scheduled to come, Storm threw the infant's mother out of the abode. He had hired thugs to see that she left the premises and could not return.

She tried. From a window aperture, he watched her being bruised. By the time the wet nurse surmised what was going on, she realized that to leave then would be to abandon the impaired infant to the rages of an out-of-control male.

Luster-Shine tried to gain custody of the child through the legal system. But with the combination of Storm's financial power and the irrefutable fact that she had consciously endangered the welfare of her unborn child, the courts not only awarded Storm full custody, but forbade Luster-Shine to ever see her offspring again.

Half a season later, Luster-Shine was found by the police, dead of an overdose, as her bloated body began to float almost out of sight in the atmosphere.

Storm was asked to identify the corpse before the membranes burst and she lost all definition. It was only then that his hidden guilt and shame broke forth, and he started spinning erratically out of control while crying hysterically. He had to be hospitalized for dozens of cycles before he was fit to leave.

Now here he is. He's doomed, he knows, to outlive his child. He will have to endure her death and relive his shame and grief over and over again. Without him, Heart-Break would have no one who loved her. There are no close relatives. So it's his responsibility to outlive her. That is not just a labor of responsibility, but also of love. For he has come to love the child deeply and honestly.

He floats into Heart's sleeping chamber. The wall luminosity is turned down, and the child floats close to the floor in a small, dome-like enclosure. The cradle-entity hums soft, soothing sounds. Heart still craves the cradle's protective enclosure in an unassuming position near the floor, where she can escape notice.

Storm places the doll-entity close to her, and it clings onto her like a snuggling baby. Heart stirs, and her visual sensors come awake.

"Hello, Daddy. Did you bring me a rub?"

"Of course, Bubble. But I'll only give it to you if you give me one of your own."

"Oh, okay," she says, feigning reluctance.

Their pseudopods reach out to each other as they exchange Gazeon hugs.

"Will you tell me about my mommy again, Daddy?"

Although Storm has gone through this hundreds of times before, the question always brings a wave of regret and guilt.

"Very well. What story did you want to hear, Bubble?"

"The one about how beautiful she was."

"Oh, well, she was the most beautiful female on Gazeon. She was so beautiful that all the males she passed would stop whatever they were doing just to gaze at her. And then, long after she was out of sight, they would continue to stare, in the hope that she would return."

Heart-Break takes up the story. "The beauty beasts would turn down their lights in shame, not wanting anybody to be able to make a comparison. When she went to important meetings, the chairmen would have to give her a veil-entity to dim her radiance, or no work would ever have been done. And she was only *my* mommy, right?"

"Right."

"And you were the only one she loved, right?"

"Right." And the equivalent of Gazeon tears well up inside Storm, as they always do at this point.

"And tell me how my mommy went away."

"That's enough story for one sleep cycle. If you still want to know, I'll tell you the next time. Okay, Bubble?" He knows she will not forget, and he will have to go through the agony once again of telling her this fairy tale.

"Okay, I guess," she agrees reluctantly. "I'm tired, Daddy. I get tired a lot lately."

She closes her visual sensors and is asleep.

Storm floats out of her sleep chamber and down into the common room. He hears the caretaker going about housekeeping activities.

"I've mixed up a brew of your favorite gases," she says. "The food-keeping-entity is keeping the concoction contained and at a good temperature, if you want it."

"Thank you. Bring it to me in my study, please."

"Yes, sir."

Storm's study is equipped with all the device-entities he needs to conduct his work outside his regular office. There are computational-entities, stenographic-entities, communication-entities, and the like. There are also picture-entities. Mercilessly, there is one of Luster-Shine and one of Strong-Presence. This time, he pauses to regard Strong's likeness.

He would not be where he is if not for me, he thinks. Harmony knows that and I know that. And by God, I will not take that guilt with me to the afterlife. We will succeed.

The next cycle at the institute, Dark-Lights is alone with Mind-Storm in his office.

"So here we are again," she says, "after all this time."

"Yes, after all this time," he responds. "But I always knew this cycle would come."

"I'm not sure how I feel about redirecting my job as a mind communicator. I thought I was doing a pretty good job as an administrator," she says.

"You're an excellent administrator, Dark. But you're an even better telepath and mind-melder. I'm glad we both insisted that you stay in practice with our other aliens."

"Why haven't you called Harmony back to work?"

"It's too soon. I don't think our initial progress will go quickly. I don't want her confronted with the frustration of day-after-day failures in contacting him. Constant failure to get him to recognize her would quickly lead to burnout. If that were to happen, Harmony would not be there when we need her the most."

"And when exactly will we need her the most?"

"When we're very close to succeeding. When their familiarity and close emotional bond will make the difference between success and failure. It may mean the difference between Strong's sanity and insanity, or even his life and death."

"Why did you invite her to the staff meeting?"

"It's a delicate balance we maintain. I need there to be enough hope to keep her interested. If she fully accepted Strong's loss, then bringing her into the program might be even crueler than raising her hopes a little bit."

"That was cruel enough, Storm."

"I know."

"Does it bother you?"

Storm doesn't answer, but Dark can detect the slightest dimming of his vital signs. She remembers his breakdown and realizes that her question itself was cruel. She has known for a long time that part of Storm's impervious shell is an act. She isn't helping anyone by attacking his façade. She knows better than anyone that the staff needs the tough, unassailable image he projects.

"There's another reason, too, isn't there?" she asks softly.

"Yes. We need the emotional energy that her presence and plight will create in the media. The public has to maintain an emotional connection to the project in order to maintain funding."

Dark wants to call him a bastard, but she knows he's right. Perhaps ruthless, but also correct.

"Okay," Dark says. "Just as long as my shifts are short and I can continue with my administrative duties the rest of the time."

"That's our agreement," he confirms.

Dark-Lights floats out of Mind-Storm's office and heads toward the focus chamber. Mind-Storm follows. When they arrive, they see that it's Bright-Spot who's monitoring.

"Anything to report?" Dark asks.

Bright answers with the part of him that is not engaged. "Just what is to be expected. I can roam around in the creature's brain without impediment. The mind flow there is meaningless to me. It's like the old records indicate it was in the early days."

"What about mind-melding?" Dark inquires further.

"There's no recognition on the part of the creature, and the mind-meld doesn't provide any more cogency to the material. You guys won't let me go any further into its mind structure."

"You'll get your chance, Bright, but you won't be the first to try. I will. I'm going to take your place for just a little while this cycle. I want you to anchor me," Dark says matter-of-factly.

A shock goes through Bright-Spot's system. Dark-Lights affects his concentration. Her beauty is too severe, and he's had too many fantasies about her. In telepathic contact, some of that stuff might leak out, and he's more than concerned about that; he's thrown into a near panic. The panic swirls into the part of Bright which is in the creature's mind, and there's a reaction similar to a vortex storm in the creature's thought patterns. Bright quickly withdraws most of himself and waits. The storm subsides, and Bright feels a deep sense of relief. Then he remembers why he was panicking in the first place.

"Uh...Dr. Dark-Lights, I'm not sure it's a good idea for me to anchor you," he says quietly, almost stammering.

"And why is that?" she asks brusquely.

"I—I'm not sure how to explain it. You see... Well..."

"Oh, come off it. I'm old enough to be your mother. Men having a crush on me is nothing new," she says brazenly. "I can tell immediately. So tighten down your reproductive pseudopod and do your job. It won't distract me if you're a little uncomfortable, and I won't try to look into your fantasies. Believe me, after a short while, you'll forget all about it."

Bright is flabbergasted. He was totally unprepared for such a direct and confrontational approach. He's mortified that he's been so transparent. But at least now he doesn't have to worry about what she might sense. However, she's wrong about his feelings subsiding. He's sure of it. His outer membrane is flushed with a purple glow of embarrassment.

Dr. Mind-Storm, who has been quietly observing the interplay between the two, is fighting very hard to contain the equivalent of human laughter. Nevertheless, small points of exploding lights cascade ever so slightly throughout his entire body.

Dark-Lights follows the silver cord up and into the creature's mind. The cord loses definition there as it mingles with the host's consciousness. It's difficult to discern the differences between Strong's mind and the alien's mind.

There are discrepancies that differentiate this individual's mind from the minds of the other specimens Dark has explored. But these differences are probably due to species-specific characteristics rather than Strong's influence. At this point, it doesn't appear relevant that a Gazeon mind is fused and melded with the creature's mind. At her present level of crude awareness, it doesn't seem to really matter.

Dark tries to find a sign of Strong, but nobody is home. Yet she's able to perceive that Strong's silver cord is present and blended into the mind matrix. The stem of his consciousness must have permeated the core of the alien's existence.

Dark changes slowly from the objective, probing mode of telepathy to that of the subjective, personal mode of melding. The slow, gentle process is not noticed by the creature or by Storm.

Does Strong even exist any longer as a separate entity? she asks herself.

At first, Dark confines her presence to the central region of undecipherable thought. Then, gradually, she explores the individual mind areas. She's very familiar with the locations and shapes of human minds. She finds that, except for subtle variations, this creature's mind is organized exactly the same way. She searches for Strong and eventually becomes aware of a subtle kind of presence. It's a barely discernible quality, a kind of non–alienness.

I know better than to try to pry out and separate this quality from the rest of the creature's consciousness, she tells herself. We have a plan. Stick to it, Dr. Dark–Lights. First, explore as cautiously as you have with other creatures. Learn what you can. There will come a time to make a bold move.

"You are doing very well, Mr. Bright–Spot," she says with her physical body. "I feel your presence, but it's quiet and non–intrusive. Those are excellent skills."

Bright has a moment of disorientation, which belies what she has just said. But he calms himself quickly and maintains professional focus.

Dark is studying the figures projected by a computer entity. Suddenly, she tenses. Her visual senses focus on a narrow band of numbers.

"Computer," she thinks at it, "do those numbers represent a pattern that designates a sleep cycle?"

"Affirmative," it thinks back.

"Give me a readout of similar patterns going back twenty cycles. Separate each grouping by a number representing the time units between each designated pattern."

In just a few moments, the computer entity has completed its task, and the numbers are displayed as a projection in the room.

"Copy," Dark commands.

A small bubble is expelled from the computer entity. Dark sticks it onto her body, where it flattens and stays. She twirls her way out of her office in Building A and goes directly to the focus chamber, where Bright-Spot is on duty. He's anchored by Clear-Lights.

Bright is no longer limited to just telepathic monitoring. He now does mind-melding work himself. He's allowed to meld into any area that has been previously explored by Dark as long as she has given approval. Those parameters also apply to the other qualified technicians.

"Mr. Bright-Spot, can you disengage for a moment to talk with me?" Dark asks.

"No problem."

He feels much more at home with Dark now than he did when they initially started working together. However, he finds her as alluring as ever.

"What's up?" he asks, as he maintains just a light telepathic contact.

"Have you noticed changes of any kind lately?" she asks.

"Not that I can think of off-pseudopod. Is there anything in particular you have in mind?"

"I'd rather leave the question open-ended," she replies.

Bright is perplexed. He tries very hard to come up with

something. There is nothing he would like better than to impress Dark with his perspicacity. But try as he might, nothing comes.

"No, still nothing," he says, feeling as though he's let her down.

"Thank you for trying. If something comes up, you can call me at any time," she says, and leaves.

Bright wishes that he could give that last invitation a more literal and liberal interpretation, but he knows better.

As Dark is halfway back to her office, she's assaulted by a shout that is both audible and telepathic.

"Wait!" Bright yells. "Wait! There might be something!"

Dark-Lights pivots and spins her way back to the focus chamber. Then she waits for Bright to explain.

"The creature's sleep patterns are becoming more erratic," Bright says simply.

"That's what I thought. The computer analysis confirms your observation. I needed you to confirm the computer."

"Oh, well, I'm happy to do that for you any time, you know."

Dark twinkles with amusement.

"So what does it mean?" Bright asks.

"It may mean, Mr. Bright-Spot, that our alien's mind is in another stage of deterioration," she says, obviously happy.

"Oh, well...that's good, I think. Ah...why is that a good thing?"

"Because after all this time, its mind may be beginning to loosen its hold on Strong-Presence. If this is a function of aging, it would seem that we have a much longer lifespan than do they," she says.

"Does that mean we can begin to pry him loose?"

"Yes."

The change in scheduling interferes with Bright-Spot's social life.

It's not healthy, he says to himself. The creature's sleep cycles are ridiculous. How can they cycle in and out of sleep so fast? It's ruining me. I can't make a date. My female friends look at me like I'm crazy when I tell them what time I'm free. If it weren't for the fact that I'm a young, budding scientist who's willing to make sacrifices to further Gazeon knowledge, I'd tell them all to block their ram jets.

Bright knows that Dark-Lights is dozing in her office, ready to replace him as soon as the creature's thought stream indicates that it's in a state of sleep—although the creature's sleep cycles are becoming increasingly erratic. One moment it's awake. The next, it's La-La Land. It's even getting hard to tell the difference.

"Uh-oh, there he goes." Bright recognizes the telltale qualitative changes. "Dr. Dark," he calls telepathically, "he's asleep."

Dark jerks into half-consciousness. She spins out of her office even before she knows where she is or what she's doing. Nevertheless, she heads directly for the focus chamber. She nearly careens into a staffer, who throws herself to the side at the last moment. Dark doesn't even notice. Upon arrival at the focus chamber, she instinctively tries to slip her mind into the silver cord, but Bright stops her.

"Hold on there, Doctor."

"What?" Her voice is confused and annoyed at her subordinate's presumption.

"I just think it might work out better if you're awake before you get involved, Doctor." The deferential use of her title is not congruent with Bright's tone of voice, which seems to be making fun of her. But now, fully alert, she recognizes that he might have just averted disaster. Despite his flippant, sometimes disrespectful shenanigans, he has already proven himself to be among the most competent and reliable of the staff.

"Thanks, Bright. Anything new?"

"Yeah. If this Zeke thing doesn't settle down and decide if it's asleep or awake, it's going to drive us all batty. How does it manage to do that without going vapors itself?"

"That's the point, Bright. It probably *is* going vapors, as you say."

"Yeah, I know. But it's going to take us all with it. Are you sure it's not doing it on purpose? We could be at war and not even know it."

"Be careful what you say. Some politician is likely to hear you and declare war on the alien home world."

"We don't even know where it is."

"That doesn't matter. They'll declare war anyway."

Dark curtails further discussion by slipping her mind into the alien consciousness, which is relatively quiet. Then she moves quickly into the visual and auditory senses, where she can directly experience what the creature is hearing and seeing.

The Gazeons have not been surprised to learn that the creatures dream, just as Gazeons themselves dream. It seemed reasonable to assume that all beings that evolve to a certain point of sentience have new structures that are built upon old structures that harbor basic psycho–physical and psychological material. The new structures will always function to quell and control the more primitive tendencies. When the conscious part of the mind is relaxed, those primeval qualities can express themselves while the superior levels are partially submerged. The opportunity to communicate with these creatures might be precisely at these times when their conscious and unconscious minds are in balance.

Dark-Lights waits in darkness. The creature's mind has slipped deeply into a dreamless shadow. But Dark knows that, sooner or later, the alien's mind will open to internal images. She knows how long it usually takes, although this creature's patterns have become erratic.

Suddenly, there is light and sound. It takes a few moments for Dark to interpret the sensations. The creature is not rooted to its solid world the way it is in waking life. In fact, it's floating like a Gazeon. There are puffs of white gases suspended in the otherwise clear atmosphere. The alien moves quickly. Sounds of glee come from its body.

This is not the first time she's been with it in a dream, but Dark has never dared tried to make her presence known. She has always held her consciousness back and unnoticed. She remembers her discussions with Mind-Storm.

"You know, Dark," Storm had said, "we're getting to the point where we're going to have to take a chance and get right in its senses."

"How do you know I won't get sucked up and trapped, like Strong?"

"I doubt that the creature has the power of mind to do such a thing in its present condition. Besides, it isn't the same. In the dream state, your presence would be externalized. It won't see you as invading its mind."

"Are you sure?"

"No."

She looks at him as though he were crazy. "You're crazy. Do you think I'm ready to end up like Strong?"

"We already know I'm crazy. But you aren't foolhardy, the way Strong was. I'm not urging you to take the chance until you feel comfortable—relatively comfortable, anyway. I'm trusting that your sense of vulnerability will protect you from making a stupid decision."

Dark-Lights now sees the creature the way it would see itself. In its dreams it doesn't always perceive itself in the same way. In fact, it often experiences itself in many different ways at the same time. But this was an average projection. Dark keeps waiting to witness the weird pods retracted into its body in order to make it look more like a Gazeon. She has to keep reminding herself that it's stuck in that ridiculous shape. Another thing she has difficulty getting used to is the odd, bumpy bulb between the two lesser appendages.

"How does it get along with most of its senses stuck on the end like that? Disgusting. But it's floating in the atmosphere like a Gazeon. I wonder if that's Strong's influence. Maybe this is the time to take that chance, to make that leap of faith and jet in, as old Strong would do."

Dark readies herself to make that leap of faith. She wills that he see her floating with him.

"Hello, little bird," the creature says.

Dark sees through the senses of the alien's mind and knows what a little bird looks like. She has an understanding of its language through cycles and cycles of study and practice.

"What's your name?" the creature asks.

"Dark-Lights," she answers.

She feels her body humming with excitement in the focus chamber, and she struggles to contain her emotions during this first contact. She is absolutely amazed and relieved that there's no sign of hostility.

"What is your name?" she thinks to him.

"My name is Zeke, and I'm five years old," he says proudly. "How old are you?"

The concept of a year is not clear, but Dark knows that it's related to a growth cycle. She also knows that five is not a large number. The feelings being conveyed by Zeke, however, indicate that he thinks it's a large number. She looks more closely at the creature. She notices that his membrane is smoother than normal. Its stature is smaller, though there is little with which to compare its size.

I must remember that this belief of its age is compromised by the dream state and a degrading mental capacity, she thinks.

"I can fly," Zeke says gleefully. "I'm not a bird like you, but I can still fly just like you, little bird."

"Does it feel good to fly, Zeke?" she asks kindly.

"Yeah. And I'm not even scared that I could fall. I'm a big

boy."

Dark takes the equivalent of a Gazeon deep breath before taking the next chance.

"You are big, Strong–Presence," Dark dares to say.

"Who's that?" Zeke asks curiously.

"It's a friend of yours."

"No. Don't know him," Zeke says stubbornly. "Oh, no!" he cries in horror.

"What's wrong?" Dark asks, looking around.

Another creature, one with a tall, pointed head and black membranes streaming behind it, has materialized at a distance. It's flying toward them at a menacing speed.

"It's the witch! She's going to get me!" Zeke screams.

Even though Dark is not connected to the emotional parts of the creature's mind, she feels his terror.

"Help me! She's going to get me!"

A maternal instinct that Dark didn't even know she had now takes hold of her, and she turns on the witch to intercept its pursuit. Suddenly a flame shoots out of the stick that the witch is perched on, and Dark sees herself in Zeke's mind as a blue-winged creature bursting into flame. Muffled sounds, as though someone is trying to scream through a thick membrane, are heard in Dark's disembodied mind.

The dreamscape disappears abruptly, and Dark finds herself looking out of Dr. Isacks' eyes. She waits to see if he remembers his dream. Lila is now in Isacks' field of vision.

"What's wrong, Zeke?" Lila asks.

Zeke struggles to remember. "I guess I had a nightmare. Something about a—a— I just can't remember. Go back to sleep, Lila. I'll be fine."

"I think you should see the doctor again about your Parkinson's. It seems to be getting worse," she says.

"What do doctors know?" Dr. Isacks quips half-jokingly.

Dark, who understands a small proportion of what is going

on, beats a hasty retreat.

"Wow!" Bright-Spot exclaims. "That was some trip."

"'Wow' is right. But it's just a beginning. Just a beginning. Bright, I've finished contact work for this cycle. Just keep monitoring the creature—I mean Zeke."

"Sounds like you're getting up close and personal with the creature," says Bright. "Ahem, I mean Zeke."

"I can see the need," says Dark. "It's important for me to relate to the entity on a personal level. I've had a tendency to look down on it as inferior."

"Isn't it?"

"Not really, Bright. If you think about it, it's only different. In some ways, it *is* inferior. But in other ways, it's superior."

"Oh? How is a creature stuck in one ridiculous shape and almost completely unaware of the essence of thought transference in any way superior?"

"You sound disdainful, Bright. Where is your humility?"

"Don't know. Never had any. Am I missing something?"

Dark's visual sensors make circular gyrations, just as human eyes might roll in mock dismay. "Never mind, Bright. But to answer your question, these *people* have an understanding of physics far beyond our comprehension. Their material world is far less limited than ours. They have liquids, solids, gases, and God knows what else to contend with. If we could genuinely and openly communicate with them, there's no telling how far our race could go."

Bright abandons his flippancy at hearing the earnest fervor in Dark's demeanor. "If we could retrieve Strong-Presence, he might be able to tell us a lot."

"Now you're being a bright Gazeon, Bright. That's what the project is all about."

"Plus, it's the Gazeon thing to do," he added.

"Right. Now I'm going to my office to dictate some notes. Then I'm going home to get some uninterrupted sleep. When is

Dr. Mind-Storm due back?"

"He's due back in five mini-cycles."

"Good. I'll be waiting for him in his office. Call me if it's important. I'll tune myself to your telepathic signature."

She floats out of the focus chamber, leaving Bright-Spot reveling in the growing familiarity with which she talked to him. He's thrilled at the idea that she's attuning herself to hear his telepathic summons even at the distance of her dwelling place.

Dark's dwelling place is not actually that far away. Her modest dwelling entity is situated within the Other Worlds Project conclave. She could afford much more elaborate home entities, but all she really wants is a place of privacy with décor and feminine amenities, one of which is the squibish entity.

Gazeons dwell in what would be for humans a highly toxic, acidic conglomeration of gases. They inhabit this atmospheric environment, which sometimes seems to be crisp and clear to their senses and at other times smoggy and even sooty. Just as humans often feel grimy after spending some time in smog, so do Gazeons. And just as humans then often seek a bath or shower afterwards, so do Gazeons.

The squibish entity filters the impurities from the atmosphere and deposits these impurities in little globular packets that have a density greater than the surrounding gases. Thus they sink toward the planet's core. The squibish entities are trained to excrete these pellets outside a domicile, with the net result being a cleaner indoor environment. In addition, they can exude a purified flow of very slightly corrosive gases from certain organs on their enclosing membranes. These they expel at will while massaging the bodies of their masters. The end result is a cleansed and refreshed master.

Dark luxuriates in this activity, which must feel much like a massage for a human. She orders a dimming of the abode's lights and floats off into her own dream world, populated by strange yet pleasant creatures.

In the morning, she's in Dr. Mind-Storm's office, waiting for him to arrive.

"I assume you have something important to tell me," Storm says in a slightly officious manner.

"You bet. Here's the report." She hands him a recording entity.

After going through the material, he says, "So you took that chance we were talking about. Congratulations."

"I'm not sure congratulations are appropriate. What went on there?"

"I agree that it isn't perfectly clear."

"That's an understatement, Doctor. I was hoping we could discuss its possible meaning and ramifications. I don't want to proceed any further before I at least have a well-thought-out theory."

"You're absolutely right, Dr. Dark-Lights. So let's talk. Do you have any starting point?"

"The first thing that concerns me is that when I identified him as Strong, it took only a few moments before I got attacked by a fire-shooting monster."

"According to your report, you put yourself in the way of that monster to protect the Zeke."

"I was only trying to protect our investment."

"That's a bunch of flatulence. You were being a mother protecting a child. Don't be embarrassed. It's a good thing."

"Regardless, Storm, Zeke was terrified by this creature, which I believe I somehow instigated by mentioning Strong's name."

"I agree. There must be tremendous conflict going on in that subconscious mind. Remember, it was fear and the desire to kill Strong that caused the problem to begin with. Whatever is left of Strong in that hybrid entity must also be frightened of exposure—though I doubt that there's conscious understanding in that conglomerate. I think there was a dual purpose to that thing that the Zeke called a witch."

"Which is?"

"One was to get the entity out of the dream state so it would not have to confront this conflict."

"Hmm, makes sense. Especially when he totally forgot what the dream was about when he awakened. What was the other purpose?"

"To kill you."

"What? Why?"

"Because you were the one who brought on the conflict."

"But as you pointed out, I put myself in the way."

"The Zeke didn't stop the attack. Nevertheless, he was in conflict about hurting you. Some level inside that thing realizes what you must be, and he doesn't want to destroy you."

"Could have fooled me!"

"Dark, I'm actually pleased about the whole thing. You got to him. He's reacting. There's hope."

Dreams of Hell

Dark sits on the grassy knoll, a picnic blanket spread out before her. The leafy branches of a single beautiful chestnut tree offer cool shade on a hot summer's day. Zeke, in farmer's overalls, sits beside her. Laid out on the blanket are a loaf of bread and a jug of wine.

"Have we met?" Zeke asks.

"Yes. Many times," Dark answers.

"If you will permit me to say, you are quite beautiful," Zeke says with a drawl.

"Why, thank you, but I must tell you that you're dreaming. I don't really look like this."

"Well, if I'm dreaming, I don't want to wake up. You know, it's strange, but there's something familiar about you. Something I can't put my finger on. Something very, very old, yet quite new."

Dark takes the equivalent of a deep breath before saying, "Look at me very closely. Concentrate."

Zeke stares. He scrunches his brows together in mock concentration. Suddenly he sees Dark transform into a spherical ball of gas held together by some form of membrane. Swirling, blinking, bioluminescent lights pulsate within the orb. Fluctuating, swirling gas eddies glow with undulating patterns.

"Argh, no!" Zeke screams.

Suddenly, he is immersed in a world like the inside of that horrifying alien bubble that used to be the beautiful woman he had been complimenting. Eddies of noxious gases wisp around him. Tiny storms threaten to tear him apart. An unbreathable, burning atmosphere sears his lungs.

Dr. Isacks jerks awake with a terrifying start. His heart pounds away at his deteriorating rib cage. He sits alone in his easy chair. Half-familiar objects surround him.

"Lila, Lila!" he calls in a croaking voice.

"Just a minute, Zeke," Lila's voice comes from another room.

Her slight form appears around the corner as she comes from the hallway to the living room.

"What's wrong now, Zeke?"

"I don't know. It seems that something frightened me. I can't remember what."

"You were sleeping in your chair. You probably had another nightmare. Can I get you something?"

"Yeah. Help me out of this chair."

Lila stands in front of him and extends her arms and hands, which he grabs. She pulls hard while bending her knees. Ages ago, as a young woman in nurse's training, she learned how to do that without hurting her back. She remembers when she and the young intern, Dr. Isacks, were first in love. He was so handsome, so shy. She thinks fondly of those times as she puts her back into lifting the old Dr. Isacks to his feet. She looks at him now and she still sees a young, handsome man.

"There are a bunch of bills in the mail today. Do you want me to put them on your desk?" she asks.

"Okay."

Zeke shuffles to his small, rolltop desk next to the large picture window facing the Potomac. Lila brings him the envelopes. He realizes it would be best for them to do the bookkeeping now, while his mind is clear. He knows he can no longer depend upon clear thinking to do this work.

"Lila, I wish you would learn how to do this. I'm not sure I'll be competent to do the bookkeeping much longer."

"Of course you'll be able to do the bills. You've always done them," she says, shaking her head.

"In case you haven't noticed, I'm not always that sharp now."

She frowns at him. "You aren't that bad."

Zeke shakes his head. I don't know what's worse, he thinks to himself, my dementia or her denial. I can only hope that the kids will help us out when the time comes.

"Humph," she says. "I don't want to hear any more of this doom and gloom. We're not going to need help. We're fine."

Zeke shakes his head slowly, knowing there is nothing he can say to get through to his wife.

Dark's own vital signs had spiked chaotically as she experienced Zeke's transition from blissfulness to terror. She had infiltrated not only his visual and auditory centers, but also his emotional mind. She is now full of confusion.

When Zeke saw his earthly environment change to that of a Gazeon cloudscape, she witnessed a beautiful Gazeon day, but the creature saw it as a horror. Dark felt that horror, and it overwhelmed her. Yet it was horror of something she herself loved. She had withdrawn from the creature's mind almost in panic. With a thump, she had found herself in her own body once again, in her own world, in the focus chamber.

Bright-Spot had managed to stay with her as well as with Zeke, but only at the telepathic level, which gave him the protection of objective distance.

"Calm down, Dr. Dark-Lights. It's all right. Everything is fine," he says gently.

Dark grabs him mentally and reaches out with pseudopods to make physical contact. Bright consoles her as a parent does a child. He feels awkward, with mixed emotions. He tries desperately not to allow his own carnal feelings to interfere with what Dark needs right now.

Gradually, Dark's emotions calm. She becomes aware of clinging to Bright, and the impropriety and embarrassment of this scenario becomes stronger than her neediness. She withdraws her mind and pseudopods from Bright and makes sounds reminiscent of a human clearing her throat in embarrassment.

"Forgive me. That was just a little more than I'd bargained for. That creature can respond in alarming ways," she says, trying to turn attention away from her recent loss of professional objectivity.

"Yeah, that's putting it mildly. Next time, you'll be ready for him."

"There may not be a next time," she says. "I'm not the person for this job anymore."

Bright's lights dim suddenly at Dark's pronouncement. He has enjoyed many aspects of his close collaboration with her, and her statement threatens that relationship. In the recesses of his mind, he has held a hope that their relationship might become something more than just a professional venture. Now those hopes feel severely wounded.

"Why is that?" he asks.

"It's time for Strong's wife to become involved."

Before he can ask further questions, Dark turns and propels herself toward the exit of the focus chamber. "Hold your contact for the remainder of your shift," she tells Bright as she's leaving.

Just like that, he thinks, I'm dismissed, and beautiful Ms. Mighty can get on with her important work. What the hell was I thinking?

Dark makes her way to Storm's office plus lab. As she approaches, she sends out a soft telepathic signal that she's on her way and asking for time.

"Good timing," he sends back. "I was about to suggest a consultation."

Dark is not surprised. Both of them know that the time is rapidly approaching when Harmony should be contacted.

As usual, when Dark floats into Storm's room, he's surrounded by various kinds of communication and research entities. Storm is almost lost behind a swirling cloud of them.

"Just give me a few moments," he says.

Dark floats there patiently, realizing that "a few moments" is not the accurate phrase for how long it will be before he can turn his full attention to her.

Eventually, the entities scatter to their stations and clear a space.

"You're here to talk about Harmony, aren't you?" he asks.

"You must be a mindreader, Dr. Storm."

"Yes, but not as good as you." His expression changes to a more serious one. "So what happened in the focus chamber to bring you to this discussion?"

Dark gives him a thorough description, minus her embarrassing emotional reaction.

"It must have been quite jarring to see our world through the eyes of an alien and to feel his horror upon this encounter."

"Quite."

"So now you want Harmony to deal with it?"

"Come on, Storm. You know why she has to get involved at this point of the project."

"As you say, quite. You proved that Strong is very much alive as part of that alien–Gazeon hybrid mind. It was Strong that recognized the Gazeon that was talking to him in the dream, but it was the human who was scared out of his sleep. Now we need to exploit the affection and love which the married couple developed years ago."

"Not to mention that Harmony is at least as good a telepath and mind melder as am I," Dark adds. "Strong is much more likely to respond to her mind than mine. It should increase his sense of identity as a Gazeon and urge him to separate himself from the human side of the hybrid."

"We're in accord," Storm concludes.

"Now the only problem is how to approach her."

"Good point," Storm agrees. "She was at the general meeting when we announced our initial ability to get a reaction from Zeke, but that was quite a while ago. Nevertheless, it shows that she's still open to some level of involvement—even if it's only at the level of staying informed regarding the most basic progress reports."

"That's a long way from wanting to become a part of the project again," Dark says.

"Maybe, but in the long run, I can't imagine that she could stay out of it when there's so much hope, now."

"Who's going to approach her?" Dark asks.

"As much as I'm not looking forward to it, I know it has to be me. I'm going to be her boss. We have to be able to work together again. I know she'll have to get beyond a lot of bad feelings for me that she probably has left over. We might as well start out dealing with it right from the beginning."

"You're right, Storm."

"Will you back me up if I need you?"

"Of course."

When the call comes, Harmony has a combined sense of foreboding and yearning. Although she has not had any contact with the project for many seasons, some kind of intuition tells her who's going to be on the other side of the communication.

"Hello," Harmony says, her voice quavering slightly.

"Is this Dr. Harmony–Lights?"

Dr. Mind–Storm's voice has gained a craggy quality since she last spoke with him, but it's as authoritative as ever. There's a long moment of silence before she responds.

"Yes, it is."

Harmony knows very well who's on the line, but she doesn't

acknowledge the fact. She needs time to collect her thoughts and feelings.

"This is Dr. Mind-Storm, your old boss," he says, trying to convey a spirit of cheerfulness.

Harmony's dominant emotion is anger. She's angry because she has never forgiven the doctor for pressuring her and her husband to join his research project in the first place. She also blames him for not discouraging Strong from taking unnecessary risks. It's his fault that she's been a widow all these seasons, a widow without the means of finding closure. After all, her mate is not technically dead. But he's also not really alive. The seasons of living in limbo come crashing down on her in an instant.

"Yes, I know who you are," she says acidly.

The hostility is not lost on Storm. His voice becomes neutral and more businesslike.

"Do you have any idea why I'm calling?"

"Let's not play games. Is Strong's body finally dead?" she asks bitterly.

"On the contrary. We've begun to make progress toward bringing him back."

The information is not totally unexpected, but just hearing it brings Harmony almost to the point of blacking out. There's a long pause as she recovers.

"Are you still there, Harmony?"

"Yes," she says huskily.

"Are you okay?"

"Hell, no."

She says nothing more. Her silence hides her racing thoughts and chaotic feelings. Questions run through her mind, questions whose answers she's afraid to hear.

His voice becomes gentle. "I can't imagine what you must be going through. I only know that if we're going to succeed, we'll need your help."

"And what if I refuse to help?"

"Then your husband will have less chance of returning and recovering. Your failure to help may condemn him to death."

"Damn you, you son of a bubble blister! Don't you dare play on my guilt! He's dead, and you are responsible. Now you want me to assuage your guilty conscience. I've managed to live an almost normal life, and you want to drag me back to that hopeless grind of helplessness, wondering every cycle if this is the time when he'll show the light of awareness in those dull eye spots."

Her body is a mass of chaotic swirls and broken patterns as her voice cries with pain.

"It's far from hopeless," Storm tells her. "I wouldn't have spent all these seasons risking my reputation by pouring these resources into Strong if I had thought it was hopeless." His voice is emphatic and calculating. He is purposefully baiting her to let out all her emotional poisons.

"Your *reputation*!" she screams in rage.

Dr. Mind–Storm hears Harmony break the connection. He's not surprised. He tries to relax as he floats in his office next to the communication entity. He wonders if Harmony will just show up at his office or whether she'll call. He's certain that she'll be back in touch.

Three cycles later, Dr. Mind–Storm arrives at his office. Harmony-Lights is waiting for him. Her countenance is steady. She gives no outward signs of her emotions.

"I'm glad you came," Storm says in a warm but businesslike way.

"I'm glad you're not pretending to be surprised."

"Yes, well, we both know you don't really have a choice." He hesitates, regarding her. "Look, Harmony, I know 'sorry' doesn't do it, but I'm truly sad that I reawakened your pain. I really didn't have a choice."

"I haven't been sleeping soundly for a very long time," she tells him. "Your call didn't destroy my wonderful life. But I won't apologize for the scene I made. It was not helpful. I'm ready to go to work now. Bring me up to date."

For the rest of the cycle, Storm briefs Harmony on the rough and fine details of the project. Toward the end of the cycle, other members of the project are brought into the process. There are many scientific details, such as factor-analyzed qualities that indicate different mind statuses.

Eventually, Harmony finds herself alone with Dark-Lights.

"I don't know if you've kept up with any of the developments and discoveries we've made over the seasons. Or have you?" Dark asks.

"I've made it my business to *not* keep up. It's part of my defensive system of denial," Harmony says without humor.

"I think I understand. In that case, you have a lot of work to do. I'll have a summary of the important stuff drawn up. Storm can't know *all* the important details of what goes on in the focus chamber. You have to have minds-on experience for that."

"I appreciate that, Dark." Harmony gazes deeply at her colleague for several moments before continuing, "You know, in all the briefings I've had this cycle, no one has told me why I'm so indispensable. I think I know, but it would help if you gave me your personal opinion."

"Has anyone informed you that it was me who made the original declaration that it was time to bring you back into the program?" Dark asks.

"No."

"All right. Let me tell you about my last encounter with Zeke."

"Wait a minute. Who's Zeke?"

"Zeke is the name the creature calls himself. At least it's one of his names. Others of his kind call him by various other names," Dark explains.

"You mean like nicknames?"

Dark can perceive that Harmony is beginning to relax with her.

"Yes. But some of the names are titles. Or at least that's what we surmise. If—I mean when—we get Strong back, he can tell us all about it, and we won't just be guessing."

"So Zeke is the creature."

"Yes and no. Zeke is also Strong. I can't tell where Zeke and Strong are separate."

"Are you sure Strong is there at all?"

"Oh yes, I'm sure. Let me go on and recite my last encounter. It will explain a lot."

Dark gives a detailed description of that encounter. She tries not to leave out a single nuance of perception or emotion. Harmony listens with rapt attention.

"As you know, all of our contact work with the creature, I mean Zeke, is recorded. You may want to go through the transcripts of that last one in particular," Dark suggests.

"I will, but you haven't answered my question as to why I'm so important."

"Isn't it obvious? Strong is there—or at least his memories are. Otherwise, Zeke would not have been able to spontaneously remember Strong's world. But other than that, there was nothing of Strong that was obvious in that experience. We need you because historically, he's had the closest bond with you. Most of his emotional memories, and we hope present feelings, are connected to you, and you to him. Those things can have a powerful effect in waking Strong and bringing him back to his real self."

Harmony looks at Dark for a long moment. Her gaze is both pensive and penetrating. "It's what I thought," she says, "but I needed to hear it said by someone who would most likely know. If I'm to reinvest myself in my relationship with Strong, I need to have all the reinforcing justifications for it that I can get."

There's another moment of poignant silence. Then Harmony asks the essential, pivotal question. "Do you really think that Strong can be brought back?"

It's Dark's turn to look, with her own considerably penetrating perceptions, at Harmony.

"Yes. There is a chance. But don't ask me the percentages. I just don't know."

"Thank you for your honesty, Dark."

"Harmony, can you do this?"

"I have to. I must."

In Harmony's last involvement with the Other Worlds Project, her primary responsibilities were supervisory and administrative. Now her duties will be carried out almost entirely in the focus chamber, working as a telepath and mind-melder with Zeke. Dark-Lights was administering her own program within the agency before being recalled to the Zeke project. The original plan was for her to go back to her own program if and when Harmony rejoined the project. But her hands-on experience with Zeke is too valuable to permit her to leave the project, which is now dubbed the Bring Back Strong Enterprise. She has taken on additional administrative functions within that enterprise and brings Harmony up to speed on all that's been going on in the focus chamber, which includes new techniques.

Bright Spot continues to maintain his anchoring and monitoring assignments, although Dark eventually does a great deal of the anchoring, as she works directly with Harmony. Bright is given additional supervisory and training tasks for the other anchoring personnel, both in the Bring Strong Back Enterprise as well as other programs in the Other Worlds Project.

Harmony has just anchored Dark for the first time since she returned to the project.

"Okay, Bright, take over. Harmony and I are going to debrief in my office."

When they arrive there, Harmony can barely contain herself. "Wow! You guys have come a long way. You were actually seeing the alien world through their sense organs. How do you make sense out of all that crazy input?"

"By this time, I consider myself part alien," Dark tells her. "But we aliens prefer to be referred to as humans."

"You mean you can actually think a little like them?"

"A lot like them. You will too. But it's going to take a little time, and we don't have much time."

"Why not, Dark?"

"Because Zeke is dying. If we're to get your husband back, we'd better do it before the human part of him dies."

"But if the human part dies, won't that free Strong?"

"Strong has been entangled with Zeke for so long that he's as much a part of the alien as he is Gazeon. He's got to make the separation before the human dies, or he might die with him. We just don't know for sure."

"But you've had cycles upon cycles to acclimate to the human senses and the human world. How can you expect me to do that in just a short time?"

"You're a quick study, Dr. Harmony–Lights. You're going to accompany me every cycle into that so-called alien mind until you know your way around. Then I'm going to anchor you. Hopefully, your learning curve will be fast enough."

Harmony gives the Gazeon equivalent of a frown. "I guess it had better be!"

"Harmony, did you pick up any of Strong's essence in this first excursion?"

"Are you kidding? All I picked up on was dizzy. Everything in that world has a floor. It has a bottom, just like inside a building entity, even when they're outside, and they're all stuck to the floor like glue. How do they move around?"

"Actually, not all the species on that world are glued to the floor. Some of them can fly."

"Fly? What's that?"

"They use wings to defy gravity."

"Wings? Gravity? What are those?"

Dark stares at Harmony, trying to figure out how to get these concepts across to her in a few words. They've become so much a part of her own general experience that she's underestimated how alien these concepts are to a beginner. The last time Harmony was inside Zeke's mind, it was far from the holistic experience that today's reintroduction afforded her.

"Never mind, Harmony. You'll learn quickly, I hope."

"Me too."

Harmony does prove to be a quick study. She has frequent debriefings with Dark and thus has the benefits that Dark's experiences can afford her. On one such debriefing:

"Water is so interesting," Harmony says, her lights blinking excitedly. "It's a solid, but it's not a solid. Moving through it is practically like moving through gases on Gazeon. It's comparable to moving through a gale that's blowing in every direction at once, but it also gives you something to almost grab on to. I could see those things they call fish in the water. In some ways, the water is akin to the Gazeon environment."

"You'll find other earthly environments even closer to the Gazeon habitat," says Dark. "The water that Zeke was looking at runs past his property, where he lives. The water there is called the Potomac River. It's a continuous wind of water that stays between its banks."

Harmony's lights turn inward for a few moments as she tries to fathom these new concepts of a river and banks.

"Never mind for now, Harmony. You'll catch on. Trust me."

"What did you mean that there are environments on—on—

Earth that are even more Gazeon-like than water?"

"The Earth's atmosphere is made up of gases equivalent to the part of Gazeon that we live in, only Earth atmospheric gases are a lot thinner. The humans have learned how to contain lighter gases in membranes they call balloons, or sometimes bigger things called blimps. Because these gases are lighter than the gases around them, they rise off the ground. The humans have equipped the blimps with rotors, just like the ones that nature has provided our bodies with so we can move through our atmosphere."

"Wow! These humans aren't so dumb."

"When you learn just how smart they are, it's going to make you glad they don't know where we live."

"Why's that?"

"Because they have weapons that can destroy our biggest towns with the push of a button."

Harmony stays silent as she tries to understand the ramifications of what Dark has just divulged.

"Dark, do these creatures ever move their towns?"

"That would be highly impractical. Remember, their buildings are not alive. They're made of things that might have been alive at one time but never mobile. Some of their materials have never been alive. The mass of a building is immense. Gazeon gales that would force a town to move on Gazeon would leave these structures unharmed and unmoved. Occasionally they have storms powerful enough to destroy their homes, but then those just lie around in broken pieces. Sometimes the water gets so big that it overflows its boundaries. In that case, parts of the buildings are carried downstream, just as a building entity would be carried downwind on Gazeon. Also—"

"No, stop! You're making my membrane ache. It's too much. Let me sleep on it."

Dark looks at her sympathetically while hoping it doesn't take too much time for Harmony to get a feel for the new world.

Finally, during one cycle:

"Harmony, it's time for you to mind meld with Zeke."

Harmony's lights start blinking out of phase. "I'm not ready."

"You won't do any interaction. I just want you to have the holistic experience. It's the only way you're going to get to really understand the human world."

With Dark closely anchoring her, Harmony starts to experience the world of Zeke firsthand.

"Dark, I don't understand. Zeke's senses are giving me one set of experiences, but I'm picking up that he's experiencing something quite different at times."

"There are two reasons for that. Zeke is senile while in the waking state. You're seeing the outer world from a relatively non-demented point of view. I've been filtering that information to you when you were anchoring for me. Now you only have the conditioning I've given you as a reference for what's real. Much of the time, Zeke is only seeing through his damaged brain."

"Then why isn't he demented in his dreams?"

"We don't know. We think it might be Strong's influence. Besides, it's difficult to distinguish the dreams of a sick mind from that of an intact mind, both on Earth and in Gazeon."

Gradually, over many cycles, Harmony becomes acclimated. She realizes that the process has been similar to learning a new language without the benefit of telepathy.

Am I Dead?

"Am I dead?" Zeke asks.

"'Why do you think that?" Harmony inquires.

"Because I'm in the clouds. I'm in the clouds with an angel. All I need is a harp and angel wings."'

Harmony is a little disappointed. She and Zeke have spoken many times in his dreams, and he has yet to recognize that he's spoken to her before. But there is a growing familiarity that she can pick up from him.

"You're not dead, Zeke. You're only dreaming."

"I don't remember going to bed," Zeke says. "I was in a car going to my daughter's house. Did I have an accident?"

"I don't think so, Zeke. I don't really understand much about what happens to you when you're not dreaming. You'll have to tell me about it."

"There's not much to tell. I'm an old man, and I'm losing my mind."

"You don't seem like you're losing your mind now."

"It's strange. Sometimes everything is clear for a little while. Then I lose it. I think I'm going to die soon."

"Tell me what you see, Zeke."

"'Well, I'm floating here in the sky. There are funny-looking clouds swirling around me. Not really like the usual kinds of clouds, but colored ones. They're all around."

"What do I look like to you, Zeke?"

"Oh, you're one of the most beautiful angels that I've ever

seen. In fact, if you weren't here, I would think I was in Hell. These clouds don't look all that friendly. More like steam from brimstone."

"Have we ever met before, Zeke?"

"I don't remember, but there's something strangely familiar about you. Something very nice, and something that makes me very sad. I don't know why."

"Tell me more about how I look," Harmony urges.

"Are you my guardian angel? Is that why you look so familiar to me? Have you been looking after me?"

"In a way, yes, I *have* been looking after you. But Zeke, why won't you tell me how I look?"

"It's confusing. I can tell you that there's a beautiful light in your eyes. Not just one color. It scares me a little bit. But I feel love from you, so I can't be too frightened. Sometimes I see a beautiful woman with flowing hair. A perfect, sexy shape with a flowing gown. At other times, you look like an aura. An aura in the shape of an egg."

"Which do you like better?"

"I think I like the woman's shape. The aura is somewhat scary. It does something to me that I don't understand."

"Have you ever been here in the clouds before?"

Zeke pauses to think. Slowly, his expression changes from one of bliss to one of fright.

"Stay with me, Zeke. There's nothing to fear here. I promise I'll look after you." Harmony's tones are soothing.

"I'd better not. Lila's waiting for me. She needs me. I think I'd better go back to her."

Harmony sees through Zeke's eyes, but the scene that includes her is fading. She feels the familiar sense of frustration, along with a sense of abandonment. It's the sense of a promise not quite kept. They are her feelings, not Zeke's.

Dr. Isacks opens his eyes to the interior of a car. Lila is behind the wheel, and she looks very cross.

"Who were you talking to?" Her lips are tight, and her voice is threatening.

Zeke's memory is already fading. What is now a normal pall of confusion blankets his mind. He is mentally and emotionally defenseless.

"I was talking to Angel," he answers.

"Who's Angel?" Her lips are hard, and her voice is acid.

"She's just a beautiful woman," Zeke says in a poorly enunciated and barely audible voice.

Lila is thinner than he remembers ever having seen her. Her own mind is awash in uncertainty and anxiety. She has given all her energy, all her time, and all her strength trying to keep her husband out of the hospital. She has fought to hide his deteriorating condition from the community, the children, and above all, from herself. Her own body and psyche are breaking under the constant stress, and now she learns that Zeke is having an affair with Angel. It doesn't occur to her that her husband has been in the car with her and could not possibly have been talking to another woman.

Lila finds a strip mall and pulls off. She parks hastily in a slot at the edge of the parking lot.

"After all I've done for you, you've betrayed me!" she yells at him.

She doesn't remember that her husband can't get out of the house without her, or that he's a decrepit old man who would not appeal sexually to any healthy woman. She forgets that he can't even tie his own shoelaces, let alone carry on an affair.

"I'm sorry," wails six-year-old Zeke. "I'm sorry. I won't do it again. I promise," he whimpers.

"Sorry is not good enough, you bastard."

Lila raises her fist like a hammer and starts pounding on the old man's left shoulder. But her frail body and awkward physical position in the vehicle don't allow her blows to carry much force. She quickly becomes winded and is left gasping for breath.

Automatically, without further word, she stops hitting him, puts the car in reverse, and drives out of the parking lot. She rejoins the highway traffic and proceeds down the road to her daughter Dodi's house to celebrate Easter with her daughters and their families. The rage has left her as suddenly as it had begun.

"Why are you crying, Zeke?" she asks.

"Be—be—because you hit me, and I didn't mean to do it," he sniffles.

"What are you talking about? Why would I hit you? I'm driving us to Dodi's house for Easter. Don't you remember?" she asks earnestly.

All memory of the incident has fled her mind.

Back in the focus chamber, Harmony is fuming. "Did you see what that monster did to Zeke?"

Dark extends a pseudopod to comfort Harmony. "Her own mind is deteriorating, obviously. We've been watching that for some time now."

"She's a bitch."

Dark stifles a chuckle. Harmony has become so immersed in human culture and language that she's using curse words spontaneously. She's thinking like a human.

"I wish I had arms, and I wish I could get their fingers around her scrawny little neck."

"Easy, Harmony."

"Stop calling me Harmony. I'm not feeling very harmonious."

Dark, who has been holding the connection to Zeke intact while Harmony fumes, calls for a backup team, so she can give full attention to her colleague.

"Why is it getting to you so much, Harmony? Are you losing your objectivity?"

"Of course I'm losing my objectivity! It isn't my objectivity that got me this job. Strong is in there. I feel him. He wants to reach out, but he's afraid."

"Harmony, it's not just that. You have to face the fact that he has divided loyalties. He's been mated to Lila for most of Zeke's adult life. You are the other lover."

"He is not married to that bitch!"

Harmony's ovoid body begins to quiver, and Dark can't help but notice that the wailing sounds that break out from it are very reminiscent of the way that humans cry.

After a while, Harmony regains her composure. "I'm sorry."

"I can't imagine what you're going through, Harmony. It gets to me, and I'm just a bystander."

"Oh, Dark, do you think Strong will ever come back to me? Is he lost in that world? Will he die when Zeke dies?"

"He'll make his way back, Harmony. As the human brain continues to lose integrity, the only thing left will be Gazeon." She wishes she felt as confident as she sounds.

"But Dark, it's only the Gazeon mind that's holding it together when Zeke dreams. He's absolutely logical in that state. Why is there this conflict in him?"

Dark knows that in any other circumstances, Dr. Harmony-Lights would know the answers far better than she does. But Harmony is not acting as a professional. She is a distraught female fighting to save her mate.

"He still can't recognize his separateness from Zeke," Dark says. "He is Zeke. But he's coming closer. He was able to see you as a Gazeon, and he wasn't frightened. He said he knew that you loved him. If he can feel that, his own feelings of love toward you are intact."

Harmony wants to probe Dark telepathically to test the conviction of her statements, but that would be a serious violation of Gazeon ethics and etiquette. Besides, she realizes that even that would not assuage her fears.

Dr. Isacks is helped down the six-stair flight of steps off the veranda of Dodi's house. He has one daughter on each side as he attempts to walk down the stairs. He is dimly aware of his total dependence on them to get to the ground safely. He has become used to falling by this time, but he has never fallen from this height.

"There we are, Dad. Can you make it yourself now?" Dodi asks.

Zeke says nothing, but shambles toward the long picnic table beside the huge old house. His body is bent forward ten degrees, as though he's trying to make progress against gale force winds. His hands and arms shake. His steps are short and shuffling. The women amble patiently beside him. The youngest grandchildren are engaged in strenuous play. The older grandchildren and Ralph, Dodi's husband, have just come back from shooting skeets on Ralph's property. Leo is taking pictures of the procession.

All settle down around the feast-laden table, which has been prepared by Dee and Dodi.

"Would you like some turkey, Zeke?" Lila asks.

"Yeah. That looks mighty good," Zeke says in a light spirit.

"Dodi cooked the turkey," Lila adds. "Dee made the salad. Doesn't it look pretty?"

"Sure," he says. But there's a confused look on his face. He hasn't been able to concentrate long enough to really understand what's being said. His mind is distracted by a flight of disconnected thoughts and a barrage of stimuli from the outside.

"Your father is getting more and more hard of hearing," Lila says to Dee. "We can't get his hearing aid to work. He won't even bother to use it."

"I know. I bought him a pocket sound amplifier. We can try it after dinner."

"A what?" Lila asks, mystified.

"It makes things louder," Dee explains. "You put earphones around your head. The earphones are attached to a little box that makes sounds louder. The closer you put the little box to the thing you want to hear, the better it is," Dee tries to explain.

Lila continues to be confused, and no matter how hard Dee tries, she can't seem to help her mother's comprehension.

Zeke is oblivious to the conversation. He focuses on the food, which he seems to be thoroughly enjoying.

After dinner, Dee attempts to demonstrate the amplifying device. Zeke remains disappointingly uninterested. It appears that he comprehends most of what is being said and complies with the requirements of the demonstration. He wants to make his daughter happy. But he considers all the wires and gadgetry a nuisance and can't imagine himself using it in any kind of public meeting, including church. For a short while, Dee is encouraged because her father's hearing appears to be improved when she talks directly into the little box, but then the indications of his understanding vanish. She wonders whether it's really his hearing or his comprehension that's the primary issue.

Lila and Zeke agree that he'll give the device a trial, but Dee knows that it will probably be put in a drawer and forgotten. She knows about the hearing aids that he's had for many years that no longer seem to be adequate. She had hoped that the new device would help him stay in social contact with people.

"I'll race you back to the house," Zeke quips in a wispy, barely audible voice.

The other diners marvel at these flashes of his old sense of humor. Dee knows that there are still times when her father is momentarily focused and is as competent and intelligent as ever. These times are unpredictable, short-lived, and becoming increasingly rare.

Zeke gets off the picnic table bench unaided and makes his shuffling, shaking way back to the steps up to the porch. The sons-in-law help him get up them.

He makes his way into the living room and falls without help onto the couch. There, he gazes at the gas log fireplace and somehow feels comfortable floating in the gently swirling gases. The angel floats there with him.

"Oh, there you are, Zeke. I missed you," Harmony says.

"Are you here because I'm going to die?" Zeke asks.

"You're not going to die just yet. You're not ready to die."

"Why not? I feel like death warmed over, especially floating here in these flames with you. I knew I wasn't perfect, but I didn't know I was going to Hell," Zeke laments.

"This is not Hell, Zeke. This is just gas. It's hotter than the world you live in now, but not the one you came from."

"What do you mean?"

"I mean it's time for you to remember your name."

"But I know my name. My name is Zeke. I used to be a doctor, and then people called me Dr. Isacks."

"Your name is Strong-Presence. Try to remember, please!" Harmony almost pleads.

"You know, it's very strange. I know I'm in Dodi's house, sitting on the living room couch. I know that most of the time I can't put two words together in my mind. I know that I'm dreaming, and for some reason, I know that my mind is perfectly clear at this moment. Yet my subconscious is telling me utter nonsense. What's your name, anyway?"

Harmony gathers her courage, because she has never been asked that. She believes that if she tells him her name, there will be a bolt of denial that will cause him to flee. She is even more petrified that there will be a total lack of recognition.

"Harmony."

"I guess that's an appropriate name for an angel. Glad to meet you, Harmony."

Zeke sees tears forming in the angel's eyes.

He Is Not Responding

"He is not responding," Harmony says emphatically.

"That's not true," Dark counters.

"And just how do you see him responding? He doesn't show one iota of recognition. I tell him my name, and it's like I've told him the name of a total stranger."

"Strong's sleeping mind recognizes you as what he calls the angel," says Dark. "He's becoming comfortable with you, and he doesn't panic when he finds himself in a gaseous medium. You said it yourself."

"Yeah, well, not panicking in a normal environment and recognizing me are not really the same things, are they?"

"Remember, you didn't suggest that he experience a gas world. That's a first. Strong sent himself there," Dr. Mind–Storm insists.

Harmony is distracted by a decoration entity sliding gracefully across a wall. She feels disjointed. In one part of herself, her emotions are raging out of control, violating a world of logical thinking. Another part is looking analytically and dispassionately at inconsequential things in her surroundings.

Whoever chose that entity demonstrated good taste, she thinks. I never thought Mind–Storm had an aesthetic molecule in his body. I wonder if someone else picked it out for him. It certainly couldn't have been his daughter. Who had such a powerful influence over the doctor that he would allow such an impractical contrivance into his working space?

"I don't feel Strong's presence," she says to Dark. Her tone is petulant. "All I encounter is Zeke. As far as I can tell, Zeke is completely alien. Maybe Strong was there once, but if he's buried in that foreign consciousness now, he's in so deep that nothing will ever dig him out again."

Dark looks at her in amazement. "That's not what you've been saying. You're just hurt because he didn't recognize your name."

"I was fooling myself before. It's a load of shit."

"Listen to yourself, Harmony," Dark insists.

She receives only a challenging look from Harmony.

"You said 'buried,' Dark says. "That is not a Gazeon word or concept. There is not a Gazeon in this world who would know the meaning of what you just said unless they were involved in this project. Then you said 'load of shit'. We don't have shit. We have flatulence. These creatures can't be so different from us when your own thinking is influenced in that way. Strong may be buried deep, as you say, but he's still there."

"All that means," Harmony replies, "is that I'm becoming confused whether I'm a human or a Gazeon, just like Zeke. He's neither Gazeon nor human, but a hybrid. Maybe there is no Strong and no creature, just a Zeke. Maybe if we continue to press for separation, it will merely kill it. Well, I don't want to hang around for the funeral."

"The alien's body is growing weaker," says Storm. "It's approaching death. The weakening alien mind is losing contact with its world. Strong's body remains relatively young and healthy. The periods of cogency for the Zeke are happening more frequently in its dreams. Doesn't that indicate to you that the Gazeon mind will eventually prevail?" he persists.

"No, no! Harmony shouts. "When the alien body dies, whatever is left of Strong won't remember it has a body to go to. It doesn't even belong in that body anymore. Strong isn't a Gazeon anymore. He's a freak!" She screams the last words.

Storm knows that Harmony is beyond reason, but he's been made so alarmed by the threat of her abandoning the program that he can't help pushing his point. However, he has enough control to keep his voice calm.

"It's true," he says. "Strong may die when Dr. Isacks' body dies. But that's only one possibility. I honestly don't think Strong will die."

"How do you know?" asks Harmony. "You don't know. You only pretend to know."

Dark puts out a pseudopod to get her attention. "Listen to him, Harmony. I want to hear what he has to say."

Grudgingly, Harmony holds her peace while she gives the equivalent of a scowl.

"The minds may separate just before or at the point of physical death," says Storm, "leaving Strong to return to consciousness in his own body. It may take the shock of death to jerk Strong into it. It's also possible that the entire Zeke may come and inhabit Strong's body with him."

The females are dumbfounded at this last possibility.

"Harmony," says Storm, "we don't know when the change will come. The more the Zeke comes to know you and the safer he feels with you, the better the chances are of bringing Strong out of this entrapment. The line between success and failure, I fear, is going to be an extremely thin one. Please try to live up to your name and overcome your pessimism. The Zeke will depend on its relationship with you more than any other factor. The Zeke must feel your strength and confidence."

Harmony tilts her body slightly downward. She turns slowly away and retreats from Mind–Storm's office. She continues to float out of the building without knowing her destination. Her mind and feelings are a jumble of discordance.

She wanders without apparent purpose until she realizes that she's in a major park that has been in their city for as long as she can remember. In front of her is their vegetative entity, which serves a purpose similar to that of an Earth-dwelling tree. It has been bioengineered to maintain its relative position in the ever-floating city state. It has been there at least since Strong and she began to bond.

Its huge lobed protuberances oscillate in varying hues of green and blue as bioluminescent energies are absorbed through fleshy membranes that maintain permanent shapes. The huge main lobes sprout slightly less permanent and smaller lobes in random positions. For reasons she doesn't understand, they tend to sprout blossoms of symmetrical color designs that they hold for many cycles. The whole arrangement of major lobes grows out of a central globe.

Damn it, why did I come here? she thinks.

Her mind becomes awash with images from the past, memories of better times. She sees herself and Strong touching intimately as they floated close to the tree, hidden from public view by its colossal lobes. They promised each other they would be together forever.

"How many lovers make that promise?" she murmers. "Well, Strong, you didn't keep your promise. But you didn't break it, either. Zeke thinks Gazeon is Hell. He's right. I am in Hell. I can't abandon you, even if you have abandoned me. But I don't know how much more I can take. Every cycle, I look at your body, hoping you're still inside, hoping to see you move. Sometimes I want to tear that empty membrane apart and let the life gases float away, to end this place of the non-living and the non-dead. But I can't do that. Please, Strong! Please come back!"

She floats hidden in the lobes of the tree, sobbing until it's time to go back to work.

Lila gathers this week's mail and puts it in a heap on her husband's desk by the living room window. She gazes out the window and sees a gathering of seagulls circling their back yard and sweeping along the surface of the Potomac. Her body makes a slight jerk of remembrance before she goes to the refrigerator and takes out a greasy bag of table scraps. She walks out the breezeway door and onto the newly mown grass of the back yard. Magically, the seagulls multiply in numbers and jockey for position in the sky above her. Lila lets out a yodel intended to raise the awareness of every gull within five miles. She is keenly successful in her efforts.

"You thought I forgot you, didn't you?" she says to the flock as she tosses carrion into the air and yard.

The seagulls dive and swoop acrobatically, catching every morsel they can before it falls with a fatty plop into the grass. Lila drops the rest of the mess out of the cellophane bag and steps back a few paces. Promptly, the gulls land, grab, and zoom away. Lila watches with amusement and satisfaction until every last morsel has been claimed. That accomplished, the seagulls vanish as miraculously and quickly as they had materialized.

The strong, vibrant air has turned quiet and empty. A fear she does not understand, or will not allow herself to contemplate, is somehow stirred awake, like a half-sleeping serpent.

Where do the seagulls go? What happens to them? she asks herself.

She turns and walks back to the breezeway, feeling somehow shaky and insecure. She opens the side door and steps into a faint smell of stale urine. Her olfactory fatigue has been partially alleviated by the fresh air. She goes back to the writing desk and calls out.

"Zeke! Zeke! Where are you? It's Thursday. It's time to do the mail."

She waits impatiently.

"Oh, where is he?"

Suddenly, she remembers that he's still in bed. It's 11 a.m., and he's still asleep.

That's not like him, she thinks. He's an early riser.

Another jolt of memory, and Lila recalls that it's actually been years since her husband was an early riser. In fact, he probably needs help to get out of bed. The terror returns. Then fear turns to anger, and she stamps into the bedroom. Zeke is under the covers, curled up in fetal position. She grabs the blanket and yanks it off his emaciated body. She grabs his shoulder and shakes him as violently as she can.

"Zeke, Zeke! Get up, damn you! You have to do the mail and pay the bills. You have to do it. You have to..." Her voice breaks, and for a moment it seems as though she will break into sobs. Instead, she gathers more anger and drags him to the edge of the bed. Zeke stirs, and a terrified little boy looks out on a foreign world. No intelligible words are uttered, just sounds of fright. Lila grabs his legs and swings them over the edge of the bed. As his feet hit the floor, the fright leaves, and a slight light of recognition shines through his eyes.

"Do you have to go to the bathroom?" Lila asks.

"No."

"It's Thursday. You have to do the mail and pay the bills. You know I can't do it. It's your job."

Her voice has a desperate kind of conviction that he will do the paperwork and the family business, just as he has always done.

She helps Zeke stand up.

"Can you walk today?"

Zeke shuffles forward while Lila supports most of his weight. Even now, in his diminishing body, he weighs far more than she does. Gradually, he's able to take more responsibility for himself. Together, they proceed through the house to the desk by the large window that overlooks the back yard and the Potomac. Together, they position Zeke over his chair and lower his body into it. Zeke almost falls. With great efforts of side-to-side movements, the two ancient people manage to get the chair close enough to the table for Zeke to reach it comfortably.

Dr. Isacks sees the envelopes before him, and the fire of intelligence becomes brighter. With Lila's help, he gets the bills out of their envelopes and makes out the checks.

During this period of lucidity he thinks, Doesn't she realize that I'm not competent to do this? What will she do when I can't manage this at all? I don't even remember when the last time was that I paid the bills. She just won't allow herself to see it.

Zeke feels something warm and wet running down the inside of his left leg. A pungent smell assaults his nostrils. He is ashamed.

"Damn it!" Lila screams. "I asked you if you had to go to the bathroom. You purposely wait, so that I have to clean it up!" She's like an angry mother scolding a disobedient child.

Fear is breaking through the surface of her denial, but she will shout it down. If she admits that Zeke can't help himself, then what will become of her? What will become of them? As she glances inadvertently out of the window, one lone seagull shrinks to a dot of nothingness as it flies away into the distance.

Going Down Fast

Dr. Isacks lies on the cold, black examining table. Underneath him is a stretch of white paper. His ribs show plainly through the skin of his bare chest. His stomach sinks into a deep pit, threatening to show the spinal column beyond. Floating ribs splay out like the gunwales of a wooden dory. He's vaguely aware of the murmur of voices around him, but he doesn't focus on the words and is not even aware that they *are* words. He has only the vaguest idea where he is, and the concept of time doesn't even occur to him.

He stares in reptilian-like curiosity at the patterns the ceiling tiles make. Thoughts come not in words but in feelings and images. The texture of the ceiling tiles describes grottoes, and in the grottoes are people, people that seem somehow familiar. A worm-like creature pokes its head over the top of a crevasse and smiles at him. Zeke smiles back and chuckles.

"Oh, don't mind him," Lila says. "I don't really know what he's laughing at. One thing I will say about Zeke is that he never loses his sense of humor. So, is he all right?"

"Well, Mrs. Isacks, Mr. Isacks has an advanced form of Parkinson's disease," Dr. Houseman reports.

"That's *Doctor* Isacks. You do know that he's a doctor and I'm a nurse, don't you?" Lila reminds the physician in a noticeably peeved voice.

"Oh, yes. I'm sorry. I'm sure he was a very good doctor in his time," Houseman says, unconsciously condescending.

"He's still a good doctor. He diagnosed these fainting spells, you know."

"Yes. That's right. You say he told you that he was responding to a too-high dose of his medicine?" Dr. Houseman asks for confirmation. He finds it difficult to believe that the senile old man lying before him could have performed such an amazing mental feat.

"Yes. So you see, he's still a competent doctor."

Dr. Houseman hesitates before he speaks again. He decides to avoid the issue. He's torn between saying nothing to the woman about his patient's condition and duking it out with her.

"Would you like to know what our findings and diagnoses are?" he asks her.

He holds several sheets of records and test results in his left hand as he stands before Lila and looks at her expectantly.

"I know he has Parkinson's disease," she says, "and now that his medicine is adjusted, I'm sure he'll do just fine."

She turns to Zeke and says, "Zeke, get your shirt back on and let's go. It's getting late."

But Zeke doesn't respond. The worm is not smiling anymore, and he's wondering about a black spot on the tiles that seems to be moving.

"Zeke, please listen. It's time to go," she says edgily.

She wants to get out of the doctor's office and head home before Houseman has a chance to brag about how much he knows. Her annoyance is turning to anger, and Dr. Houseman hears it.

"Mrs. Isacks, he can't understand what you're telling him right now."

"That's nonsense. He understands perfectly well. He just won't listen. You don't understand what I have to put up with. He doesn't pay attention to me just to be annoying. I'm getting sick of it."

"Mrs. Isacks, he has more than Parkinson's disease. He also

has advanced dementia. In fact, he suffers from Alzheimer's disease as well. You can yell at him all you want, but you won't get through to him," Houseman says, his own voice becoming irritated.

Zeke's brain and senses begin to refocus. He tries to sit up. Lila is there in an instant to help him.

"Where's my shirt?" he mumbles.

Lila fetches it for him and helps Zeke don the button-down garment. At the same time, she prevents him from falling over on the table.

"You see?" Lila says to Houseman triumphantly.

Together, Lila and Houseman assist Zeke off the table. With Lila doing at least fifty percent of the work, the old man shuffles out of the office.

The receptionist and the nurse look on with great concern as Zeke and Lila struggle their way precariously through the reception office.

"Please, Mrs. Isacks, let me get Mr. Isacks a wheelchair," the nurse implores.

"It's *Doctor* Isacks, and I'm a nurse. I know what I'm doing. He won't use a wheelchair. If he did, when we got to the elevator and back to the car, he would just have to get out of it again. It isn't worth the bother." Her irritation at the busybodies is obvious.

The distraction causes Lila to stumble, and the two of them teeter on the verge of falling into a heap. The nurse rushes forward and prevents the disaster.

"Don't!" Lila screams as she recovers her balance. "Get your hands off him! He's my husband! Why don't you get your own husband?"

The nurse steps back, her mouth open in shocked amazement. She stands by helplessly and watches the couple continue their agonizing, stumbling progress out the door. She's thankful that another patient has opened the heavy glass doors for them. Dr. Houseman has come into the area and is watching the whole procedure. He shakes his head slowly.

"Shouldn't we be calling adult protective services or something?" the nurse asks.

"You're welcome to try," Houseman says, "but I don't think it'll do any good. Nothing really spectacular has happened yet. If you had let them fall and he had broken his neck, well, maybe then they would do something." He turns around and goes back to his examining rooms.

Lila and Zeke arrive back at their car. Zeke musters a little more control and gets in without further mishap. Lila slams the door hard. Her posture is severe and her movements brusque. Zeke can feel her disapproval and rage seeping through his closed door, as though they were palpable fluids. His body curves into the shape of a C. His head is down, and his shaking shoulders are hunched, as though he is a little boy about to receive a severe punishment for doing something naughty.

Lila unlocks the driver's side door and swings it open. She slides into the seat and slams the door shut.

"Why were you flirting with that woman? After all I've done for you. This is the last time, Zeke. I'm not going to take it anymore. I'll take you home, but I expect your bags to be packed in the morning. You can go live with that hussy. I don't really give a damn anymore."

"I'm sorry, I'm sorry," Zeke sniffles.

Lila drives the car out of the parking lot and heads the vehicle in the wrong direction. After half an hour, her anger gives way to anxiety and confusion.

Shouldn't I be turning soon? she thinks.

She comes to an intersection and makes a left turn. After another thirty minutes, her confusion and anxiety become unbearable. Suddenly, she is aware that a police car has pulled alongside her. The policeman in the passenger seat has his window open. He motions to her to lower her own window. Lila feels a sense of relief. The police will help her. She pushes the window control button.

"Please pull over, ma'am."

"Can I pull over in that parking lot?"

There's a strip mall just ahead, and the officer nods.

Lila pulls into the parking lot, and while she's deciding whether or not to get out of the car, one of the policemen comes to her door.

"May I see your driver's license?" he asks politely.

Lila fumbles in her purse.

"Is it in my wallet?" she asks.

"Is that where you usually keep it?"

"I guess so. Isn't that where you're supposed to keep it? I hardly ever have to use it."

"If you hand me your wallet, I'll check," the officer offers.

The officer finds the license, checks it out, and returns the wallet.

"Everything seems to be in order. I stopped you because you were driving so slowly, and you seemed confused. Are you lost?"

"I think so. I know I'm in Virginia Heights Beach, but I can't manage to find my street."

"Ma'am, Virginia Heights Beach is two hours from here."

"What?" Lila says with disbelief and alarm. "Oh, dear. How is that possible? Well, I do get a little confused with directions sometimes. Two hours! What will I do?" she implores.

The policeman tries to give instructions for how to get back to her home, but it becomes obvious that she doesn't understand.

"Mrs. Isacks, just follow us. We'll get you there."

"Oh, thank you so much. You are very kind. You won't have to take me all the way. Just until I recognize where I am."

"Is that Mr. Isacks?" he asks.

"It's Dr. Isacks. I'm a nurse."

"Is he okay?"

"Oh, yes. Just tired. He hasn't been well lately."

When Lila tries to follow the squad car, she finds the task of following while also concentrating on the traffic and the signals to be beyond her. This becomes very obvious to the policemen, and they pull over at the earliest opportunity.

"Perhaps it would be better if you let one of us drive your car, Mrs. Isacks," the officer standing outside her window offers.

"Are you sure you don't mind? Just until I recognize where I am. I'm usually pretty good about these things. It's just that I've had a hard day."

"I'm sure," the officer says.

Two hours later, the policeman parks her car in her driveway. He copies down her address before he leaves. It's nighttime.

During the trip home, Zeke sits slumped in the passenger seat. He has a sense of foreboding. He's done something wrong, and he's going to be punished. He doesn't know why. That makes the fear worse. He looks out the window as the world rushes by. At times, that world comes together in meaningful patterns, depicting a universe he knows vaguely. At other times, the patterns on his retina have no more meaning than random scattered leaves blowing in the spring breeze. The fear leaves as he floats on the edge of sleep.

Suddenly, he feels a sharp pain in his chest. His mind becomes alert. He tries to speak, but words won't come.

I'm having a heart attack, he says to himself. There is a clinical calm about him. Is this going to kill me? he wonders. He feels an arrhythmia in his heartbeat. He tries to breathe slowly and not panic. There's an abrupt sensation of weakening, and the pain goes away slowly.

It's an infarction, he thinks. Some of my heart will be damaged, but it might not be too bad. If the doctors were doing their job, they would have put me on blood thinners. I probably won't remember, but I could at least take a daily aspirin. Why doesn't Lila carry aspirin in the car?

He feels a deep fatigue, and he falls asleep.

"Strong! Strong! What's happening?" Harmony asks, alarmed.

"Why are you calling me Strong? My name is Dr. Isacks. Zeke to my friends. But never Strong."

"Don't you remember my calling you that before?"

"Angel, you are the only one who ever did—even though you're a figment of my subconscious calling myself that," Dr. Isacks analyzes.

"What's happening?" she demands.

"I think I'm having a heart attack."

"What is a heart, and how can it attack you?"

Zeke laughs. "It's no laughing matter, but just to humor myself, I'll tell you. The heart is a vital organ, and it pumps blood through the body. An attack is when it malfunctions for one reason or another. That's it in a nutshell."

"If it's a vital organ, that means you'll die if it fails."

Zeke becomes vaguely aware of the gentle jostling motion of the car.

"I think I'm waking up. Too bad you can't come with me."

"But I *am* there. I just don't understand everything I see, and I can't be with you all the time."

"I don't remember seeing you when I'm awake."

"I know. I wish you could."

Zeke is back in the car. Although a feeling of pressure in his chest is alleviated, his heart races unevenly. He remembers only that Lila is upset with him, and there's a sense of panic. She opens his door with a smile.

"I'm sorry," he whines.

"Sorry for what?" she asks pleasantly.

"You're mad at me," he sniffles.

"Wherever did you get that idea?" Lila asks in surprise. She remembers nothing of her explosion in the doctor's office.

They struggle together, extricating Zeke from the car and getting him into the house. Then she helps him out of his soiled clothing and into the bathroom, where she cleans him up. Shortly after that, they're asleep in their bed.

The next morning, Zeke is feeling better. He knows where he is and wants to look at the river. He manages to get out of bed by himself and without waking Lila. He has vague memories of a dream in which he spoke with his angel.

Zeke shuffles toward the living room. As he crosses the threshold from the corridor to the living room, his dragging foot catches on the rug piling. He teeters off balance and falls sideways, banging his ribs against a wooden armrest of the couch. There's a sharp pain in his ribcage, accompanied by the surprising sound of something breaking, like a dry piece of wood being snapped in two. He slides off the armrest and lies on his back. Ignoring the pain, he tries to rise, but his coordination and strength are woefully inadequate. After several exhausting attempts, Zeke lies there and eventually dozes off.

He finds himself once more with Angel. She sits on an examining table in his old office. Dr. Isacks is wearing a lead X-ray vest.

"Well, hello again, pretty lady."

"What's happening out there, Strong?" Harmony asks. "I'm sorry I missed your last sleep cycle."

A crease of worried concentration furrows Zeke's forehead. "I fell down. I think I broke a rib."

"What's a rib?"

Dr. Isacks touches her rib cage to answer the question. A surprising thrill of satisfaction and pleasure runs through him.

Angel smiles in surprise. "I see. Do you remember the last time we met?"

Zeke concentrates. "It had something to do with you calling

me Strong. That's a name, isn't it?"

"It's your name."

"If you say so. You said there are two of me. Something like *The Invasion of the Body Snatchers*. Then something happened, and I got scared."

"That's good, Strong. I'm sorry that you got so upset, but you have to get acclimated to your real home before it's too late."

"Too late for what?"

"Your physical body is dying in this world. But you have another body waiting for you in your old world."

"That's sacrilegious. I'm a Christian. My heavenly body waits for me in Heaven. That is, of course, if I make it there. Are you telling me that I'm going to Hell?"

"What is Hell?"

Zeke rolls his eyes. Surely she must know what Hell is. "Hell is where bad people go when they die. Heaven is where good people go when they die."

"That's curious," Angel says. "Some of my people believe the same thing. I wonder if they're the same places. But Strong, your home is neither Heaven nor Hell. Your body is not dead. Even now, you're connected to it, although you don't remember."

"You're taking advantage of an old man with an addled brain. I'm decidedly confused. What do you want me to do?"

"Let me show you what I really look like. Try not to be scared away this time."

Zeke vaguely remembers the last time he witnessed the transformation.

"But it was so ugly," he complains.

"Am I ugly, or is it just so divergent from what you've become accustomed to? At one time, you thought I was beautiful." There are tears in Angel's eyes.

Zeke feels sympathy and a strange longing. "I'll try to stick it out this time, but I can't promise. Can you keep the rest of the stuff out of the picture? All those fiery clouds look like Hell to me."

"Zeke, as you've pointed out before, I'm in your mind. If you concentrate exclusively on me, maybe you can keep the rest of the environment out of the picture."

"Okay. Let's give it a whirl."

Slowly, the image of Angel blurs, and an aura forms around her. The aura is not ugly to Zeke. Gradually, the aura becomes dominant, and the human body fades behind it. Before the transformation is complete, Zeke hears Lila's voice.

Two hands grip his shoulder as it's shaken back and forth. Zeke is staring at the side of the living room couch as he lies on his right side. He mumbles some sounds as he's pulled over onto his back. Lila is staring down at him concernedly. For a brief instant, Zeke's mind is clear. Then the clarity fades as the memory of Angel dissipates. In that last glow of cogency, he realizes that he has soiled himself.

Storm, Harmony, and Dark are floating in the equivalent of a Gazeon restaurant.

"I don't believe it," Harmony says. "This is actually on you, Storm."

"Are you calling me cheap?" he retorts.

"Well, not exactly. But when was the last time you treated us to a meal?"

"Thirty cycles ago. You ordered pink swirl and bursting bubble fantasia. It was rather expensive."

"What did I order?" Dark asks.

"Something less extravagant. It was hardly worth remembering."

A restaurant hostess floats toward them as they wait in the reception area.

"A party of three?" she asks.

"Yes."

"Would you like the open area or an enclosed one?"

"Enclosed, please," Storm responds.

The hostess floats slowly through the open area as they follow.

Groups of patrons are clustered in designated spots, where they dine sociably. The individual dining spots are situated in a complex three-dimensional pattern. Each location is marked by a cluster of glow entities that illuminate their respective dining areas with a specific color. Some of these areas accommodate more patrons than others and so have more color glow entities that illuminate larger areas. There are at least seven different colors.

As they pass through, one of the diners signals for the hostess's attention.

"Can I help you?" she asks.

"I'm sorry to be a pain," the Gazeon says, "but my eye spots are sensitive to yellow. Can you change our spot more toward blue or violet?"

"I'll attend to it immediately, sir. Just let me get these folks situated."

"Thanks."

They continue to float toward a group of booth entities situated along the far wall.

"Do you want your booth completely enclosed, or would you like one side open?"

"Completely enclosed, thank you," Storm says.

They float into the adequate but cozy enclosure. The opened access side slowly fills in.

"The service is usually fast. Let's wait to give our orders before we start our shop talk," Storm suggests.

In a short interval, the booth begins to pulsate with lavender light.

"Enter," Storm says in his officious voice.

The wall dilates, and a waitress enters.

"Are you ready to order?"

Harmony responds immediately. "I'd like pink swirl and bursting bubbles fantasia on the side, please."

Storm's sigh is obvious.

"You know, I've never tried pink swirl before. I think I'll try a flask of that. But I'll have red splatter on the side," Dark orders. She knows perfectly well that red splatter is very expensive.

"An excellent choice," the waitress says. "And you, sir?"

"I'll just have some black goop gas over a white cloud."

"I'll be right back with your orders." As she floats briskly off, the chamber closes again.

"I've invited you out to celebrate the noticeable change in your morale, Harmony," says Storm.

"It's only a small change," she replies. "I'm still not what you might call optimistic."

"Your lights have been a lot more harmonious these last few cycles than they've been in a long time," Dark says.

"Well, it's not hopeless anymore. Zeke is showing less fear and more cooperation. He even shows rudimentary signs of recognition."

"Then why the remaining pessimism?" Dark asks.

"You know as well as I do that Zeke might die and take Strong with him. It's a race, and there's no reason I should believe we're going to win it."

"But you do believe we will?" Storm urges.

"I have *hope* that we will. That's enough for now."

The booth pulsates again. According to custom, Storm doesn't have to say anything. After a few discreet moments, the opening appears, and the waitress floats in, pulling gas flasks in a serving net. Her pseudopods reach in and extract the flasks one at a time.

"Two pink swirls, a black goop over a white cloud, bursting bubbles, and red splatter."

She places each flask in a proper pattern before the patrons.

"Anything else? An intoxicant, perhaps?"

"We're fine for the moment," Storm says.

The waitress leaves, and the booth closes.

Harmony puts one end of the gas flask to a portion of her ovoid body. The membrane that encloses the nutrient gases and the membrane that makes up her skin seem to merge. A tiny opening develops between the flask and her body. A slow hiss of pink, swirling gas can be seen spurting into her body through the translucence of her skin. A dreamy look comes into her visual organs.

"Mmm. This is absolutely delicious."

"For what it costs, it certainly ought to be," Storm grumbles.

The pink color of the gas is gradually absorbed throughout Harmony's body, leaving an ineffable appearance of pleasure and health.

"Why are you constantly hollering at him?" Dee asks.

She and Lila are in the Isacks' living room.

"Why are you always criticizing me? I'm not always hollering at him." Lila's voice is tight and loud.

"Just listen to yourself. You're screaming at me, now."

"You just don't know what it's like. He won't do anything I ask him to. I ask him if he has to go to the bathroom, and he says no. Then I get him dressed and out here to breakfast, and he wants to go to the toilet. I ask him to talk to me, and he won't say anything."

"Lila, he's not doing it on purpose. He can't help himself."

"What do you mean, he can't help himself? Of course he can help himself!"

"No, he can't. He has dementia."

"No, he doesn't. He has Parkinson's disease."

"He has more than that. Let me tell you something, Lila. Your yelling at him and treating him roughly, and the way you do it, is abusive."

"Abusive? *Abusive?!* I'll tell you what's abusive. It's abusive when he hits me. It's abusive when he kicks me."

"If he's actually doing that, and I doubt it, he either doesn't know what he's doing or it's because he doesn't have control over his body."

"I'm sick and tired of your criticism, Dee. You never have anything good to say about me. If you're just going to come here and tell me how awful I am, don't bother to come at all."

"I don't think you're awful. I think you're under tremendous strain and you need help."

"I don't need help. There's nothing wrong with me, nothing at all."

"I didn't say there was anything wrong with you. I mean you need help taking care of Dad. You need someone to help move him, to clean him, to do the housekeeping, the cooking."

"No busybody is going to come here and interfere with my business. You and your sister want to take over my life. Well, I won't have it. You can leave right now."

"Okay. If that's the way you want it, then I *will* leave now."

Dee turns and walks to the breezeway door. Leo, who has been standing silently by, careful not to get caught in the middle of the fracas, follows closely behind her with a feeling of satisfaction that Dee has finally said what was concerning the whole family. They get into their car and drive away. They've been there less than thirty minutes.

The following weekend, Dee and Leo are once again in the Isacks' home.

"I can't get him up," Lila says. "Will you help me?"

Dee goes into the bedroom. The smell of urine is very strong. She gets on her knees so that her head is level with her father's. She has done this many times before. She talks to him in a cooing voice, the way a mother would to a three-year-old child. She smiles as though looking down at an infant. Zeke has always responded to this. But today there is nothing. He lies curled in a fetal position without movement or sound.

Leo stands in the doorway, watching. He feels useless and uncomfortable, so he leaves.

A few minutes later, Dee comes out of the bedroom.

"Leo, will you help me get my father out of bed? He can't help us do that the way he normally does. We need your muscles."

"Sure," he says, trying not to show his squeamishness at handling the urine-soaked and unwashed body of his father-in-law.

They go back into the bedroom. Leo has no experience with this sort of thing. He helps Dee maneuver the body to the edge of the bed. Zeke is as limp as a sack of potatoes. Leo puts his forearms under Zeke's armpits, while his wife grasps her father around the knees. He lifts the old man over the arm of the wheelchair, which is sitting parallel to the bed. They settle him into the seat. Zeke lets out a groan as he's lifted.

Leo leaves the bedroom and goes to wash his hands and forearms in the hallway bathroom.

Five minutes later, the two women come into the living room where he's waiting.

"Dee, I've never seen him this way," Lila tells her daughter. "I think there's something seriously wrong. I'd better get him to the hospital."

"I think maybe you're right. Would you like us to take him in our car?"

"No, I can handle it," Lila says emphatically and peevishly.

Dee knows it will do no good to argue with her mother.

"I'll lock up the house after you."

"Thank you."

"What's happening?" Angel asks.

"I'm not sure. Maybe just the running down of this old clock. But this could be the big one."

They are sitting on a huge boulder. Beyond the rock is a swirl of fog. A barely perceptible noise emanates from the featureless surroundings. The noise sounds like all the keys depressed on an organ at the same time.

"Stay with me, Strong."

Harmony wills for Zeke to see the transformation into her natural form. Again, the beautiful aura spreads out from her human guise. It is a golden, translucent hue. The Gazeon gaseous orb becomes gradually preeminent. It fills with obvious and subtle flows of translucency and points of light. Harmony consciously projects the most appealing countenance she can muster. She floats above the barren rock, a glowing specter against the featureless backdrop.

"You are beautiful, Angel."

The featureless, surrounding void takes on color and movement, slowly metamorphosing into the typical, ever-changing Gazeon gas-scape.

"Strong, do you know me?"

"Of course. You're Angel."

Somehow, Zeke detects disappointment within the creature's expression. He has no idea how this knowledge comes to him.

Harmony sees a slow transformation in Zeke's own projection. A secondary face with a secondary expression is mingled with the calm, confident Zeke that she's been talking to. It fights for dominance. First there's one Zeke, and then the other. One is frightened and mistrusting; the other is rational and accepting.

"What's happening to you, Strong?" Harmony asks.

"I feel so strange. I'm almost of two minds. One would gladly go with you. The other fears you as an alien."

Zeke desperately presses the palms of his hands over his temples. His brows knit together as he squeezes his dream eyes shut. Deep wrinkles crisscross his forehead as his lips curl back in agony. The internal conflict tears at Zeke's mind.

"I...can't...control...it," he hisses out through clenched teeth.

A frightened old face gains sway in the inner war, and the beautiful images give way to hellish ones. Zeke spirals off his rock into the Dante-esque landscape with screams of terror.

Harmony races after him, but Zeke fades from view, and the dreamscape fades along with him. She is left alone in the quiet.

At first, she is petrified that the Zeke has died, and Strong along with it. But then she realizes that she's still in his mind. She backtracks down the silver cord and into her waiting body.

"I need a conference immediately," she demands.

As Bright-Spot takes over from Harmony and monitors the Zeke, Harmony, Dark, Storm, and a few others spin to a conference room.

"What's going on?" Harmony asks, her lights blinking dim and frenzied. "He didn't wake up. Yet the alien mind still overpowered Strong. I thought that couldn't happen unless the waking mind gave more power to the human's mind."

"My guess is that the alien's mind is becoming detached from its physical anchor and is now groping for purchase in Strong's mind," Storm hypothesizes.

"You mean, turnabout's fair play?" says Dark.

"So why isn't Strong able to overcome the human's mind?" Harmony asks.

"The fear factor, probably," Dark says. "Its body may be dying, but it's still dominant and producing lots of emotion-intensifying hormones. My God, if the creature's body had died at that point, I would have lost Strong. He would have gone with it to oblivion—or to whatever the human afterlife is."

"Unfortunately, that's probably right, but not necessarily," Storm says. "You went after him, and I'm not so sure that you couldn't have caught up with him and still brought him back."

"Harmony, I think you ought to start sleeping at the facility," Dark suggests. "The Zeke can die at any moment. We can't miss a single opportunity to communicate with it."

"I agree," Harmony says. "But what can I do differently? This strategy of exposing him to the Gazeon environment doesn't seem to be working."

"That's not quite true," Storm corrects. "His comfort with the representation of our world is decreasingly foreign to the human psyche. You need to keep strengthening that familiarity. Hopefully, the alien xenophobia will eventually be overwhelmed by this comfort. He even referred to you as beautiful in the latter stages of the transition process."

"But he shows no signs of recognizing me or anything Gazeon."

"It's been a long time for him, Harmony," Dark points out. "Strong has been in a kind of coma for all these cycles. He's been through the ultimate identity crisis and mental shock. It's not surprising that he suffers amnesia."

"Just keep plugging away with what you're doing, Harmony," Storm urges. "From now on, all operatives will sleep in, not just Harmony. That includes Bright. He's the best monitor we have outside of you, Dark."

"I think you'd better be the one to tell him, sir," Dark ventures. "It's really going to mess up his social life."

Lila has been in Zeke's hospital bedroom the entire night. She has refused to leave and has been only partially successful in falling asleep on an uncomfortable chair. Her anxiety has reached a fever pitch and has become unbearable.

The early morning nurse's aide comes into the room. She gives Lila a perfunctory "Good morning."

Lila watches her change the sheets as she rolls her husband one way and back the other. Later, Lila observes a nurse give Zeke a cursory sponge bath. Her mind is befuddled by the stress and lack of sleep. As Zeke's arms and legs are moved about, she sees something else.

When the room is again cleared, and she finds herself alone with him, Lila gets out of her chair and approaches the bed.

"You son of a bitch. Why did you make out with that woman?" she screams at him.

She shoves Zeke's shoulder violently. His whole body reacts reflexively, and an arm flails out and strikes Lila on the breast.

"You bastard. You son of a bitch!" she yells as she begins to hammer strike his chest with both fists.

At that moment, a nurse enters the room and grabs Lila from behind, trying to immobilize her arms while shouting for help. Before help arrives, Lila twists out of the nurse's grasp with surprising strength and starts to kick and strike her wildly. A nurse's aide and an orderly rush into the room and pull the two women apart.

"I saw you making out with my husband, you cheap piece of shit. I was right there. You did it right in front of me."

By this time, the head nurse bursts into the room. "Hold her down, Millie. Are you all right?"

The other nurse is shaking, and there are scratches on her face. "I'll be all right," she gasps.

"Call security, and then check yourself into the emergency room," the head nurse orders.

Three minutes later, the uniformed security guards have Lila in handcuffs and are escorting her to a secure room on the psychiatric ward.

"Leave me alone! Leave me alone! I'm a nurse! You have no right to treat me this way!" Lila shouts as she's forcefully led down the halls.

After they reach the secure room, the guards stay with her.

In time, Lila runs out of energy. She becomes quiet and docile and sits down. Eventually, with caution, they remove the cuffs.

In the meantime, the hospital social worker is brought into the situation. Hospital records are searched, as well as Lila's handbag. Her daughters' names and telephone numbers are found.

At Dodi's home, the phone rings.

"Hello. I'd like to speak to Dodi, if I may."

"That's me. Who is this?"

"My name is George Krimpwell. I'm a social worker at Colonial City Hospital."

A sudden twinge of panic flashes through Dodi's body.

"What's wrong??"

"Is Ezekiel Isacks your father?"

"Yes. What's happened to him?"

"He was admitted to the hospital early yesterday and is staying here for observation."

"Please," she interrupts, "tell me what's happened."

"You'll have to talk to the medical staff about that. But I need to talk to you concerning another matter."

"I want to know what's wrong with my father."

"That's being evaluated right now, and I'll have a nurse or doctor talk to you right after we communicate about the problem with Mrs. Isacks."

"Good Lord! What's going on?"

"Right now, we're trying to keep her quiet. She's in a secure room with attendants."

"What? Why?"

"She attacked your father as well as hospital personnel."

"Oh my God! What made her do that?"

"We think she's not thinking clearly. It's too early to know what's wrong with her."

"What are you going to do with her?"

"We don't want to press charges. We want you or a member

of your family to request a temporary detention order so that she can be held for observation and possible treatment for a psychiatric disorder. The alternative is to press charges for assault and battery."

"This can't be happening. First my father, and now my mother! Are you sure she wasn't provoked?"

"I'm sure. She is definitely a danger to herself and others."

"What do I have to do? I—I don't know anything about getting a person committed."

"It isn't very complicated. You just need to come down here to fill out some papers and be present at a hearing set up with a magistrate."

"Good Lord. A hearing? Why?"

"The magistrate has to decide whether your mother is safe to be on her own. A mental health worker will make a case that she is not. A lawyer will make sure her rights are not being violated and act as an advocate for her."

"Oh, Lord. I'll have to cancel some things I was supposed to do, then it is an hour's drive down there. I can't get there in less than three hours. Can you hold her until I arrive?"

"I understand she's cooperative right now."

"Is my father all right?"

"I'm told he's resting comfortably. That's all I know. You can talk to a doctor when you get here."

Schizoid

"Do you remember the last time we talked?" Angel asks Zeke as they sit on the sands of a misty beach. The water of an opaque ocean laps gently at their feet. It's calm water, with no breakers and no rollers.

"Most of it. I remember you changing into this ball of gaseous light. It didn't bother me this time. What you call your world didn't bother me either. I even thought it was attractive, but something came over me, and I was terrified. I thought I was dying and going to Hell."

"I also think you were dying, but you were not going to Hell. Believe me, Strong."

"There's that name again. You really are tenacious, Angel." Zeke hesitates and seems to become lost in his thoughts as he gazes out over the placid waters.

"What's that thing you're sticking in your mouth?" Harmony asks.

The question jerks Zeke's attention back from his gaze.

"I'll be darned. It's a toothpick. Actually, I haven't had teeth to pick for a dog's age. I guess that proves I'm dreaming."

"What are you doing with it?"

"Right now, I'm just chewing on it. But generally you use it to pick food out from between your teeth."

"Ugh, that's disgusting."

Zeke chuckles. "Oh, we humans can get a lot more disgusting than that. Want some examples?"

"I think not, Strong."

Zeke becomes pensive again. "You know, I really am dying. It's not what I expected, though."

"What did you expect?"

"I didn't expect to be talking to a figment of my imagination. I especially didn't expect to be mentally functional in my dreams. I haven't really been awake since the last time we spoke. I have no idea of the passage of time."

"We have so little time, Strong. If the body you inhabit dies and you haven't come back home to us, you may be lost forever."

"I still don't understand, Angel. If I die, I die. I hope to go to Heaven, but nothing that I've seen of your so-called world reminds me of Heaven. Maybe I shouldn't indulge myself with these dream fantasies. Maybe I should just let go and die, so I don't subject myself to these excursions into terror—which is the way these meetings always seem to end up."

"These are not simple dreams, Strong, and I'm not a figment of your imagination. You've become a healer in the world you've come to call your home. You must know something about the mind and dreaming. Do your experiences here reflect what you know about normal dreaming?"

"I was never a student of that sort of thing, but this returning over and over again to the same personality in order to continue an ongoing cogent discussion doesn't seem to fit the common lexicon. It certainly pushes the idea of recurrent dreams to the max."

"Strong, I never told you the story of who you are and what circumstances you find yourself in. We were hoping that you would recall these things through your exposure to me, but since that doesn't seem to be happening and time is running out, I'm going to tell you."

Zeke sits quietly, waiting for the story to unfold. Harmony gives a synopsis as he listens attentively. She doesn't know when they'll be interrupted again, so she doesn't waste words. As she finishes, she scrutinizes Zeke for a reaction.

"Angel, if that isn't one of the most unbelievable, farfetched science fiction yarns I've ever heard, my name must be Strong. You must be crazy to think I would go for it. Since you're a projection of part of me, I must be the crazy one."

"Please, please indulge me, Strong. Every time we've tried to show you reality, the alien part of you becomes agitated and overcomes your Gazeon mind. So I want to see if you can separate the two minds in this dream state."

"Wow! Is that even possible?"

Harmony continues with an air of urgency. "You keep saying that everything in this dream is a projection of a part of you. If that's true, then you can separate the parts that you yourself have identified as the rational versus the frightened self."

"I understand what you're getting at, but I don't have the foggiest notion how to split myself into two people. Not on purpose, at least."

"That's okay. I'm here to help you. I'm a master of the sciences of mind, but I need your complete cooperation. I know you have a great curiosity as to the nature of things. That was true of Strong, and I believe that it's true of both parts of Zeke."

"I suppose you're right about that. Okay, what do you want me to do?"

"Just have an open mind. Look and listen very closely. The procedure will be close to what you call hypnosis."

Harmony wills the aura that Zeke has witnessed many times before. It begins to appear. She manipulates the flow and quality of colors so as to induce a sense of wellbeing. After a period of this, she begins to describe in words and images what she's seen of the old man as he had manifested himself in the past. But she doesn't include elements of horror. She suggests the existence of such an entity biding silently inside the younger, more vital persona which is Zeke's current presentation. She calls this persona Strong. She suggests that the old man's curiosity is being drawn to the surface of Strong's face and body.

Slowly, that image of the old man does begin to superimpose itself over the features of the younger, healthier person. With Harmony's urging, the old man she refers to as Zeke and the younger man separate gradually into two separate beings, until they're standing independently. There remains an umbilicus that stretches from navel to navel.

"Strong, I want you to remain quiet and watchful while I talk to Zeke. Zeke, what do you see?"

"I see a beautiful angel with a halo around her."

"How do you feel about me?"

"You are a beautiful lady, but I'm a married man. Lila would be very angry if she saw me talking to you."

"There's no reason to worry about that. You're not worried about that. Everything is going to be all right. You are all right."

Zeke smiles.

"What do you see standing next to you?"

"A young man. A man like I used to be."

"I'm going to go for a swim with him," she says. "You'll be fine here while you wait. We will return. You feel good about that, because you can sit here and enjoy the beach while we're gone. Is there anything you want while you wait?"

"Yeah. I'd like to have my Gordon Setter with me. It seems as though I haven't seen her for a long time."

"She's right behind you, Zeke. Turn around, and you'll see her," Harmony says matter-of-factly.

Zeke turns, and as he does so, Harmony sees the image of a Gordon Setter manifest. Excitedly, Zeke bends down to hug his tail-wagging, tongue-lapping old friend.

"Strong, give me your hand and follow me. We're going into the water. You'll have no trouble breathing. This is a dream, after all."

Strong takes Harmony's hand and walks confidently into the water. It doesn't feel like water. It feels like gas.

"I've taken you into this medium so that what you experience will not be experienced by Zeke."

"I'm still attached to him by this umbilicus," Strong says.

"That's okay. Just ignore it. The umbilicus will take care of itself. I'm going to expose you to what I've led you into before. This time, you won't be frightened away."

"Will I return to the beach?"

"That's up to you. It would be better if you didn't, but you're the only one who has the power to decide."

"I'm ready," Strong declares. He almost feels enthusiastic.

He feels a little queasy, like a boy on a roller coaster, but the feeling dissipates as he becomes increasingly comfortable in the environment. For the first time, Strong feels a slight sense of familiarity with the gas world.

"Now, Strong, I'm going to take you one step further. The form you see me in is your form as well. Your real form. I'm going to allow you to know what it feels like. Any moment you need to go back to being human, just let me know, and it will happen immediately. Try not to panic."

"Wow! That's a tall order. I'm not sure I'm ready for it."

"We don't have much time, Strong. The human body is dying. We don't want you to be faced with this change at the moment of crisis. You must be prepared."

Strong takes a deep breath. "Okay. Let's go."

Through her powers of mind-crafting, Harmony directs the transition as gently as possible. When she detects the buildup of tension in Strong, she slows the process down to a standstill, even to the point of going backwards on a few occasions.

Strong feels sensations that are exceedingly foreign to him. He begins to see, but not with human eyes. He gradually senses in other ways, ways that are similar to but somehow different from his human means of knowing the inner and outer worlds. As strange as it all is, there's a far-off sense of recognition. The Gazeon body is a useless thing to him in terms of maneuverability.

It's like a newborn human who must learn to use its body, or like a man who's been in a coma for a decade—who, coming out of it for the first time, must learn to walk all over again. After a short time, Strong notices that the umbilicus is still attached.

"I think I've had enough exposure for one time," he says to Harmony.

"You don't have to go back at all. I can lead you to your corporeal body, which is just like this, and you can be safe from the danger inherent in the human death."

"As much as you would like to believe that I'm a Gazeon," Strong tells her, "you must remember that I'm human. Even if the story you told me is true, I've spent most of my life being human. Even if that old man out there is separate from me, he's also part of me. It's a symbiosis. If his body and mind have been host to me, I owe him something. If I were to abandon him now, it would be the same as abandoning myself. I'm not whole without him. I wouldn't abandon him in his time of crisis."

"Even if it means your own death?"

"Even if it means my own death. If he dies, I die."

Though he's in a strange form, Strong can perceive that Harmony is sobbing.

"Why are you taking it so personally?"

"Strong, what do you think I am to you?"

"You're probably part of a team that's trying to get me back for scientific reasons."

"Damn it, Strong, I'm your wife! I've been abandoned by you for your so-called whole lifetime. You wouldn't abandon this creature, but you have no qualms about abandoning me," she says through the equivalent of angry tears.

Strong has the shock of sudden understanding. He feels a flame of sympathy run through his new form. It's more than sympathy. It's something else, something more personal.

"I don't want to die, Angel. I—I actually am beginning to believe your story, and I want to go with you, but I have to go back to that old man up there."

"He will never be able to adjust to this world and this form," Harmony protests.

"Don't sell him too short. I adjusted to *his* world. I made it mine. Given our help, he might surprise you."

Harmony's emotions of hurt and abandonment are alleviated as she realizes that Strong is talking as though he accepts that he is a Gazeon. Her hopes are lifted. Maybe Strong is actually coming back to her.

"Strong, you were always willing to take chances. You'll never take a bigger chance than this."

"I won't be taking it alone. You'll be there helping me, Harmony."

Strong uses her proper name on purpose. There's a sense of connection and appreciation about her, perhaps more than appreciation. His mind quickly encompasses all that she must have been through and all the devotion that it represented.

"I have a hunch that this is coming down to the wire. No matter how bad it looks, please don't give up on me until the umbilical cord is broken, Harmony."

"I won't. I never did," Harmony says through sobs.

Strong feels a tug on the umbilicus.

"I think Zeke is being called to wakefulness. I've got to go."

Humoring Lila

Lila has been sitting in the cushioned chair in the lobby of the hospital. Two guards sit nearby, keeping a watchful eye on her. Lila gets up and walks to the receptionist's desk. The security man follows at a discreet distance.

"Can you please tell me what room my husband is in? I'm here to visit him. His name is Dr. Isacks, and he came here yesterday."

The receptionist, who has been briefed as to how to handle this situation, responds, "Dr. Isacks isn't receiving visitors right now. He's undergoing an examination."

"Oh, that's all right. I'm a nurse. The nurses here asked me to come and look after him."

"I'm sorry, Mrs. Isacks, but you'll have to wait."

Lila returns to her chair. The security man remains standing for a few minutes and then returns to another chair. He doesn't want it to be obvious to Lila that she's being dogged. Besides, the chair he was occupying is no longer available.

A few minutes later, Dodi walks into the main lobby from the parking area.

"Dodi, what are you doing here?" Lila asks as she walks over to her daughter.

"I was told you were having a hard time, Lila."

"Who, me? I'm not having a hard time," Lila says, surprised. "I just got here, and I'm trying to see your father. But they're not letting anyone see him now because the doctor is examining him.

Why do you think he's in the hospital, Dodi?"

Dodi doesn't know quite what to say. "I don't know any more than you do," she manages to get out. "I...uh...I have to talk to someone."

"Oh, well. Go ahead, then."

Dodi goes to the receptionist and identifies herself. She tells the woman that the social worker is expecting her. The receptionist calls the social worker's office and is lucky to find that he's in his office and not on the telephone. Dodi is told to wait in the lobby. She goes back to sit next to her mother. It's 11 a.m.

Lila begins to talk a blue streak. She talks about her neighbors, about the man who mows the lawn, and tells stories about Zeke that seem improbable to Dodi.

"So, Lila, why did you bring Daddy to the hospital yesterday?"

"I didn't bring him here. He decided to bring himself. The nurses called me to come in this morning to look after him, but I haven't been able to get in to see him yet."

"Daddy can't drive himself. You must have brought him here."

"What do you mean, he can't drive himself? Of course he can drive himself!"

"No, he can't, Lila."

"Well, I'm not going to argue with you about it. You never believe anything I say." Her lips become tight, and she glares into space.

Before anything else can be said, the social worker walks up to the two women and introduces himself.

"What do you do here?" Lila demands.

"I try to help people."

"Good, can you help me to see my husband? His name is Dr. Isacks."

"I have some business to attend to with your daughter first. Then we'll see."

He turns to Dodi, "Will you come with me?"

"He's my husband," Lila says angrily. "You have business to do with *me*."

"It's okay, Lila," Dodi says soothingly. "I'll be back in a little while."

The security guard begins to get to his feet. He moves slowly so as not to create alarm.

"Oh, okay. But don't take too long, Dodi,"

The security guard relaxes and slips back into his chair.

"Will my mother be okay out here by herself?" Dodi asks the social worker.

"Ah...yes. Everything is under control."

Dodi reads the man's body language and knows there are things that he can't speak openly about. She follows him to the elevator. Lila waits in her chair. When they're out of earshot, the social worker speaks.

"Your mother is being watched closely by the security guards. They'll take care of things if there's a need."

When they get to his office, he explains everything to Dodi in detail.

"What we need is your signature so we can get on with the temporary detaining order. The form will have to be signed by the magistrate as well. After that, your mother will be examined by a mental health worker, and if he agrees with us that she's dangerous to herself and/or others, she will be assigned a guardian *ad litem*, who will make sure that her personal rights are not being violated and that she's given a fair hearing. If the magistrate agrees with the mental health evaluator that she needs more extensive observation, your mother will be required, with or against her will, to undergo hospitalization."

"You mean she might be locked up?" Dodi asks, wide-eyed.

"Only until she's under control and no longer a danger to anyone. That probably means a couple of days, until she's stabilized under medication."

"She won't take the medication."

"I don't really know what will happen, but her behavior certainly shows potential for dangerous activity."

"Are you trying to tell me my mother is a danger to society? I can't believe that. She's never harmed anyone."

"Do you want me to put in my records that your mother has never exhibited any irrational behavior?"

"Everyone acts a little weird at times, but that doesn't mean they're dangerous."

"Are you sure that's an accurate description of your mother's most recent behavior? Do you want to take the responsibility for your father's wellbeing while under her care? Are you sure she's capable of taking care of herself?"

Dodi's mind goes back to recent incompetencies that Lila has exhibited, such as serving rotten food.

"Let me tell you the details that make us think she may be dealing with some sort of senility," the social worker says.

Dodi flinches at the word, but she listens to the man's narrative. When he's finished, she sits numbly for a few minutes, allowing herself to digest what suddenly seems unmistakably clear.

Then she sighs. "I'll sign those papers, whatever you said they're called."

As she signs her name in several places, she has difficulty concentrating on the legal jargon.

"Now can we see my father?"

"You can. But your mother may not. We are afraid of another outbreak, and we can't take the chance of subjecting anyone to that abuse again."

"But my mother is the only link to the outside world my father has. It would be crueler to cut him off from that."

"I'm sorry. It's not my decision." His voice has hardened.

So Dodi visits her father without Lila. On the bed lies a semi-conscious, sick old man that she barely recognizes and who she is not sure recognizes her or is even aware of her presence.

In the meantime, Lila strikes up a number of conversations with other visitors and staff members. She appears to be enjoying herself. There is not the slightest hint that there is anything amiss in her universe.

Time ticks by, and Dodi is called into the social worker's office once again.

"It's about time. I've been waiting here for five hours," Dodi says.

"I apologize. We've only just now been able to get in touch with the magistrate to give him the papers. He's refusing to verify the temporary detention order, even though the mental health worker clearly sees the need."

"What does that mean?"

"It means we can't hold your mother. We have to let her go."

"What?!" Dodi explodes. "After getting me to come down here because we had an emergency, first you tell me she's dangerous,, then you keep me here for five damn hours, and now you say you're just going to let her go home without treatment? I'm sorry, but there's something very, very wrong here."

"She can still get treatment if she's willing to. We're going to present that option to her, and we need your help to do that. I'm extremely sorry about the magistrate. Off the record, he won't accept the recommendations of the professionals because he thinks old people that act strange are just misunderstood. We're as frustrated with the situation as you are."

At that moment, Lila walks into the office, accompanied by a man in a doctor's smock and another man in a business suit.

"This isn't the hospital room," she says in confusion. "Zeke isn't in here. Dodi, what are you doing here?"

"Lila," the doctor says, "I've tried to explain to you why we think you should stay here for treatment, at least overnight. I've tried to explain why we think you need it, but you've refused. This is Mr. Belasco." The doctor indicates the man in the business suit.

"He's the hospital administrator. He has something to tell you."

Mr. Belasco, looking both officious and uncomfortable, says, "If you do not agree to undergo treatment, we will not accept any responsibility for your health and safety. We cannot allow you to see your husband in this hospital if you do not receive treatment, for fear that you will demonstrate further abusive behavior. For that reason, we also cannot permit you to enter the hospital grounds ever again until such time as you are a patient, or we deem that conditions have changed. We cannot discharge Dr. Isacks into your care for the same reasons. Also, he needs the care of a nursing home. We will be making arrangements to transfer him to an appropriate facility as close to your home as possible. We will be reporting your abuse to protective services. It is possible that your contact with your husband at the nursing home he is discharged to will also restrict your contact with him. I'm sorry, but you give us no choice."

"Well!" Lila huffs. "I don't ever want to set foot in this place again anyway. It's the worst hospital I've ever been to, and I've never been treated so badly. Those accusations are nothing but a bunch of rubbish. You will be hearing from my lawyer."

She turns and stalks out of the office. Dodi, whose sentiments toward the hospital are not that different from her mother's, is right behind her.

Lila is halfway down the hallway before she realizes that she has no idea where the exit is.

Let's Get Cracking

In the focus chamber, Dark, Harmony, and Storm confer while Bright-Spot monitors Strong. Strong's body floats off to one side, attached to life-maintaining entities.

"Okay, so now what do I do?" says Harmony. "Strong feels at home and is willing to go with me, but not without the human. The human is terrified of anything resembling our world." Her orb vibrates with exasperation.

"Obviously, you've got to appeal to the human," Dark-Light says. "Get him isolated and help him become used to Gazeon phenomena."

"How can I appeal to the human when it's senile?" Harmony's lights drop a half-tone, into a splotchy red.

"You might consider talking it over with Strong," Storm suggests.

"Good idea," Dark agrees.

"I'm also considering another possibility," Storm continues. "There may be a point of diminishing returns, in which the human consciousness becomes less dependent on the physical brain after it deteriorates sufficiently."

Dark's lights blink in a confused pattern. "I thought you said that as its brain deteriorated, the human was becoming more dependent on the Gazeon side of its consciousness."

"Up to a point," Storm replies. "Remember, this joining of Gazeon and human minds is unprecedented. As far as I know, most humans don't have Gazeon minds upon which to lean when physical life is ending. If the Gazeon and human minds are split, as they were in the last encounter, the human mind might do what I'm suggesting and regain a cogency that its weakened brain can't diminish. According to Bright's report, the Zeke was reasonably lucid when it was separated from Strong's mind."

"That's right," Harmony says, her lights suddenly shifting to a higher and lighter hue. "Why didn't I notice that? I just took it for granted that the human's mind was becoming more enfeebled." Her membrane takes on a slightly wrinkled appearance. "But even though the human was cogent, he was also very simple."

"Who knows how complex that alien mind will become when the process of physical deterioration is complete?" Dark submits.

Harmony's lights dwindle in their brightness. "How do we know there will be any mind at all if there's no brain? How do we know whether Strong will survive the death of the human brain?"

"Talk it over with Strong," Storm directs. "He's our expert on the human brain and mind. Ask him about the normal process of the physical death and mind."

Suddenly, Bright Spot's voice breaks into the discussion. "He's beginning a new dream cycle."

The creature that is a hybrid of Gazeon and human sits crossed-legged in a church in front of a gold cross. A statue of a Buddha sits on the left side of the cross, and Mahatma Gandhi, in a business suit, stands on the right. The human entity contemplates the triple image with a mixture of thoughts and emotions.

Then, in the forefront of the trinity, Angel manifests herself.

"We meet in the strangest places, Angel."

"Am I talking to Strong or Zeke?"

"Mostly Strong, I suppose. Anyway, I'm the rational one. It's strange, but if I hadn't experienced what I experienced in our last lesson, I would have sworn there was only one of us. Yet I'm still Zeke. I'm the retired Dr. Isacks. I know it will make you happy to call me Strong, so go ahead. Be my guest. I've been sitting here giving it some thought. When Zeke was healthy, I guess I was part of his subconscious. Now, in the dream state, when Zeke's brain is a mess, I'm the conscious part, and Zeke is the subconscious part."

"Do you have any memory of me yet?" Harmony asks hopefully.

"Not exactly. All I can tell you is that I feel a growing sense of connection with you. I still prefer my females with long, shapely legs, breasts that aren't too large, and blond hair. But you make a very attractive soap bubble."

Harmony considers that for a few moments, not knowing what to think or feel about that comment.

"The team has just been discussing where we are with this whole thing," she says. She summarizes the recent discussion and says, "So what *does* happen to the human mind as the brain deteriorates?"

"Damned if I know."

Harmony's luminescence takes on amoeba-shaped black spots. "Is that all you have to offer? Remember, this is a matter of life or death. Not just yours, but mine as well. If you turn your back on my needs, I'm not sure I'll be able to handle it. Everything I've ever experienced about you has shown me that you're not a quitter."

"I didn't say anything about quitting. I suppose Zeke is still pretty influential. He's not a quitter, either, but he believes in accepting the inevitable. Death is inevitable. I'm a real doctor, not a psychiatrist." The creature chuckles at his last statement.

The humor is lost on Harmony, but she's pleased with one aspect of the conversation. Strong is exhibiting some of his old jauntiness. That's an encouraging sign.

"Please try," she says softly. "Any insights you have might be crucial."

"Okay, I'll try. But it'll be completely unscientific. For many dying humans, at the very end, they report seeing and talking with people who have been very close to them emotionally and who are already dead. There actually have been studies indicating that only dead people make this alleged contact. This apparently happens even when the dying individual does not have any obvious way of knowing who's alive or who's dead. These discussions often seem more lucid than the talk between the dying person and his survivors, even though the bystanders can only hear one end of the conversation. There are also reports of people who have been out of it for a long time, such as patients in a coma, who have come back to waking awareness and are perfectly logical for a short period before they die. So maybe your Dr. Mind-Storm is right. Maybe the consciousness becomes disembodied at the very end and functions competently. Many people believe that the mind is returned to perfect health in the afterlife. Tell me, Harmony, do your people believe in an afterlife?"

"Our people," Harmony corrects him. "Yes, we do. We're not as connected to physical things as you humans are, probably because our living matter is not as dense."

"Then you shouldn't be so shocked at the prospect of my dying, Harmony."

"Death before one's time is more than a waste. It's a travesty, and you and I are relatively young. If the part of the Zeke that is Strong dies, it would be a tragedy."

"Ouch. Okay, do your hypnosis thing, and let's talk to myself. I understand shrinks make their patients do that all the time."

"First," Harmony begins, "tell me what's going on outside."

"I'm dying. Big surprise. What more can I tell you? The heart's gone. The brain is gone, and the rest of me is leaving. I'm not even sure where my physical body is, but I think it's in either a hospital or a nursing home. I could probably hang on for a while, but not for long. So let's get cracking."

Death Vigil Begins

Zeke lies in a nursing home bed. His daughter, Dee, keeps vigil at his bedside. Nothing has been said between them for two hours. Dee wonders why she's there. Her father is apparently unaware that anyone else is present. His eyes are closed, and his breathing is slightly ragged.

Then suddenly he says, in a rusty but clearly understood voice, "What do you think of Jesus?"

Dee's body jerks. She's dumbfounded. Then she offers something that she hopes his enfeebled mind can grasp. "Jesus is good."

"Yeah, I guess he's just a regular guy. His Father is awfully confusing, though." Zeke goes back to his ragged breathing, leaving Dee with her mouth open.

In the silence, Dee's memory goes back to the last few days, in which there was contentious wrangling with the nursing home authorities. Even Leo got into that one. She remembers his conversation on the phone with the nursing home administrator, who was not going to allow Lila to see her husband. Leo told him that not allowing Dr. Isacks to see his wife was tantamount to abuse. It was a cruelty to both of them.

"I don't care what social services says," Leo said angrily. "They're being far more abusive to your patient than Lila could ever be. Regardless of the past behavior, she is his main support system, his primary contact with the only world he knows. You're signing an early death sentence if you follow that stupid dictum."

The administrator made a poor attempt to avoid seeming condescending. "I understand what you're saying, sir, but we can't take the risk that she'll attack him again."

"Be reasonable. First of all, that old woman drove her dying husband to the hospital. She sat upright in an uncomfortable chair at his bedside for over twenty-four hours. She's been under tremendous stress for well over two years as his sole caregiver. And she's been having difficulty with her own dementia. She cracked. You might do the same under similar circumstances. Now that she doesn't have the responsibility of caring for him, she has a lot of that stress off her back. You can have someone there with them when she visits."

"We can't spare that kind of personnel for one person."

"What kind of facility are you running, anyway? You would keep two people apart who have been together for over sixty years? He may not have much longer to live. You have some nerve calling Lila abusive. If you stick with this decision, we'll investigate our legal options."

The administrator lost his condescending air.

Later in the day, the nursing home administrator called back. "I've been thinking about some of the things you said, and I believe I've come up with a solution. Your mother-in-law can visit her husband in the common room. In that way, there will be personnel around all the time without our having to delegate one of our people to monitor them exclusively. Will that be acceptable to you?"

"Well, it's much better than what we had before," said Leo. "I think you should make your proposal to my wife."

Leo handed the telephone to Dee, muttering under his breath, "Asshole."

It was a reasonable compromise, Dee thought. Actually, she wasn't so sure that Lila wouldn't do a repeat performance given the right set of circumstances.

Right now, Lila is at home getting some sleep. She has no

recollection of what she had done at the hospital and has no idea that she's barred from going back. She can't understand why she's not allowed to visit her husband.

Dee notices that her father's eyes are moving rapidly under his eyelids. She knows that means he's dreaming.

Zeke is sitting on a grassy knoll. Harmony is in her guise as a beautiful human woman. Following the same hypnotic procedure that she used previously, Harmony separates the two entities. She and Strong are facing Dr. Isacks.

Harmony first turns her attention to Strong. "How do you feel, Strong?"

"Not any different than I did a moment ago, before you did the voodoo."

"Dr. Isacks, how do *you* feel?" She has decided to refer to her husband as Strong and address the human as Dr. Isacks.

He shrugs. "I guess the way I felt before you did the voodoo."

"Dr. Isacks, do you remember how you felt when I became a bubble?"

"The bubble wasn't so bad. But when you took me into Hell, that was a different matter." He shuddered.

"Do you know anything about Strong? The one who's facing you now?"

"He's my sharper self, before I got old and sick. It happens, you know."

Harmony smiles despite herself. "Do you know anything about Strong's origins?"

"I remember something, but it's not a clear recollection."

She turns to Strong. "I think this might work better if you tell him."

Strong shrugs. "I'll give it a try."

Strong recites the story that was told to him.

Dr. Isacks listens carefully. "One thing is undeniable," he says. "My thinking here, in this state, seems to be clearing up. I'm still not as sharp as I used to be, but I'm not really demented right now. So some of your story checks out. I do have vague memories of being in a hellish place, which you insist is not Hell but a different world of aliens. It's too fantastic for me to swallow hook, line, and sinker, but it's interesting, and while I'm dying, there doesn't seem anything better for me to do than explore the notion."

"Are you willing to come back with me?" Strong asks.

"If what you say is true, you're in my head. I'm not in yours. When my body and brain die, I'm not so sure I can go with you."

"Are you willing to try?" Strong asks.

"When my time comes, by rights I should move on to where I'm supposed to go, and I don't think that's to a gas planet where I would be floating around like a bubble making sweet talk to another bubble of gas."

"But Dr. Isacks, Strong isn't old. He's not chronologically ready to die. If you don't go with him, he probably won't survive."

"Well, Strong—or me, or whatever you are—if you really are some sort of symbiont, why can't you go alone?"

"Because, although my origins may be different, you and I have come to be the same. We even have the same bizarre sense of humor. I can't abandon you any more than I could abandon our right foot."

"You would if it were a matter of life or death," Zeke retorts.

"In Strong's body, you would be young again," Harmony says.

"In Heaven, I'll be eternally young, young lady, or whatever the hell you are."

"You know you're not that sure about Heaven, old friend," Strong says. "Remember, I know exactly what you believe. You used to pray all the time to Jesus and God, but a lot of that was for family and for show."

"I guess Jesus is all right. He seems like a pretty good guy.

But God? I'm not so sure what to make of him. Anyway, I'll take my chances. It would only be postponing the inevitable. The difference is that I would be spending a lot of unnecessary time in a place that looks like Hell to me. If you want to come with me, that's your business. If you don't, that's still your business."

"How can you be so callous about the life of someone else, someone who would give their life for yours?" Harmony asks incredulously.

"Zeke, cut the bullshit," Strong interjects. "All that fake callousness. The truth is that you're really scared. You're no different from me when it comes to valuing human life."

Dr. Isacks stares directly into Strong's eyes for a long moment and then turns away. "I guess you've got that right. You know me pretty well. But if you've gone through the same sort of degrading, humiliating, undignified, and abused life that I have lately, why aren't you ready to die?"

"The more we talk," says Strong, "the more convinced I am that what Harmony says is true. I'm different. I'm younger, and I want to keep living."

Dr. Isacks says, "Now it's time for *you* to cut the bullshit. You won't go without me because you're afraid to go it alone. You've been tied to me for so long that you don't know who you are without me."

Strong looks away from Zeke's accusing gaze. "I admit that. Look, Zeke, will you at least go along with the program and let us try to acclimate you to the gas world and its people? You're still in charge and will do as you like when the time comes."

"Now that we're being more honest with ourselves, I'll cooperate," says Zeke. "But I doubt that I'll agree to become imprisoned in a ball of gas. Do you know what's interesting, Angel? Strong and I are fast asleep, and this discussion is making me tired. We either have to wake up a little or slip below the dream state of consciousness." Dr. Isacks yawns.

Harmony is alarmed to find herself stifling her own yawn.

She wonders how a Gazeon can be compelled to yawn when it's not something that her species does.

"Can you try to stay separate?" Harmony asks.

"It's okay with me if it's okay with him," Dr. Isacks answers.

Despite the promise, as the grassy dreamscape begins to fade and the Gazeon world comes into focus, the two separated entities begin to merge again.

Can't Tell the Difference

"Hello, Dee. This is Dodi."

"Oh, hello, Dodi. Is anything wrong?"

"Yes, something's wrong. I just thought you should know, I tried to visit Daddy today, and they aren't letting in any visitors."

"Can they do that? What's going on in that place?" Dee's voice is tight, irritated, and anxious.

"The whole place is in quarantine. There's some kind of bug in there that has most of them sick."

"Oh my God! Is Daddy sick?"

"They won't give me a straight answer. They say it's too early to tell. I don't believe them, Dee."

"How is Lila doing?"

"She seems to understand and isn't making a fuss. She's doing okay, I guess. You know they started to let her visit Daddy alone in his room without any restrictions. I think she'll be okay as long as she doesn't see any other females attending to him."

"Does the staff there know about Mom and her problem with paranoia and jealousy?"

"Yeah, I let them know. They thought it was amusing, even cute. I don't think they would still feel that way if they ever saw her in action. I just thought I'd better tell you in case you were planning to visit anytime soon."

"Thanks."

"I'm glad to see only see one person here," says Harmony.

"I didn't stay split the way you asked me to when we left. There's something new that you should know about. There's no dominant consciousness in here anymore. Zeke and Strong, as you refer to me, are of equal strength now."

Harmony feels uneasy about that. She would rather Strong be dominant. However, an intact Zeke intellect might not be a bad thing.

"That might have some advantages." Harmony pauses to collect her thoughts. "Will you try to separate without my help?"

In answer, the hybrid entity furrows its brow for a few moments and then says, "I'm afraid I still need your help on that one."

Hiding her disappointment, Harmony leads them through the hypnotic procedure and also suggests that they'll remember the process and be able to accomplish it on their own. The transformation is successfully completed, and standing before Harmony are two identical twins. There is only the slightest difference in appearance between the two of them. Zeke is slightly older, but it would be more accurate to say he looks more mature. He is virile and alert. The light of intelligence shines through his eyes, and despite the obstacles that Zeke represents to her, Harmony feels a tear in her human–form eyes to see this decrepit old man restored to his sound, younger self.

"Okay, Zeke. I'm going Gazeon," Harmony warns. She makes the transformation slowly, watching for any signs of panic on Zeke's face. None appear.

"Are you ready for Strong's world to manifest?" she asks Zeke.

"Ready or not, here you come," he responds.

Harmony wills the gas world into appearance. It's as if a movie is coming into focus on a flat screen. As she detects no extreme reaction on Zeke's part, she allows the movie screen to become three dimensional, so that gradually Zeke is enveloped in a pleasant Gazeon gas-scape. Zeke himself is standing on a solid rock foundation.

"Zeke, is it all right if I refer to you as Dr. Isacks? You deserve the proper respect for your achievements in life."

"Doctor or Zeke—it's all the same to me. I've never stood on ceremony. I'm just a country doctor from Missouri. But thank you. It feels good. It's been a long time since I've felt a measure of dignity."

"How do you feel physically?"

"Oh, I'm enjoying the show. What comes next?"

"Well, you're standing on solid ground. The next step is for you to be floating."

"That reminds me of my flying dreams. The landscape is a little different than I remember, but let me give it a try by myself. Give me room."

With a slight brightening of her lights, Harmony floats back a few body lengths.

Zeke takes a deep breath, bends his legs, and springs off in a swan dive into the gently blowing breezes of the multicolored atmosphere. He soars into the gases and executes a banking left turn, using his arms as wings, then circles back to the rock upon which Strong, in human form, still stands.

"Whee, wow, what a gasser! I haven't had so much fun since skinny dipping at the old pond in Missouri. It's your turn, Mr. Strong," Zeke says with a courtly bow.

"No problem. This should come naturally to me."

Strong, in human form, duplicates the performance of his twin. When he comes back, he doesn't alight on the rock but remains levitated just above it. Zeke mimics this, and he too remains floating.

"Now, Strong," Harmony urges, "you first. Morph into your true form."

Slowly, ever so slowly, Strong's shape becomes ovoid. His solidity becomes translucent, and the other Gazeon characteristics manifest and become dominant. Although Harmony is controlling the change, Strong feels himself more than passively cooperating. He anticipates the changes and fits into them comfortably.

"Dr. Isacks, are you ready for this?" Harmony asks.

"Probably not. It's strange enough talking to two bubbles. To be one is an entirely different matter. They're apparently natural forms to you, but to me, it's almost inconceivable. Take it slow—very slow, please."

Zeke's arms and legs shorten until they're only half their normal length.

"How are you doing?" Harmony asks.

"I feel a growing helplessness and vulnerability. I use my arms and legs to do almost everything. At least I used to," he adds as an afterthought.

Strong suggests, "Zeke, just as you soared before, practice flying now just with what you have."

"I'll give it a try." He takes a deep breath. Tentatively at first, but with increasing confidence, he flies about in gentle circles.

"Is this the way you people get around in your world? You just will yourself? Don't you have to do something physical?"

"Yes, we do," Harmony replies. "But in the end, it's still just a matter of willing. You will your arms and legs to do what they do. We will our body parts, parts that you don't need to know about yet, to spin, to undulate, and to change shape in order to achieve what we need to do in our physical gas world. So using your will in this dream state is good practice."

"Okay, let's make the appendages smaller," Zeke says with determination.

His arms and legs diminish to stubs as he continues to soar in circles and figure eights.

"Now just hover, Zeke," Strong says.

Zeke hovers just above the rocky island. He begins to feel queasiness in his stomach as he dissolves into a gaseous state.

New, strange inner forms begin to manifest. A severe disorientation descends upon him, creating the worst vertigo and seasickness of his life.

"Stop!" he shouts, trying to hyperventilate without lungs to do so. The world around him starts spinning wildly. From an outside perspective, his ovoid, half solid body spins and lurches out of control.

Hastily, Harmony restores solidity.

Zeke has managed to maintain a hold on his sanity. At first, he tries to flail with arms and legs that don't exist, but then he forces himself to slow his breathing in newly restored lungs.

"That's a bit too much," he says. "If you change one little part at a time and let me get used to it before going on to the next one, it might work out better."

"I'm sorry we went too fast. I'm motivated to go as quickly as we can because your body is dying quickly. We don't have time."

"Angel, don't assume that I have any more intention of becoming a citizen of your world than I did during our last meeting. I'm doing this out of curiosity and a sense of adventure."

"And I'm determined to stick with you wherever we go," Strong says.

"Okay. Let's just do as much as we can," Harmony says.

As the metamorphosis resumes, Zeke feels an emptiness developing in one small part of his oval body organs. He believes it must be a gallbladder or some other nonessential contrivance. He feels ill.

"Wait a minute. We're still doing it wrong. As long as I'm a mammal, I need a mammal's physiology. I can't have part yes and part no. Therefore, I can't have a gradual change at all. It would prove fatal. I know this is all a dream, but it's real to me."

"What can we do, then?" Harmony asks, discouraged.

"I just don't know," Strong says. "Maybe we could switch you back and forth for split seconds at a time, while gradually trying to expand your tolerance time," he suggests.

"That sounds just lovely," Zeke remarks. "Oh, what the hell. Let's go for it."

Harmony wonders whether she can pull this off. But she makes the effort. Zeke feels a split second of total otherness, but it's like the blinking of an eye. It's like taking one short, normal step only to find that the ground beneath you has turned into a sidewalk curb. For a moment, there's nothing beneath your foot.

"Is everything okay?" Harmony asks.

"Yeah, I guess so. But I'm getting mighty tired. I'm going to fade out at any moment."

And with that, his ovoid body begins to fade. An almost imperceptible umbilicus that attaches Strong and Zeke tightens, and Strong finds himself being pulled into the void along with Zeke.

Ventilator

"Oh, hello, Dodi," Dee says, answering the telephone. "What's up?"

"What are you doing?"

"Just some housework. Why?"

"They took Daddy back to the hospital last night."

Dee carefully leans the broom against the closet door and sits down in a nearby chair.

"Did he get that disease that was going around the nursing home?"

"He sure did. They sent him to that damned place, and instead of helping him, they made him sick." Dodi's voice is bitter. "He was ill before he went, but he didn't need their help to make him even sicker."

Dee looks out the living room glass door and watches a small wren pecking at the bird feeder. A squirrel eats sunflower seeds off the round picnic table, and she notices that leaves are beginning to fall in earnest from the apple trees.

"How bad is he?"

"I think he's pretty bad. It's his upper respiratory system. He isn't breathing very well, and they have him on a ventilator."

Dee's breath catches in her throat for a moment. She pauses, clears her throat, and asks, "Is he conscious?"

"They didn't tell me. Mom and I are going down today to see him if they'll let us in. Dee, do you think he's going to die?" The question comes out broken, forced.

Dee looks out the window and sees a lonely, V-shaped flight of geese. The sounds of their honking come, grow louder, and then fade into the distance. When she speaks, her voice is firm and resolute.

"Yes. How is Lila taking it?"

"I don't think it's really dawned on her. She knows he might die, but she doesn't seem terribly disturbed by that. Maybe she even seems a little relieved."

"So am I," Dee says.

There's silence on the other end. Dee has said that which Dodi would never dare say or even admit to herself. But somehow, Dee's saying it is a relief to her.

The old man lies in the hospital bed. The many tubes sticking into and out of his head and body make him look like an extension of some macabre machine. There's no outward motion.

An old woman sits quietly in a chair by his iron-railed bedside. She's waiting—waiting as though she expects a train to come and take her husband into a dark tunnel, never to return.

A young woman sits in another chair. She's too young to be accustomed to waiting.

Why doesn't something happen? Dodi wonders. But she fears the happening. She also fears the not happening.

"Come on, Zeke. You can do it!" Strong is cheering Dr. Isacks on as the doctor struggles to cope with the feeling of his ovoid body, which lacks a digestive system.

"Oh, God. This is a horrible feeling. Let me rest."

"There's no time to rest. You have to do it now," Harmony demands.

"I'm not going with you people anyway, so why am I doing this?"

"You're doing it for me and for you," she says. "You know that if you don't give it everything you've got right now, you won't be able to live with yourself later, regardless of the outcome and where you happen to be living."

"That's assuming there is life after death." Zeke slurs out the words between softening gums as his physical parts dissolve slowly into gas.

Dee walks into the hospital room. She bends over the quiet form of her father. The respirator has been removed, and she hears his breaths coming further and further apart. Each breath is increasingly shallow. Dee holds his left hand in her two while kneeling on the floor beside his still body, as though in prayer.

"It's okay, Daddy," she whispers.

There's one more breath. Then she feels a change of some sort, and Zeke's body begins to cool.

Train of Death

Meanwhile, Zeke struggles valiantly to tolerate an increasingly alien body.

Harmony is the first to feel a mysterious change. She's been directing the images being experienced by Strong's and Zeke's minds, but a subtle loss of her control begins to pervade the scenery. The gaseous environment gradually takes on solid characteristics.

A silvery train track materializes, running beside a lonely train station platform. A green, weather-beaten wooden bench stands alone beneath a faded, tin-roofed wooden lean-to. The mournful sound of a distant train cuts through a sunless winter day.

Dr. Isacks' ovoid form sprouts arms and legs until he's standing in front of the old bench, dressed in an overcoat and worn fedora pulled down on his head against the late December cold. Another shadowy human figure stands next to him. An orb of glowing lights and undulating fluorescence floats behind them.

Frantically, Harmony tries to draw Dr. Isacks' attention. He doesn't seem to hear her. The shadowy figure, which is Strong, hears but can't respond. Harmony wills herself into human form and screams at them.

"What are you doing? What are you doing here? You have to get back to work. There isn't time!"

The mournful sound of the train whistle gets louder. The rumbling sound of the locomotive's approach, at first barely audible, becomes stronger and insistent, until the platform shakes as though in fear. Harmony's voice cannot be heard above the roar.

The speeding, irresistible force of the engine slows, and its intention is clear. This is its station, and it will stop here. This is obvious even to Harmony, who has never seen a train before. Her feelings of panic and desperation mount even as the roar of the engine diminishes. The air brakes hiss like a thousand angry cats as the train rumbles to a jerky stop.

The doors to a passenger car open, and Dr. Isacks walks toward it. Harmony sees the umbilicus connecting Dr. Isacks and Strong. She grabs it in her two human hands, trying to tear it in two, but only succeeds in stretching it. She pulls the strand into her human mouth, trying to gnaw it apart, but the cord slips like phantom jelly between her teeth. Dr. Isacks steps into the open car. The umbilicus tightens, and the shadowy Strong is pulled along.

"No! No! Strong, don't let it take you! For God's sake, please don't!"

But Strong is drawn into the open doorway, with no more ability to resist than gossamer in the wind.

Harmony sees the doors begin to close. In movements born of desperation and terror, she tries to enter.

"No, Harmony, you can't. Don't!" The voice is Bright-Spot's. He has been monitoring dutifully and becoming increasingly alarmed.

As Harmony steps through the sliding door, Bright does what no monitor should or could supposedly do. He manifests within the scene and wraps gaseous arms around Harmony's waist. But she moves right through them. The doors slide shut behind the three of them, and the engine begins to chug-chug into motion, leaving Bright-Spot alone on the platform, hopelessly looking on.

The train gathers speed. In the distance, a swirling tunnel

appears, into which the silver tracks disappear.

In a daze, Strong begins to understand the meaning of these events. He's willing to go with Dr. Isacks into the abyss. The umbilicus makes them one. Then he sees the human form of Harmony, and he realizes that she's willing to go with him to his fate rather than give him up. A trickle of memory begins to flow into his consciousness, gradually coating his mind with a tapestry of forgotten feelings and images. As the now torrent of memories gushes over him, he finds himself shouting to his mate, "Harmony! Oh God, Harmony!"

She knows immediately that her partner is once more beside her. There is a desperate, longing embrace that is both human and Gazeon. The death tunnel looms closer as the locomotive continues to gather speed.

Strong tries to break the bonds of the umbilicus, like a rat chewing to free itself from a trap. But the cord remains unbroken.

The tunnel looms, its opening gaping like the maw of a monstrous worm. A sudden light of insight shines from Strong's eyes, and he whirls to face Dr. Isacks.

"Zeke, Lila needs you. Only you can help her. Don't abandon her."

For the first time, Dr. Isacks recognizes that he's not alone.

"How can I help her? I'm dead."

"Not quite yet. There's still time. You can live through me, as I've lived through you. We have the means. You know we do."

Dr. Isacks scrutinizes Harmony with penetrating eyes intensified by death. "Will you support this? Do you think you can convince the boss to pour in the resources?"

"Yes! Yes! I'll make them listen. They've spent resources spanning almost your entire life just to get Strong back with his knowledge. They're not going to give him up now."

Dr. Isacks turns to the side and finds the emergency stop cord that all old trains had when he was a boy. He yanks down hard.

The locomotive air brakes suddenly hiss. The train lurches violently as metal wheels screech. The gaping maw of the open tunnel draws nearer. To Harmony, it resembles a violent, churning storm on Gazeon that's seeking to pull lost souls into its vortex. The front of the engine is lost in the maelstrom before the train lurches to a squealing halt. The doors open halfway as Dr. Isacks, Strong, and Harmony squeeze out. They stand alongside the tracks, dwarfed by the hungry, wild tunnel, which seems to yearn for them.

"Okay. What do you have in mind?" Dr. Isacks asks calmly.

Strong looks puzzled, not knowing what to suggest.

Harmony's human form gasps for breath. A detached part of her mind thinks, They process metabolizing gases just as we do. I wonder whether it feels the same to them.

"Your body is probably dead by now," she says. "You're a disembodied consciousness. The umbilicus attaching the two of you is keeping you from being engulfed by that thing. Strong, try mind-melding with Dr. Isacks."

"How can I mind-meld with him when I'm already mind-melded with him?"

"I don't know whether you are or not. His physical body is dead. You're not bound to the physical aspects of his mind anymore, and neither is he. He can't make the transition to our physical way of being, but he can be in you as you make the transition into your own body."

"I'll try."

Strong-Presence begins a procedure he hasn't attempted for over eighty years. Dr. Isacks feels the familiar sensations of two personalities blending and becoming one. But this time, it's Strong's personality that's dominant. Then Strong begins a slow transition into his natural form. He goes slowly, because he feels what Zeke feels. No matter how slowly he goes, Zeke's reactions are violent. In mutual agreement, Isacks' consciousness goes dormant. It finds comfort and protection in the unconscious recesses of Strong's mind, just as Strong found refuge long ago in Zeke's mind by losing his own identity.

The yawning chasm that threatened all of them moments ago fades. Strong and Harmony feel themselves to be alone in a void.

"You are not alone." Bright's voice is heard somewhere unplaceable.

"Where the hell are we?" Harmony asks.

"I have no idea. But your silver cords are intact, and if you just follow them down, you'll end up in your own bodies."

Strong is shocked to be reminded of the fact that he's not in his real body but in some kind of dream image of his corporeal gaseous self. He seeks for awareness of the silver cord, which is something he has also not been aware of for eighty years. It's with a strange sense of relief and dread that he finally sees it and allows his consciousness to flow through it and into something else.

When he lands in his own body, it feels less real to him than the imaginary one he had recently created. It's very stiff. Maintenance entities are attached to him, further encumbering his movements. Strong focuses his visual perceivers to see several Gazeons staring at him as he floats in the center of a circle of gas beings.

"Do you know who I am, Strong?"

Strong sees an aged, wizened Gazeon.

"Dr. Mind-Storm, you've gotten old in one cycle."

"He's going to be just fine," Mind-Storm says sardonically to the others floating around the resurrected Strong.

"Take everything very slowly," Dark-Lights says. "It'll be a while before you're vortex surfing again."

"Oh, I think I have a few promises to keep before I get into that sort of thing again."

Strong and Dr. Isacks are standing near the prow of a thirty-foot sloop that somehow needs no crew. It's a beautiful blue-sky day, with cumulus clouds decorating the skyscape with moving puffs of textured cotton. A stiff breeze propels the vessel forty degrees off windward through a choppy surface in Biscayne Bay as it was in the 1950s. An invigorating spray tingles against their bare chests. Both men are in the prime of life and close enough in appearance to be twins.

"Gazeons dream just like humans," Strong says. "Long ago, as a Gazeon, I mastered lucid dreaming. So it's through my dreams that you and I can meet and plan."

"This is a nice place you've picked out. When I was in the Navy, it was one of the few times we actually got to see water."

"Do you remember what happened here, Zeke?"

"Of course I do. This is where I met Lila."

"Excuse me. This is where *we* met Lila."

"Strong, can you bring her back here as well?"

"I could. You have some say here also. Do you want me to bring her into the picture? If I remember correctly, she should be swimming at Matheson's Hammock with her brother and father."

"Yeah. They chose to vacation here just when we were on leave ourselves. Isn't it strange how we chose to go sailing on our vacation away from the Navy?"

"Not so strange when you consider that we rarely got near the water."

"I would like to see her again as she was back then, Strong. Just to look. Not to touch. How do you feel about that?"

"Well, remember that my feelings for Lila were the same as yours. However, now I have my memories about Harmony and being Gazeon, and it's changed my attitude about Lila. So this is your call."

"Then Shazam. Do your stuff."

Strong concentrates, and they find themselves standing on the sand facing a ring of boulders that form the protected swimming area called Matheson's Hammock. Children are playing in and out of the water.

A blonde, beautifully shaped woman stands laughing at the antics of the kids. There's a quality in her laugh that makes Zeke feel extra good, while at the same time tears well up in remembrance. There's a gentle carefreeness that lightens his own heart. He finds his resistance melting and walks over to her. He recalls and says the line, the line that changed his life.

"Are those your children?"

She looks up at him in surprise.

"Oh, no. I'm too young to have children like that." She hesitates, looking into Zeke's eyes with a strange expression. "But I'd like to have some like that one day. Do you like children?" She smiles.

Joy and pain occupy the same place in Zeke's heart, and it's more than he can bear.

A moment later, they're back aboard the sloop. Zeke holds onto a mast sheet and stares blankly into the distance.

"Strong, have you convinced the powers that be to help Lila?"

"No problem. They knew better than to even hint at denying me that. We hold the trump card. I've got what they want, and they can't get it without my enthusiastic cooperation."

"What do you have, Strong?"

"My people must seem like wizards to you. Our science of mind is of course far beyond Earth's, but we live somewhere in the outer reaches of a giant planet, one similar to Jupiter. No one even guessed that there was something like a solid core inside a planet, or even conceived of the ideas of solids and liquids. We didn't know there was a universe out there. After all, we can't see a night sky. We're embedded in rolling clouds of what are, to you, noxious gases. Try to imagine the knowledge I've gained living on the Earth as a human for over eighty years. This is the most stupendous thing that has ever happened to advance Gazeon understanding."

The import of what Strong has explained is not lost on the science-educated Dr. Isacks. But one thing stands paramount in his mind.

"How do we help Lila?"

"First, we have to find her."

Finding Lila

"How can we find her?" Isacks asks.

"Gazeons have become very good in the last eighty years at isolating individual minds from the constant flow of alien minds that streams through the focus chamber," says Strong. "It's not too different from turning the dial on an old-fashioned radio. Every individual's mind can be thought of as a separate station with its own frequency. So once we learn that frequency, it's relatively easy to tune it in whenever we want."

Isacks' eyes open wide, and his brows arch. "You mean you've been able to tune in to Lila?"

Strong puts his hand on Isacks' shoulder. "No, I'm sorry to have implied that. We don't get to choose whom we make the initial contact with. That's just dumb luck. The odds of picking up on any given individual are far worse than winning an Earth lottery."

Isacks' shoulders and head droop. "Then how does this ability to tune in on someone you've already contacted help us?"

Strong's human dream body turns away and looks back at Matheson's Hammock thoughtfully. "There's a Canadian we've tuned in on."

"How does that help?"

"We've worked through most of the dangers that I faced when I first infiltrated your mind. We can eavesdrop on the host's senses without triggering any automatic defensive reactions. We can even influence behavior through suggestion. The thing about this Canadian is that he's very suggestible and has the means and opportunity for travel."

Dr. Isacks weighs the implications of this information. "I'm listening, Strong. Go on."

"Well, if we can direct this guy to finding Lila, we've gained possibilities of influencing her life."

"How?"

"Many possibilities. Not only might we be able to get our Canadian to manipulate her social and physical environment, but we might also be able to influence her mind directly through him."

Isacks shakes his head as though trying to shake off confusion. "Explain that last part, brother."

"I can't. It's a little too technical for your Earth-based mind. It would be like you trying to explain quantum physics to untrained Gazeons."

"Yeah, I see. Since you're probably the only Gazeon that has the right kind of training, the opportunities would be limited, wouldn't they?"

"Look, this is all just speculation. We'll have to wing it as we go along. Are you game?"

Isacks sticks out his hand, and they shake on it.

"Are you going to send me back into your subconscious now, Strong?"

"I will—unless you want to hang around as a blob of gas like me."

"Uh, I'll pass on that. But I'm curious."

"About what?"

"Are humans the only other species you've tuned in on?"

"No, there are quite a few others. But we seem to have a strange affinity for humans."

"Why do you suppose that is?"

"It does seem strange, doesn't it?" Strong muses. "I mean, when you consider how physiologically different we are. Mind–

Storm has a theory about it, though. I guess he has a theory on everything. It's as though his theories beget theories."

"Get on with it," Isacks urges.

"Sorry. You get kind of mind-bound when you hang around that guy too long. Anyway, he thinks it has to do with our social structure. It must be a fluke of fate or chance that we would happen to have family and community values that are so similar. It means we think a lot alike. We have very similar emotions, even though those emotions are based on totally different neurochemical systems. We haven't run into any other species that is as close to us in those areas. There's even a species that has gas bodies, just as Gazeons do, but their mind structures are really hard to fathom."

"Strong, before you put me back to sleep, I wonder if it would be possible for me to be aware during those periods when I don't manifest."

Strong seems almost shocked as he turns to face his twin. "Why, yes. Why didn't I think of that?"

"Probably because all I wanted to do was escape from that hell fire you call Gazeon. Now I want the opportunity to think."

"I think I can put you into a dreaming state. It'll be a cogent dreaming state in which you'll know you're dreaming. But when you're in that state, you'll be on your own. I won't be able to keep tabs on you, even if you're in my mind. It would split my attention too much. You might have some nightmares."

"I'll take my chances. Don't hesitate to visit any time."

"Actually, you'll be able to signal me to let me know if you want a visit. I may not be able to leave what I'm engaged in at the moment, but I'll return the phone call as soon as I can."

"Will I be able to dream that I'm sleeping?"

"Who knows? Go back to bed, brother."

Isacks and the bay scene fade. Strong moves out of the dream and back into the home building entity where he and Harmony reside.

Dr. Isacks is dreaming that he's in his old hospital office when he was the head of the X-ray department. He's been thinking a lot about the last meeting he had with Strong. There are a lot of unanswered questions.

Now how in the world do I get Strong back here? he thinks. He said I could summon him, but he never said how.

Gradually, a smile forms on his fortyish face. He reaches for the phone intercom.

"Yes, Doctor," a secretary answers.

"Can you send in Strong-Presence, please."

"I'll try to locate him, Doctor."

"Thank you."

I guess I'll just twiddle my thumbs until he shows up, he thinks.

It isn't long before there's a knock on the door.

"Come on in, Strong."

Strong comes striding into his office, a broad smile on his face, which is a younger version of the face of the slightly graying man sitting behind his desk and wearing a doctor's white smock.

"That didn't take long," Isacks says.

"I doubt that you have a good sense of time, brother. Anyhow, how do you know it's me and not just another figment of your imagination in your dream?"

"Come on, Strong. Don't play games with me. All the cards are stacked in your favor."

"Yes, it's me. What's on your mind?"

Isacks winces at the complexities that the question evokes. Since he lives in Strong's mind but has his own individuality, he's not really sure whose mind is whose.

"Question: How exactly do you influence the Earthling minds you contact?"

"Through dreams. We make suggestions in dreams. Sometimes they remember the dreams, but most often, they don't. But in either case, the suggestion is planted. Then it's up to them and their psychological makeup whether or not those suggestions have influence. Sometimes they feel compelled to do something. They don't understand the origins of these compulsions unless they remember their dreams."

"Is that ethical?" Dr. Isacks asks.

"We try to be as non-intrusive as possible and yet still do the research."

"Do you have a kind of Prime Directive?"

Strong immediately understands the allusion to the popular *Star Trek* series, as they were loyal fans while inhabiting the same personality.

Dr. Isacks continues, "You guys aren't much different from us. We've been faced with that dilemma in animal experimentation forever."

"Yeah, we didn't enjoy those experimental method classes much, did we? But in this case, where Lila is concerned, we intend to be very intrusive. Hopefully, it won't be harmful to the subject. Do you object?"

"Tell me first how that will help Lila. Are your plans any clearer than they were the last time we talked?"

Strong takes a seat across from Dr. Isacks. He crosses his legs and leans back. "We've got to convince the Canadian to find Lila. She's a complete stranger to him. If we're successful at doing that, I can ride in the subject's visual and auditory perceptual centers when he makes contact with her. That way, I'll be able to see Lila. Since she's been my wife as much as yours, there won't be any trouble in recognizing her."

Strong pauses.

"Okay, then what?" Isacks urges.

"Well, it's a little difficult to explain the technicalities, but it might be possible for me to make direct contact with Lila's mind from that vantage point. It's not like anything we've ever done before. I won't actually be in her mind, but rather feeling some of the effects of her mind patterns. If I read them correctly, I can bring them back to the folks in the focus chamber."

"Will those patterns allow you guys to tune into Lila directly?"

"Gosh, Zeke, you're almost as sharp as me. I wonder how that happened."

"Okay, then what do we do once we get into her mind?"

"Then you and I can make suggestions through her dreams," Strong says. "That's as far as we've gotten in our planning. So what do you say? Do we have the go-ahead?"

Dr. Isacks thinks. He gets out of his chair, goes to the window, and gazes out at the small cityscape that is Waynesboro, Virginia. He looks out on a bare mountain slope where men have defoliated one side, leaving a red clay scar on the landscape. "I wonder whether anything will ever grow again on that slope," he says.

"Don't know, brother, but I get your point. Where men and Gazeons meddle with the natural order of things, there's also the chance of great damage."

"You're damned right. Let's go ahead with the plan, and may God help us."

Meanwhile, back on Earth, Lila is standing at the water line of her property, looking out at the Potomac. Far out in the water, she thinks she sees heads bobbing. Some of them are children, and she fears they're drowning. She wades into the water, which is sandy at first, but it quickly turns to mud and rocks.

"You out there! You're out too far! You'll drown!" Lila yells. Her piercing voice is heard throughout the neighborhood.

She stands there screaming for half an hour as the sun goes down.

"Zeke, is that you out there?"

Though she perceives the bobbing heads to be 200 yards

away, Lila believes she can make out Zeke's facial features. With disappointed weariness, she finally turns around and leaves the river to return to her house. She walks slowly into the breezeway, through the side door, and through the empty dining room. As she walks past the kitchen, she doesn't notice that the sink is full of dishes and a viscous brew of black water lies deep in the basin.

The old woman walks aimlessly into the living room and sits in Zeke's old chair. She sits there for three hours, staring out the window at the drowning people. She continues to gaze, half awake and half asleep. Finally, at 10 p.m., she walks down the hall to her bedroom. The house is dead. Nothing there speaks to her. She lets her garments, still damp from the river, fall to the floor. She slips on a dirty nightgown. Then she lies in her unmade bed.

At 3:00 in the morning, she turns to look for Zeke on her right side. As her arm gropes for him, a feeling of panic overcomes her. She gets out of bed and searches every part of the house, calling for him. She stumbles outside and looks for him in the garage and in the tool shed. Eventually, she looks out over the Potomac and remembers that he was out there drowning. With her heart in her mouth, she rushes to a neighbor's house and bangs on the bedroom window.

An irate woman peers through the closed window and tries to make out Lila's words. The elderly woman's own husband is in the hospital. She opens the window.

"I can't find Zeke anywhere," Lila pleads to the neighbor.

"Zeke is dead, Lila. Go back to bed," the woman says curtly and slams the window shut. The curtains are drawn, cutting off further contact.

Lila steps back, confused, humiliated, and angry. But she's reminded that her partner is indeed dead and gone.

She returns to her empty bed.

Several weeks later, Lila is again standing knee-deep in the river water, trying to coax Zeke and the children to come to the shore. It's 9 p.m., and a mist engulfs the Potomac. She stands, a ghostly figure, slight and gaunt, her white hair wild and unkempt. Finally she turns and returns to the house. She goes to the phone and calls 911.

"Hello. Is this Dee Tucker?"

"Yes. Who is this?"

"I'm awfully sorry to call you this late at night," a woman's voice replies. "Is Lila Isacks your mother?"

"Yes. What's wrong? Who are you?"

"I'm with the rescue squad. You're mother called us an hour ago to report that there were some children drowning in the river. We don't think there's anyone out there, but we're looking, just in case. Has she had trouble discerning reality before?"

"Oh, no! Yes."

"Well, we're afraid to leave her here alone. She might go wandering into the river and end up drowning herself. She's been seen and heard out there for over a month, calling for imaginary people to come out of the water. I think you should come down here."

"I live two hours away. It'll change nothing if I come down."

"Maybe she could stay with you for a while."

"We've tried to get her to move closer to us so that we could help her, but she utterly refuses." Dee's voice has a defensive edge.

"I don't think she's using good judgment. Can't you get a psychiatrist to look at her?" the rescue squad lady asks.

Dee sighs with frustration. "Believe me, we've tried. She won't go. We've attempted to get the courts to force her to go, and they think we're trying to take advantage of her. We've tried to get her home health care, but she won't accept anyone coming into her house and interfering with her life. So, at the risk of sounding callous and irresponsible, I'm not coming down there. You can ask my sister. She's a little closer."

"We've already dialed her number several times, but there's no answer."

"Well, maybe you'll have better luck getting her into a hospital than we've had."

The rescue worker's voice turns lighter. "Well, I suppose she'll be all right. Sorry to bother you."

"No bother." Dee slams down the phone and walks away in a confusion of guilt and anger.

Why Canada?

Somewhere in Canada, Matt and Maude are planning a vacation.

"But why Virginia, Matt?"

"I just think that would be a wonderful place for a vacation."

"I could see something like the Bahamas or Europe, but the thought of Virginia never even occurred to me. What's in Virginia, anyway? You never showed any interest in it before. You don't have relatives there. So what's this all about?"

"I don't know. It's just that there's this feeling that it's the place to go. Like something is calling me there. Didn't you ever get that kind of feeling yourself?"

"Nope, and neither did you before, not as long as I've been married to you. You've always been a little strange, but this is the icing on the cake." Maude turns away from him in exasperation. She stalks out of the kitchen, where they've been having their conversation.

Matt follows her, talking as he goes. "It's steeped in American history. Thomas Jefferson, James Madison, Woodrow Wilson, Civil War battle fields. What's *not* in Virginia?"

"We're Canadians."

"I know. That just makes it more exciting."

Maude throws up her hands and looks heavenward, rolling her eyes. "You're not going to let this stupid idea drop, are you?"

"Oh, come on, Maude. You'll enjoy it. I promise you that you will. There are things about that place you wouldn't believe."

She spins around to face him. "Is it going to make you happy if I agree? Will it get this stupid bug out of your ear?"

"It's not a stupid bug, but it will make me happy."

"Next year, do I get to make the choice? No questions asked?"

"Maude, you wouldn't want to spend a whole vacation with your mother."

She stares at him, as though staring him down.

"Oh, all right," he says. "Next year, you get to make the choice, even if it means staying at your parents' house."

A sly smile forms on her face. "Okay."

Matt looks like he's just been promised a BB gun for Christmas.

Dr. Isacks is fishing in his pond at the old Waynesboro farm. In his dream world, Lila is in the house with their two daughters. He can hear an occasional loud voice drift down to him from an open window. His two Gordon Setters are romping on the other side of the pond.

I know this is my dream, he thinks. So I can make the fish bite. But if I make them bite when I want them to, what fun would that be? If I don't want them to bite, that's certainly no better. So how come they bite sometimes and sometimes they don't? I guess my own mind will always be somewhat of a mystery to me. Boy, if that isn't mind-boggling. I'm going to lose my mind just thinking about it.

Suddenly, he feels a hand on his shoulder. He isn't startled. He doesn't even turn to see who it is.

"Hi, Strong. Life treating you well?"

"Well enough."

"How's your Canadian?"

"You mean our Canadian. He's coming along. Would you like to see some movies about him?"

"That's possible?" Isacks asks, intrigued.

"Why not? It's all in my mind, just as you are. Only it's under the category of memory. Would you like to watch my memory?"

"My God, this gets curiouser and curiouser. How do I do it?"

"Would you like the holographic version, or the TV version?"

"I'm just a beginner. How about TV? I can operate one of those. We can go into the house and just turn on the boob tube."

"Our family is in the house. I'm not sure I'm ready to see them," Strong says.

Within a few seconds, a middle-aged Lila and two pre-teen girls leave the house, get into a Jeep Cherokee, and drive out of the long farm driveway.

"Nobody else home but you and me, Strong."

They walk to the house and into the living room, where Isacks turns on the television. A scene unfolds in which Matt is arguing with Maude about their vacation plans. Isacks watches the whole episode, fascinated and concerned. The scenario comes to a close, and a Viagra commercial comes on.

"Very funny, Strong."

"Well, what do you think, Doctor?"

"You did warn me that you were going to be intrusive in this poor man's life. Hell, he'll be lucky if this doesn't end in divorce for him."

"You're exaggerating. Look, they're working through the difficulties."

"For now, but this little adventure is just beginning for them."

"So do you want us to back off?"

"Now, Strong, I didn't say that. Besides, it's too late. The die is cast. But I think we're building up a lot of karma for ourselves."

"Having any luck with the fish?" Strong asks, changing the subject.

"A couple of bites. Want to grab a rod and do a little fishing together?"

"I'd like that, Zeke. It's been a long time."

Before the dream ends and the sun goes down, the two beings in human form sit in silent comradeship, watching the play of evening and the dwindling light on the little pond.

One month later, Matt and Maude are driving past Fredericksburg, Virginia, toward Virginia Heights Beach, where they've rented an apartment for a couple of weeks.

"Tell me again why it is that we're staying in this Virginia Heights place," Maude asks Matt sarcastically.

"Because it's centrally located, near a lot of other important places, and small. It's right by the water. And we won't have to pay those outrageous prices just to be near the ocean. Washington, D.C., is just on the other side of the Potomac River. You know that's the capital of this country. Why, the president of the United States will be right across the river from where we are. Won't that be exciting?"

Maude yawns loudly, making sure Matt doesn't miss how underwhelmed she is. "I'm not a complete imbecile, Matt. I know Washington is the capital of this country. I even know the name of its president. Can you imagine?"

Matt winces. "Can you smell the water?"

"No. We aren't anywhere near close enough yet. Your head is full of water."

Matt gives a long-suffering sigh.

By mid-afternoon, they've reached their destination, and Maude has to admit that she can smell the brackish water of the Potomac. Despite herself, she's beginning to see possibilities in this vacation.

The next day, they start out early in the morning to visit Washington, D.C.

"Matt, you're going the wrong way."

"Nonsense. I know where I'm going and what I'm doing."

"But I remember how we got here, and this is nothing like that. We have to backtrack to get to a bridge," she says insistently.

"When you're driving, you can go any way you like. You won't find me backseat driving the way you do. Now please afford me the same courtesy, okay?"

"Okay. Boy, isn't this fun?" she says sarcastically. "Do you see what that sign says?"

"Yeah, Colonial Beach."

"When I looked at the map yesterday, I saw that Colonial Beach is east of where we're staying. We're headed toward Chesapeake Bay. I thought we were going to D.C."

After a while, even Matt has to admit that he's hopelessly lost.

Strong–Presence, who is ensconced in Matt's sensory mind, watches intently. The images he has implanted in Matt's dreams are suggesting every turn he takes, although Matt himself is totally unaware of what directs him.

"It's been a long time since I've seen this place," he says. "It brings back such nostalgia. We're coming to the traffic circle. Come on, Matt. The first left. That's it. Good."

He watches for the left turn at the gas station, excitement building as the car takes them closer and closer to Lila's house on the Potomac. He doesn't know how he will feel when (or if) he sees her eye to eye.

"I haven't seen her with a clear mind for almost a decade," Dr. Izacks says. "What does she look like? Stay focused, Strong. Don't get lost in your emotions. Gosh, he took the left, and I didn't even notice. I was so tied up with my dithering. Focus!"

Matt ends up at a T intersection.

Although Strong's thoughts were almost screaming inside

his own mind, he wasn't trying to project them in any way to Matt. He needs to trust that the dream conditioning will do the job. He doesn't want to interfere and create an unknown result.

"You're doing fine, Matt. The T intersection is correct. Turn left. Turn left! Why are you hesitating? Okay, okay, here we go. Two blocks. Just two more blocks. Good. Now right."

They're on Lila's street.

Maude throws her map on the floor. "What's the sense of my trying to read the map when you don't pay any attention to what I'm telling you? We're lost. Hopelessly lost. This is some residential neighborhood. Call me stupid, but I don't see how this has anything to do with getting to Washington."

"Okay, okay. I concede that I'm lost. Something just seemed to be leading me here. But I'm lost. Oh, that old woman across the street in her driveway. I'll ask her for directions."

"Wow, a man willing to ask directions, and from a woman, yet. Fantastic. Matt, she looks kind of out of it. Be careful. You might scare her."

"Oh, don't worry about it."

Matt gets out of the Volvo and approaches a woman who is trying to get into her car. She looks frail and confused.

"Excuse me, ma'am. I hate to bother you, but it seems that we're hopelessly lost. Perhaps you could help me get my bearings."

The slight woman looks up at him, and he feels a very strange, subtle kind of recognition.

At the moment Matt and Lila make eye contact, Strong opens his receptiveness as wide as he possibly can.

"I'm getting something," says Strong, "but it's very weak. If I didn't know and love this woman, if I hadn't lived most of my earthly life with her, I would have missed it. But I've got it. I've got enough here for us to be able to find her in the focus chambers. Harmony, did you get that?" He projects his telepathic question to his wife as she monitors his experiences.

"I got it, Strong. Now come on home."

But Strong lingers. This might be the last time he'll see his earthly mate from an outside perspective. He watches the interaction between her and Matt continue.

"Can you help me get into my car?" Lila asks.

"Of course. Do you know where your car keys are, ma'am?"

"Oh, yes. I guess that's why the door won't open. Thank you very much."

Matt leaves without getting any directions from the confused lady, but somehow he no longer needs them. The route is clear in his mind. Strong was responsible enough to include that in his dream training.

"You know, Maude, maybe this getting lost is telling us something. Maybe a Virginia vacation wasn't the best idea."

"No kidding. We can book a cruise to the Bahamas from here. Are you interested?"

The next day, he and Maude book passage for a cruise to Barbados.

Zeke and Strong are sitting on a log. They're watching a makeshift sailboat made of a curved piece of bark, a twig for a mast, and an oak leaf for a sail.

"Zeke, I always look forward to joining you in your dreams. I never know where I'll find myself."

"Do you recognize this place, Strong?"

"Well, I wasn't exactly in any condition to be objectively observing what the Earth boy was doing. But I think this was the place where you tried to annihilate me."

"Only because I thought you were a bug trying to eat away my brain. And I'm not so sure you weren't. After all, you were trying to devour all the information you could."

"I didn't know I would create such a ruckus. How could I

know how weird you creatures are?"

Zeke chuckled at their banter. "Now that I see it from your point of view, I guess we are pretty weird. How does it feel to be one of us—sort of?"

"Wouldn't have missed the ride for anything."

Zeke's demeanor changes, and he looks seriously at his counterpart. "I want to understand what the plan is. Go over it one more time."

"No problem. Now that we have her code, we can get into her brain anytime we want."

"You mean *you* can," Zeke corrects.

"But you'll be there with me. The best way to do it is through her dreams. That way you can keep your own separateness from me. You can interact with Lila as part of her dream. From there, you can wing it."

"This might be difficult for me. I haven't had any real interaction with Lila for a long time."

"I know. I've been living my own life as a Gazeon, so my emotional connections to Lila are not as strong as yours. It's going to be tougher on you than on me."

A puff of wind suddenly sends the toy sailboat skittering across the pond. Both Strong and Zeke smile like little kids. The gust subsides, and the boat settles down to a barely perceptible drift.

"Wow, that was exciting!" Strong says.

"When can we get started?" Zeke asks.

"Just as soon as Lila starts dreaming. The monitors will let me know. They tell me it's getting difficult to tell sometimes when she's awake and when she's sleeping."

"I know how that works. I was like that for a long time. Come to think of it, I'm dreaming now, right?"

"Don't ask. These states of mind are getting too complicated for description. If I try to explain it, we'll both have headaches."

"Just give me some warning, okay?"

Strong gives Zeke a thumbs-up sign.

In her dream, Lila talks to Dee and Dodi on the phone, while Zeke plays his guitar on the couch. Sometimes she's talking to them on the phone, and sometimes they're with her and her husband in the living room.

"What time will you be home from the hospital tomorrow, Zeke? I want to make sure your dinner is warm."

Sitting on the couch, next to Zeke, are several of Lila's grandchildren.

"It's time for you to go to bed now," she says. "I'll fix you all a glass of milk. It'll help you sleep."

"You don't really have to go through all of that, Lila. I don't have to go to work anymore," Zeke tells her.

"And just why would that be?" she asks.

"Because I'm dead now. I have to move on."

"Yes. I know you're dead. But that doesn't mean I can't take care of you."

"What would you do if I weren't here?" Zeke asks.

"Then I would have nothing," Lila answers in a depressed, angry voice.

"You would have the children to take care of."

"Why are you talking about not being here? That's silly talk."

The scene changes, and Zeke finds himself driving his old Jeep Wagoneer. Lila is in the seat next to him, and their two little daughters are in the back seat.

"Where are we going, Lila?"

"To visit my father and brother in Tampa."

"Are you happy?"

"Of course I am. I have my family to take care of."

"Don't you need anyone to take care of you?"

"I need you to make money, to pay the bills, and to mow the lawn. Mostly, I need someone to take care of."

The scene changes again, and Lila is in her house with Dodi. Lila is the size of a ten-year-old girl, but she has the shape of a wizened old woman. Dodi towers over her, shaking her finger at the old lady.

"You have to go to a hospital to live. You have to be locked up. They'll take care of you there, so you can't hurt yourself and get into trouble."

"I don't want to," Lila whines. "I don't need to."

"Then someone will have to come to your house every day and make sure you do things right, because you're crazy, and someone has to tell you what to do."

"No! No! No!"

The dreamscape fades away. Dr. Isacks and Strong look into the darkness of lid-closed eyes as Lila begins to awaken in the middle of the night.

Zeke and Strong sit on the dock of a bay watching the tide roll away.

"Well, old friend, what's the plan?" Strong asks.

"Why are you asking me? She's your wife too. Dead or alive, she won't let go of me."

"Zeke, she said it herself. Without you and/or children to take care of, she has nothing."

"Maybe we could reason with her better if we were more direct," Zeke suggests.

Goodbye

In the afternoon of the following day, Lila is awake and speaking with one of her daughters.

"Why can't you just *visit* Vintage Years home, Lila?" Dodi asks.

"Because I need to take care of your father and the kids."

"Lila, they're just stuffed dolls and a teddy bear. They aren't real."

"What do you mean they're not real? Can't you see them?"

Dodi rolls her eyes. "All I see are dolls and a teddy bear. They are not alive!"

"I know they're not alive, but they need to be taken care of anyway. If I leave them here, they'll get lonely and hungry."

"Lila, they are not real!"

"If they're not real, then I have nothing, nothing at all!"

Dee, who has been listening and watching from the kitchen, suggests, "Why don't you take them with you when you visit the apartments?"

Dodi looks at Dee disapprovingly.

"Why should I have to visit, anyway?" Lila protests. "I'm perfectly okay right here. I don't want to live anywhere else. So there's no reason to visit an old age home."

"You're losing weight, you can't remember how to turn on the air conditioner, and this morning you tried to cook rotten hamburger meat. God only knows what you've been eating," Dee says. She's trying to keep her voice gentle.

"It was not rotten. But I'll go to the store and buy some fresh food."

"You can't even get the car started, let alone drive it. The only way you ever get to the store is if a neighbor drives you," Dee says, her voice rising in volume and pitch despite her efforts.

Dodi interrupts, with no governor on the anger in her tone. "You can't pay your bills or do anything with your checkbook. I have to come down and do all that for you every weekend, and I'm tired of it. I'm not going to do it anymore if you don't at least look at a few assisted living places."

"You're all ganging up on me. Oh, look. Your father wants the channel changed on the TV. He's tired of watching cartoons. That's one problem I have with them. They don't always like the same program."

Lila goes over to the television and tries to figure out how to change the channels. Her efforts are futile. "All right, I'll look if I can bring them with me. But I'm only going to look."

Dr. Isacks is walking through a dreamscape field back in his old Virginia home with Strong and his dog Twiggy.

"You're getting tricky, Zeke. How did you pull me into your dream?"

"Oh, I'm learning a few things, old buddy. It boggles my mind, but right now in this state, living in your mind, I guess I'm as much Gazeon as human. It's like things are reversed. You piggybacked in my brain all those years, and now I'm doing the same to you."

"Yeah, except you don't have a body waiting for you to reanimate, as I did."

"Confusing, isn't it? I'm really a part of you who's drawn you into our collective mind."

"Please, Zeke, you're giving me a headache."

"You don't have a head, Mr. Gazeon. Anyway, how do you like my dream?"

"I like it. It's nice. I miss the old place sometimes. So what am I doing here?"

"I just wanted to share our thoughts about how things are going with Lila."

"How do you think they're going?"

Zeke picks up a stick and flings it as far as he can. "Mixed results. She's gotten those dolls and a teddy bear. She sees two kids and me in them. Which one do you think is me?"

"The teddy bear, no doubt. But you don't look much like a teddy bear."

"Funny, neither do you. The problem is that she's having more and more trouble taking care of herself, and her physical condition is deteriorating. So is her mental condition, but that could be connected in part to the physical deprivation. My daughters are trying to get her into an assisted living facility. I'm hoping they'll succeed. It would be a shame for her to have to go to a nursing home. I didn't have much luck with one of those."

"Zeke, how do you know all these things? I've been monitoring Lila in her waking state and witnessing these things you're describing. But as far as I knew, you were safely living out your own life in a dream state."

Zeke chuckles. "Maybe you've created a monster, brother. I've been doing a little exploring with mind states. After all, I am part of a Gazeon mind."

"You're scaring me. Why don't we just take a walk around the property for old time's sake?"

"Why don't we go hunting?" Zeke counters.

"Looks like the right season for pheasant. Did you bring any guns?"

"You're carrying one, dummy."

"It wasn't there a moment ago. Get to work, Twiggy," Strong commands the Gordon Setter.

A few weeks later on Earth:

"How did Mom's visit go yesterday?" Dodi asks her sister on the phone.

"She actually liked it, but we couldn't stay too long, because she was afraid it was getting too hot in the car for the kids and Daddy."

"Why are you encouraging her to think that way about those stupid toys?"

"I'm not encouraging it. I'm just humoring her. We can't talk her out of her delusions, and, frankly, they may make life more bearable for her, Dodi."

"But it's crazy."

"In case you haven't noticed, Dee, Mom is crazy. These delusions are harmless. If we can get her to go to the facility, that's all that matters."

"Does the director know about Lila's imaginary friends?"

"As a matter of fact, she does. She said it won't be any problem. She just wouldn't want her to bring the toys down to common meals."

Back in another of Zeke's dreamscapes:

"I don't believe it. Why are we in the lamp of the Statue of Liberty? We've never even visited Ellis Island," Strong says.

"I always wanted to visit it. Didn't you?"

"You know I did, of course. But isn't the lamp closed to tourists?"

"Not to these two tourists. Besides, you're an immigrant, right? So give me a progress report."

Strong looks at the New York City skyline. There's a slight, gentle mistiness that softens the hard edges. "I thought you were watching when I was watching," he says.

"I haven't got the technique down perfectly yet," Zeke says. "I want your description and assessment."

"Well, Lila is now ensconced in the Vintage Years assisted living facility. She keeps saying she wants to go back to Virginia Heights Beach, where she knows everybody. If she talks to Dodi, there's usually a big fight. If she complains to Dee, there's no fight.

"Dee is a smart girl. She knows there's no way Lila could manage it, so she just says, 'Okay,' and it doesn't go any further. Lila's made a few friends. Her memory is broken really badly. She doesn't remember important conversations she's had from one day to the next. So she ends up calling our kids to tell them some earth-shattering thoughts they had already discussed the previous day—or even that morning, sometimes. On the other hand, she looks good. She's gained weight. She's not having as many of those dark psychotic episodes."

"How is she doing with me and the kids?" Zeke asks with a wry sound in his voice.

"You mean the stuffed toys?"

"Of course."

A dark cloud passes overhead, and with it, a light rain. Strong and Zeke walk around to the ocean side of the Statue of Liberty's torch. The sun is reflected in sparkling colors off a slightly choppy sea.

"She's just as involved with the dolls as before. She's stopped trying to feed them, though, and she's spending less time with the teddy bear. I think our strategy is working. She may be starting to let you go." Strong looks pensively back toward New York Harbor. There's a hint of sadness in his human eyes.

"I think Zeke might not be there anymore," Lila tells Dee as they sit in the Chinese restaurant.

"I notice you don't speak about Dad as much," Dee says, as she tries to catch the eye of the waitress.

"He just seems to have gone on somewhere. Maybe he's in Heaven."

"How did your Bingo game go yesterday?"

"Oh, I was so embarrassed. I kept calling 'Bingo' because I saw the boxes lining up. But when they asked to see my card, the letters weren't really covered. I just thought they were. I don't know what's wrong with me."

Dr. Isacks stands on a wharf overlooking a vast, calm ocean. He's wearing a dapper business suit and carrying a doctor's satchel. Strong suddenly finds himself standing there next to him.

"Hey, I wish you'd give me some warning before you just make me pop into your dreams like that," Strong complains.

"Don't worry. I know when I shouldn't drag you away from something."

Suddenly Harmony, in Gazeon form, materializes on the wharf.

"Where are we?" she asks. Her lights flicker in a confused pattern.

"I invited you here," Zeke says.

"How?" Harmony asks in wonderment.

"I can't really explain it very well, Angel, but I didn't want to leave without saying goodbye."

"Goodbye? What do you mean?" Strong asks.

"Lila doesn't need me anymore. Mission accomplished. There's no reason to hang around."

"But where will you go? What will you do?" Strong asks incredulously.

"Go? Why, out there," and he sweeps his left arm to take in the vast expanse of the limitless ocean. "Do? I guess I'll find something to do. I notice I have my doctor's bag."

"We're attached. You can't go anywhere without me," Strong

protests. His human guts are roiling with anxiety and sadness.

"Want to bet?"

As they stand there, the umbilicus connecting the two figures begins to glow. It expands until it encompasses all three of them in a golden glow, and then it expands to include all that can be seen.

"There," says Zeke. "Now we're no longer attached to each other any more or any less than we're attached to all life everywhere."

In the distance, a tall white ship in full sail glitters in unseen sunlight.

Harmony concentrates and slowly takes on the form of Angel.

"Well, hello again, Angel," says Zeke, smiling. "You do me an honor to take on human form."

"It's the only way I can hug you goodbye."

The tall ship grows in size as it draws closer. The sea sparkles around it.

Tears flow down Strong's human cheeks.

"We'll always be connected in a special way, even without the umbilicus," he says.

"No doubt about it, brother."

"Will we never see you again?" Angel asks.

"From time to time you may see me as I am or in disguise. Somehow I know that I'll never be that far away from you."

The tall ship now draws near. Magically, it pulls up to the dock, and a gangplank materializes at Zeke's feet. He begins his walk up the ramp, turns for one last look as he reaches the gunwales, and then is seen taking a position near the bowsprit.

Silently, the tall ship's sails fill, and it moves away quietly and swiftly. It turns towards the unseen horizon. Zeke is looking outward, toward an unseen destination. A vortex appears in the distance—not dark, but white. It's a color that somehow fills Harmony and Strong with a sense of wellbeing. The vessel sails directly into the vortex. Its form is framed for a moment and thereby made more striking. Then it's gone. The vortex moves swiftly out to sea until it can be seen no more. The wharf vanishes under the feet of Angel and Strong.

Just before they find themselves floating in their sleep chamber side by side, they manage a human, "Goodbye, Dr. Isacks."

About the Author

Leonard Tuchyner was born in New Jersey in 1940. He has watched the world change dramatically—yet remain, in some ways, much the same. His lifelong studies of spiritual and human issues have been strengthened by the counseling work he did for 60 years. His own gradual path into blindness has brought him to an ever-growing understanding of disability and inequity, as well as compassion for self and others. His work as a counselor is now followed by a second vocation of writing poetry and prose, combined with facilitating writing critique groups and a long-continuing "Writing for Healing and Growth" group.

He has one published book of poetry, *Journey to Elsewhere*. *Merlyn the Magic Turtle: A Story of Love and Justice* (2022) was his first published novel. In addition, he has had hundreds of poems and short stories published in magazines and anthologies.

Leonard lives in Virginia with his wife and two old dogs. His extended family includes four adult children, five grandchildren, and two great-grandchildren. He is an avid gardener and enjoys playing the harmonica, with his wife on the piano.

Website: https://www.dldbooks.com/tuchyner/

Made in the USA
Columbia, SC
21 February 2025

c2dd9336-d740-4d44-8e17-1701bb32fa89R01